Stalking Christmas

A.L. Maruga

Copyright © 2024 by A.L. Maruga

All rights reserved.

No portion of this book may be reproduced in any form without written permission from the publisher or author, except as permitted by U.S. copyright and Canadian copyright law.

No portion of this book may be used for training AI.

This book is a work of fiction. Names, businesses, places, events, and incidents are either the product of the author's dark imagination or used in a fictional manner. Any resemblance to actual persons, living or dead, or actual events is purely coincidental.

No Copyright infringement intended.

Cover: A.L. Maruga

Editing: Furious Editing

A Note from A.L. Maruga

Hello, my lovelies,

This book is the first holiday book I have ever written, but let's be honest, I don't really do warm and fuzzy. Dark, depraved, and having you questioning your life choices is more my speed.

If you're new to me, *oh boy*, are we about to go on a ride in my dark mind. If you've been with me for a while, *buckle up*; Nic is about to blow up your world. You may even still be functioning at the end of it; no guarantee you won't have scars, though.

I take no responsibility for the rollercoaster of emotions you are about to go through or if you'll never be able to look at a man dressed as Santa again. You stepped willingly onto this ride, so get ready for some fuckery of the best kind.

This is an **adult**, dark romance and is strictly a work of fiction. I do **not** condone or approve of any behavior, actions, or scenarios which take place between these characters. This book is intended for 18+ only. All characters are over the age of eighteen, and none are blood-related.

If you haven't bothered with the trigger warnings because you're a red flag-loving warrior, there are over 40 of them. Please, for your sanity and mental health, heed my warning.

You can find them on my website at : www.authoralmaruga.com

Happy holidays, my little sinners!

A.L Maruga xoxo

Dedication

To all the booktok girlies & guys that dream about a
masked man slipping down your chimney,
and fucking you right up with a candy cane, or
stealing you for the holidays,
and tying you up with some sparkly lights.
I hope you get your bell rung!

Chapter 1

Santa

The wave of obnoxiously bright, strobing lights and thumping music hurts my head, and forces me to grit my teeth from sensory overload. My eyes slide across the patrons of this shitty establishment, that smells like a combination of puke, piss, and stale beer. I hate this fucking dirty city; why am I even here? I down my first shot of scotch, savoring the cheap taste, and the burn in my throat, before chasing it with a gulp of beer, the need to get completely wasted trying to sway me away from my desire for control. The laughing hyena to my right is pissing me off, as he sloshes his drink all over the bar counter, and gropes every stripper and server that walks by. *Pathetic*.

If I cared about human decency, I would crack my knuckles across his fat, ruddy face or, better yet, take the bottle of beer in my hand, shatter it on this worn-out, sticky counter, and use it to slice his fucking neck wide open, and watch as all his blood spills across this tacky floor. Good thing for him that I am not, in fact, a decent human being, and I don't give a shit about others.

My eyes wander around the strip club, with its dirty white and scuffed platforms, and neon signs imitating naked dancing girls, along the walls. One even looks like she's putting a cock in her mouth if you squint the right way, it might also be a microphone she's singing into, but I prefer my version better.

Floating cages hang suspended from the corners of the room, and sway with naked women gyrating inside of them to the raunchy holiday music. Who the fuck strips to *Jingle Bells*?

My eyes keep moving as I take another sip of my beer, cataloging the VIP area with its rich burgundy-colored booth, that's corded off to the left side, and the semi-sheer gold curtains that have seen better days, that block off the private dancing areas. There aren't many in that section, but I wouldn't expect there to be. No one with real money or taste would be caught dead in here. If you looked up seedy in the dictionary, this establishment's image would be right next to the description, with a health hazard warning.

My eyes return to the stage as the lousy DJ slurs his words, and announces another stripper dressed as a naughty elf. This one's name is Candy. *Pfff,* there is no originality left in the world. I snort as I look down at my own pathetic Santa costume, and scratch at the itchy white beard across the lower half of my face. *My dad's a fucking asshole for making me wear this shit.*

"She's hot, right? For forty, she'll blow you in the men's washroom, but she's got to take out her fake teeth first. I recommend it, buddy, she gums your dick like a fucking champ." The drunken hyena slaps my shoulder hard, as his voice gets even louder above the horrific version of *'Santa Baby'* that's currently playing, and he slams back what remains of his drink.

Rage instantly rises within me at his touch, and I have to take deep breaths to talk myself out of murdering this fucker, in a packed strip club, in the middle of downtown Boston. "Don't touch me again, or I'll break your fucking hand," I grit through my clenched teeth. I down the second shot of scotch in front of me, the burn helping to soothe some of the scalding fury within me, and I squeeze the glass for dear life, trying to force myself to keep my hands to myself. He's not fucking worth it, even if seeing his blood would improve my mood.

"Not very festive, huh?" He tips his head to my costume and releases a cackle. I ignore him, and once again permit my eyes to trail over the drunken inhabitants of this fucked up establishment. I need something, or more like someone, to either fuck hard or spill their blood, maybe even both. The itch in my veins is rising like the intoxication inside of this cesspool, and with it, I know it will be only a matter of time before I snap. I can't do that here, I can't allow myself to be reckless, I'm too exposed.

"Girlie, give me another drink, and don't stinge on the pour. While you're at it, let me feel those pretty tits; if you do, there's a twenty in it for you." My momentary perusal for a victim is paused, while I follow the line of the hyena's stare to behind the bar, where a new bartender is pouring drinks for a group of suits hanging out at the end of the bar. She ignores the hyena's slurred, lewd comment, and continues pouring, before carrying the drinks down to the trio. I watch intently as one of the '*stockbroker*' fuckers tries flirting with her, and she shoots him down with a polite smile.

The guy grabs his chest dramatically, imitating that she's crushed his heart, while his buddies laugh at him. She shakes her pretty auburn head and smiles demurely, coming back over to us and pouring the drink the hyena is still loudly demanding. "Here you go, that's ten dollars, please."

Her voice is soft and melodic despite the racket in the club, and I sit back and take in her features. She's got beautiful dark brown eyes with amber flecks, behind full, thick lashes, high cheekbones sprinkled with adorable freckles, and a pouty pink-stained mouth. She's wearing the barely-there club uniform. A snicker leaves my lips against the lip of the beer bottle. Ear muffs would cover more than that purple bra she's wearing across her tits, and the tiny black booty shorts with hearts across her ass do nothing, but show off her perfect peach of an ass, and long toned legs. I can't see her feet, but I would bet all the money I have in my wallet that she's wearing the same clear sky-high heels all the servers are. Like I said, this place is a fucking hazard to your health, and whether you're a patron, or an employee, makes little difference.

"What about the tits, girlie?" The drunken idiot leans across the bar, as far as his massive gut will allow him, and tries to grab onto her arm, but she remains out of his reach. A scowl mars her pretty face, and her lip curls in disgust, as her chocolate pupils narrow on him. I'm immediately amused at the vehemence emanating from her; she's just a little thing. No way she could fight off a guy the size of hyena if he decided to get rough with her.

"I'm not interested. Pay your tab, or I'll cut you off and call security." She wipes the spilled drink from the bar's surface, and starts to move away from our spot to serve someone else, after giving him a scathing look. Out of the corner of my eye, I spy hyena picking up his drink and raising it towards his lips, before he changes trajectory and throws the full glass of amber liquid at her. *What the fuck?*

His aim is a mess, and he misses her, but the glass hits the bottles behind the bar and they shatter, spilling alcohol and shards of glass everywhere. *What a fucking prick.* Her scream is loud enough to be heard above the raunchy music, and gets the attention of everyone at the bar. "You fucking asshole! That's it, you're done. You're getting thrown out of here!"

Hyena breaks out into a chortle, laughing so hard tears are running down his pudgy face, and snot comes out of his nose. *Fucking gross, asshole.* Some of us are still trying to enjoy our shitty drinks.

I can see the burly Asian bouncer heading in our direction, and I can't wait to see this fucker get thrown out of here. I might even help the guy break a few of his bones. Not because I care about what happened to the bartender, she's not my problem, regardless of her nice ass, but because he's been irritating the shit out of me for the last thirty minutes, while I tried to drown my fucking sorrows in peace.

"What's happening here, Chrissy?" The guy, who's built like a tank, questions the pretty bartender, and she motions to the mess behind the bar. *Chrissy*, that's a pretty name; it rhymes with pissy, like this whole situation and my life at the moment. What a fucking mess, the situation *and* my existence. "This asshole refused to pay for his drink, was propositioning me, and when I turned him down, he threw his drink at me."

"Listen, bitch, me and my good friend Santa here were just having a few drinks to relax, and celebrate the season. You didn't have to be a fucking, uptight cunt. Your tits are probably shit anyways." Hyena motions to me, and almost falls off the stool he's precariously straddling. "Right, buddy, she's an ugly bitch anyways. Better looking pussy in this place, fuck her."

"That's it, both of you are out of here!" Asian *'He-Man'* scowls before grabbing onto hyena's arm and ripping him from the stool, while the drunken fool swats at him, looking like a mosquito about to fight a lion. *Jesus fuck, this guy is a mess.*

"I don't know this fucker. I had nothing to do with what happened to her." I motion to the bartender, as she uses a bar cloth to wipe at the small cuts on her arms from the shards of glass. Hmmm, that's a pretty shade of red she's now wearing. Would she bleed so prettily if more of it was to be spilled? My mouth begins to salivate, with the desire to run my tongue along the cuts on her arm.

"They were chatting it up since I took over for Trish. Look like friends to me, and I want them both out of here, Angus." She gives me an angry glare as Angus comes around the bar, places his massive hand on my shoulder, and squeezes. "Come on, Santa, time to go."

"What the fuck? I didn't do anything, I was sitting here having a beer. I don't even know him." I shrug off his touch, my blood pressure rising, and a red haze beginning to rise behind my eyes. I hate being touched without my permission. This fucker is a few seconds from me shoving this bottle down his roid-filled throat. *Control, don't lose control, too many witnesses.* I force myself to take deep, even breaths, and visualize pushing this fucker's head underwater. *One, two, three... breathe.*

"I don't give a shit, you're both trouble, and you're leaving now." Angus steps back as hyena falls off the stool, and then proceeds to try to crawl between other patrons' legs, to try to get away from him. "Oh fuck, this asshole is just pissing me off now." He blares into his headset mic, and I immediately notice a few more bouncers heading in our direction. Fuck, this is about to look like a nasty version of *Wrestlemania* in here, and I have no intention of getting my ass beat for that lush.

I turn my furious glare back to the bartender, who's watching all of this go down with a mixture of horror and satisfaction across her face, her arms crossed against her chest, causing her pretty tits to squeeze together. "You're making a mistake. I had nothing to do with him, or what he did. I don't know him."

I give her a chance to correct her mistake, to apologize to me for ever thinking I would associate with someone like that dipshit, but instead, her pretty lips go into a straight line, and her milk chocolate brown eyes glare back at me with wrath. "I don't care, I want you fucking out of here, asshole."

She turns her back on me just as I am grabbed from behind by a massive gorilla of a man, and hoisted right off the stool. I lose sight of her as I'm shoved, and manhandled, toward the entrance of the club, along with hyena, who's got two bouncers forcefully carrying his drunk ass out.

With one final look back, a malicious grin crosses my face. Well, it looks like I've found my next victim to play with. She's going to regret falsely accusing me, and having me thrown out of here. First, though, I have a hyena to split open from chest to asshole, and coat the alleyway with his guts. I'm about to give the rats their holiday dinner.

Chapter 2

Santa

Hyena stumbles towards his car, his greasy shirt haphazardly hanging on for dear life, as he attempts to withdraw his keys from his stained pants pockets, and leans his substantial weight against a dark green Chevy Impala. "Fucking bitch, fucking whore, who does she think she is?" He mumbles repeatedly to himself while I watch from the shadows, the cold night air doing nothing to sober the jerk up.

Once we got kicked out of the strip club, and there was no chance of reentering, thanks to the gorilla they posted at the door, I gave up trying and walked over to my midnight blue Mustang Shelby GT500, and ripped open the trunk, looking for the blade I know I had stashed in there. Irritation, outrage, and resentment were riding me hard, first at being touched, then falsely accused, and lastly at being dismissed by that cold bitch. How dare she look down her nose at me. Doesn't she know who I am? Can't she sense the predator before her?

Once I found the blade, I wrapped my fingers around the solid metal handle, tucking and hiding it in the long sleeves of the wretched Santa suit I still wore, to disguise it from any of this lousy establishment's patrons. Then, I went in quiet pursuit of my first victim. He is the reason I had to endure any of that shit. If he had just kept his ugly, loud, fat mouth shut and drank his liquor, none of this would have happened, but no, he had to be a belligerent drunk cunt.

A part of me, the giddy part that gets off on hunting prey, thanks him for allowing us to fill our urges tonight. For a brief moment there in the strip club, I thought I might actually go home empty-handed, and have to survive the holidays without the feeling of fresh blood on my hands, but obviously,

fate has intervened, and now not one, but two, will die. *Merry fucking Christmas to me.*

As I inch closer and closer, I pull the white Santa beard up higher on my face, and the ridiculous red cap lower, to hide my features. I only spied one camera when I entered the parking lot earlier tonight. Like I always do, I made sure to park far enough away so that my car was never in the camera frame, and inside, I always kept my head down, or disguised by the stupid, itchy beard. No one will be able to connect me to this night once this pitiful excuse for a human is found, and that's only if I don't carve him up for wild animals to consume

I rise from my crouched position and take the last couple of steps, my eyes skimming over him, taking him in. It's almost too easy. I hate hunting weak prey. It takes all the joy out of the experience. I need to hear as their panicked breaths leave them in a hurry, knowing that their blood is rushing a million miles an hour, and their brains are screaming for them to run. A predator is hunting them, and about to set his teeth into them and rip them apart. I love the adrenaline, and smell of their sweat and fear; it's an aphrodisiac. It becomes a pure shot of dopamine straight into my own veins, empowering me, and also helping to soothe the savage rage that lives like a monster within me, always demanding more bloodshed and pain. It's an unquenchable thirst that keeps me perpetually hungry for the next victim.

"*Santa?*" He slurs, and squints in the dim parking lot light, as he sways on his feet. My lips quirk behind the beard. "Hey, you… want to… go party? I… know a better… place," he questions, and releases a huge burp.

"Sure, buddy, let's go party. Why don't you give me your keys? I'll drive." I reach out my white-gloved hand towards him, and impatiently wait until he manages to yank his keys from his pocket.

"Yeah, you… drive. Good idea, Santa… we might… crash the sleigh if I do it." He releases another gross, loud burp, and throws the keys at me, and I reach for them just before they would have landed on the ground. This fucker is going to pay me in screams for ruining my night.

I round his car, open the driver's side door, and almost immediately gag at the stench of body odor, rotten food, and nastiness from within. For a brief moment, I waver on my decision; is killing this piece of shit worth possibly catching something from this vehicle? My skin crawls with just the thought of how much bacteria is probably living in the confined space. "Let's go, Santa, we... can find... some hoes to jingle." With a laughing grunt, he launches his hefty weight into the car, and it makes a horrific groaning noise. His words, and the sound of his laughter, are precisely what I need to steel my resolve.

I start the ignition and pull out of the parking lot with a screech of tires, heading toward the freeway. "Hey... Santa... the bar is the... other way," he groans, as he braces himself on the dash as our speed climbs, and after a few moments of his ragged, panicked breathing, I pull off at an exit and slam on the brakes, sending his head smacking into the windshield. "Ah, what the fuck!" He groans.

"You should really put on your seatbelt, it saves lives." I reach over and grab the belt from his side, pulling it so I have enough slack, and wrapping it around his neck as he struggles. He keeps swatting at me, like I'm some kind of insect he can fight off, and it irritates me even more. I yank hard, fisting the seatbelt until his face goes beet red, and he chokes on his next breath, as my other hand snakes forward with the blade. I slam it into his protruding belly, yanking back before thrusting it again and again, as he makes sickening, gasping sounds. "Let's hear you laugh now, asshole."

My eyes meet his terrified blue gaze as the light goes out, and he takes his last shuddering breath. His warm blood soaks through the white gloves, coating my fingers, and a quiver races through my body, as my cock stands hard and ready inside of my Santa pants. Fuck. I need to cum so badly now, but I can't while we are on the side of the road.

I ease my foot off the brake, and release my hold on the seatbelt, as his head slumps forward, but I keep my fingers tight on the blade. The desire to pull my cock out right here, and fuck myself in his blood, is almost all-consuming, but I won't risk getting caught for this piece of shit. I keep going for another twenty minutes until a dirt road appears, leading me further into the rural area. *Perfect.*

The radio croons country music, helping to bring down some of my rage and relax me. Not enough to soothe the lust riding me, but enough that I don't lose complete control over myself, and I can pull back the red haze that threatens to overtake me. I turn the song up, Dolly singing something about Jolene taking her man. *Pfff, you should stab a bitch, Dolly. Then no one would take him.*

"We interrupt our regularly scheduled broadcast for a news update. Another headless and dismembered body has been found on the outskirts of Boston. This one is also believed to be female, although the body has been exposed to the elements, and is badly decomposed. This brings the total for the year to seven bodies that have now been found in a similar state. The Boston Police Department is urging anyone with any information to please come forward. The person or persons committing these crimes are thought to be quite dangerous."

A snort leaves my lips at the apt description of me. *Quite dangerous*, indeed. The general public, however, has little to fear from me; there are bigger and scarier predators out here pretending to be good law-abiding citizens. So what if I've committed a few murders? Seven have already been found, but so many more are still hiding in the graves I gave them. Most of them weren't good people, like hyena here. I just helped speed up the process of their imminent death.

Once I reach an utterly secluded spot, where I can see nothing but white snow grazing the fields, I pull the blade out of his belly, the cooling blood doing nothing to soothe my raging hard-on. I pull down the front of my pants, my rigid cock twitches in the cool air, and beads of precum ooze from the slit, as I wrap my blood-soaked gloved hand around it, and stroke myself from root to tip. *Fuck yes, this is precisely what I need, after the shitty day of playing dress up for my cunt of a father.*

My breathing begins to pick up as my balls tighten, and I grip myself more firmly, pressing against my various piercings, and increasing the speed of my thrusts until I'm panting and moaning, with only the soft music as my company. *Fuck, so good.* The squishing, wet feel of the glove against all my ridges and my metal piercings feels fantastic. My balls tighten as I release a growl, and I cum into my hand. *Fuck, I wish that had been a warm cunt or a tight asshole.* An image of dark brown condescending eyes enters my mind, and pulls a moan from my lips. Fuck yes, but I need to slit her chest open and make those vicious lips scream for me first.

I raise my cum drenched palm and slather it all over hyena's face, making sure to get some inside of his gaping mouth, before stuffing the glove inside. When I'm satisfied with the mess I've made, and my breathing has returned to normal, I pull my phone out of my pocket and check the time. Fuck, if I'm not quick, I might miss that bitch leaving, and that just won't do. She's my Christmas present to myself, after all, and it's exactly what I wanted.

I get out of the car, pull a cigarette and my lighter from my pocket, light it up, and lean against hyena's car, as I stare up at the cloudy night sky and take a deep drag. This was reckless of me. I usually don't do spur-of-the-moment kills, preferring to stalk and watch my prey, and then take them so I can play with my food. Although this was momentarily amusing, it wasn't fulfilling, and I'm left once again feeling empty and raw.

He was an exception because he enraged me, but she won't be. I want to hear her pretty screams, and the way she's going to beg me for her life. The image of her dark brown judgemental eyes and those pouty lips enters my mind, and my cock once again awakens, ready and willing to go once more. With one last drag of the cigarette, I throw it inside the disgusting vehicle, watching as a chip wrapper catches the tip, and a small flame begins. I take off, running back towards the exit of the freeway. I need to put distance between myself and his car.

The small splatter of his blood is easily camouflaged against the dark red of the Santa suit, so I don't have to worry about others noticing my state immediately. Well, I guess my father was right; the suit would get me in the holiday spirit, just not the one his rich, pretentious ass thought.

I'm coming for you, Chrissy. You've made Santa's *naughty list*, and it's time to pay up.

Chapter 3
Santa

It took me much longer than I anticipated, to get some much-needed distance between me and hyena's burning body. By the time I managed to make it closer to the freeway, and called for an Uber to take me back to my car in the strip club's parking lot, at least three hours had passed in the frigid cold. I am now frozen, highly irritated, and filled with the need to stab someone again. The night is quickly evaporating into the morning, and I don't have much hope that I will get to capture my Christmas gift.

A small Toyota Prius dropped me off near my car, and with a wave at the Uber driver, who hadn't raised an eyebrow at my choice of clothing, I got back in my baby and set in to wait, with the heat defrosting my cold limbs. It is now close to four in the morning, and, finally, the side door of the club opens up, and a bunch of employees exit the space. Some are still dressed in stripper wear, with coats thrown haphazardly over them, and their flesh exposed to the elements, and others are in sweats and hoodies.

Thank fuck, a few more hours, and I might have had to just torch the building with all of them inside. I'll save the possibility of doing something like that for another day, it could be amusing to watch them scream and try to get out, after I've blocked all the exits. Great, now I have a chub, thanks to the images my brain just supplied.

I bite down on my bottom lip, attempting to distract myself from my murderous thoughts, the itchy beard getting on my nerves, as I wait for my mark to come out. When she finally does, she's covered from head to toe in ugly red and white flannel pants, and a thick, puffy gray jacket. With her auburn hair pulled into a messy bun, and her makeup wiped from her face, she's almost unrecognizable. She looks somehow younger, less harsh, and more innocent now than she did inside, under the lights of the club. She walks arm in arm with another female, the both of them giggling conspiratorially as they follow two other women, who I'm pretty sure were the dancing elves from earlier, to a dark blue, rusted minivan. Fuck, this is going to be more challenging than I anticipated, I release a groan of frustration as I watch all four of them pile inside.

When their vehicle starts moving, I give them a head start out of the parking lot and slowly follow them at a distance. A new plan begins hatching in my head, to follow my bartender home and capture her from there. This might be even better than taking her from the parking lot, since there's less chance of me ever being linked to her this way.

The first stop drops one of the elves off at a small rundown bungalow, and she scurries inside. The next stop has my Chrissy, and the other female she was giggling with, stepping out and rushing onto a dilapidated porch of an old back-split house, with large, dirty windows and dingy siding, as they fumble with the keys. The minute they let themselves inside, they slam the door, and the minivan takes off down the street. *Fuck, she has a roommate.*

I drag my hands down my face with exhaustion and frustration. I should just give up for the night and head back to my place, and chalk this nightmare up to the fucked night that it is. I managed to get my hands bloodied after all, so some of the need has been sated. The reasonable part of me is telling itself to put the car into drive and head home, but the psychopath who lives inside of me is refusing to listen, and instead pulls around the block, parks the vehicle, and gets out.

I take a quick look around the street, keeping my eyes peeled for danger. Most of the houses in this neighborhood look either abandoned or run down, far from the glamor of Newbury Street. My Mustang sticks out like a sore thumb amongst the broken-down beaters, rotting wood fences, and trash-littered sidewalks. Fuck, I'll be really pissed if my car gets stolen, or broken into, here.

I jog around the corner, keeping to the shadows, with my eyes and ears open for anyone approaching behind me. It would be fucking hilarious to get mugged in my Santa costume, or, better yet, have a police cruiser shine its lights on old Saint Nick, and I end up in the slammer for being a peeping Tom. I can picture my dear old dad's malignant face if he received that call in the middle of the night. *Governor Brantford, can you please explain why your oldest son was peeping in women's windows in an impoverished neighborhood?* The privileged fucker would have a stroke. It might just be worth it if the fucker actually died.

When I'm three houses away, I decide to slip through backyards, rather than approach the house from the front. It's a little more tedious, having to climb over fences and hide behind different sheds, but I don't want to take any chances if someone comes out and shoots me. I doubt the residents here would have licenses to carry, or give me the benefit of the doubt. I finally make it into their back yard, press my back against the aged siding, and creep along its perimeter until I come to a window. I peer inside cautiously, trying to keep my Santa costume in the shadows. *Fuck, I should have taken this shit off. It's too late now.*

The room I glimpse into is partially dark, with only a small lamp in a corner giving off a muted glow. It's a sitting area with mismatched furniture, throw pillows on the surfaces and on the floor, and shadowed artwork that I can't make out. I don't see Chrissy or her roommate; the room is empty.

Dammit. I wait a few more minutes just in case, but when no one comes, I keep moving until I encounter another window. This one has old plastic blinds pulled down over the glass, but various rows are missing chunks, so I can still see within. It's a bedroom, the overhead lights are on, and I spy clothing discarded everywhere, piles of stuff on every surface, an unmade bed, and a small television on a dresser, playing what looks like cartoons. *What the hell, is there a kid in there?*

I try pulling on the bottom of the window to see if it will lift. After making a groaning noise, that I swear could wake the dead, and announce my presence to the whole street, it gives a little, and I'm able to slip my fingers below it. I'm about to pry it further up, and lift my body through the window, when a noise alerts me to the fact that I'm no longer alone. A deep growl makes the hairs on my arms and the back of my neck stand on end, and the fading moonlight catches the glow of two luminous eyes, and sharp white teeth. *Fuck, that's either a damn wolf, or a really big dog, but either way, I'm toast if he gets closer.*

I immediately pull my hands back, reach for my blade tucked in my pants, and start slowly backing away from the house and towards the street. The dog takes a few steps towards me, its huge paws looking as menacing as its teeth, as it snarls at me and saliva drips from its large mouth. Where did they get this thing, the bowels of hell? Fuck, its neck is wider than my thigh; this thing is going to rip me apart if I don't get out of here.

"Good *hellhound*, you stay right there, *buddy*," I whisper, the sound of my blood whooshing in my ears.

"Toothless! Where are you, buddy? It's time to go night-night, come on, little friend," a woman's voice calls from the back door, and the massive hound's large head turns on its neck to look in that direction as its ears twitch. *Toothless? Little friend? Is she fucking kidding?* This monstrous thing has nothing but teeth to rip a man to shreds. I take another step back, and he growls and moves closer to me, ignoring the woman's commands. "Where is that sweet boy?" I hear the voice moving closer and closer, and dread starts to fill me. In all the years I've been killing people, I have never been taken down by a dog, but I guess there's a first time for everything.

"Come on, sweet buddy. Momma's tired. Let's go, handsome!" The voice sounds more annoyed now as it calls again, and the dog wavers on whether to attack me. "Do you want some peanut butter? Come on, and Momma will give you some treatos!" With a final snarl, the dog turns around and lopes off toward the voice calling him, its tail wagging. I see a hint of auburn hair shining in the moonlight, before the back door opens and closes, and I'm left standing flush against the side of the house, with my heart in my throat, and so close to peeing my fucking pants.

That was close, too fucking close. I'm pretty sure I saw my life flash before my eyes, and none of it brought me satisfaction. I haven't murdered enough people yet, not to mention my pretentious asshole of a father would be relieved if I died. I won't dare give him that gratification. I slide back towards the window, peeking through the broken blinds again, and I hear her voice through the opened crack. "What a *good boy* you are, the goodiest, sweetest baby!" She croons to the giant black monster who's getting his head rubbed. A full-body shudder runs through me at the thought of those large teeth gnawing on my bones.

Fuck, there is no way I'm risking getting in there tonight, and being that beast's chew toy. I need another plan, but it will have to wait until later. The miserable sun is getting ready to rise in the sky, and any meager amount of cover I had to disguise me out here is about to evaporate. With one final look in the window, my eyes trail over the silhouette of my current craving, then I force myself to leave the side of the house, and quickly make my way back to my vehicle.

   Don't worry, Chrissy. I'll be seeing you real *soon*.

Chapter 4
The Gift

I release a huge yawn, my body riddled with various aches and pains from the lousy few hours of sleep I got, thanks to the over one hundred and twenty pounds of fur ball that hogged my bed. The clingy bastard waits until I get up, his ears perked, and then takes over what's left of the mattress as I start my day. "You're just lucky you're so damn cute," I groan as he burrows deeper into my comforter, until only one of his large black paws is visible.

My groggy thoughts turn to last night at the strip club and how, despite working every day this month, I'm still going to be short on rent, and all my credit cards are now maxed out. I need to find something else, something that doesn't involve me wearing barely there clothing, and having assholes proposition me all night. The cuts on my arm catch my eye, and a scowl crosses my lips; that guy was such a jerk, and so was his creepy friend in that ridiculous Santa get-up. I'm so glad I got those two kicked out.

"What are you doing awake already?" I question my roommate Daisy as I walk into our rundown kitchen, and the smell of fresh coffee reaches my nostrils. She usually sleeps until mid-afternoon, since we both work at the club until the early hours of the morning, but she's up after only going to bed five-short hours ago. She groans as she clutches her head, no doubt feeling the after-effects of all the tequila shots she took with patrons, after she was done performing on stage. "Shhh, your voice is too loud," she groans.

I pour myself a cup of steaming black coffee, and sit at the old, fake-wood folding table we eat on. I grin at her as I watch her in the misery of her own making. I don't know why she does this to herself night after night. Mind you, if I had to take off all my clothes, and swing naked on a pole for a bunch of drunken horny fools, I'd probably be drunk too. It's bad enough that I'm barely dressed, and have to serve them alcohol.

I reach across to the rickety bookcase we have next to the table, that serves as a pantry, and grab the chocolate cookie package. It's one of the last few things we have left to eat in the house that isn't in a can. "Here, eat some of those to help soak up all that tequila, and drink some damn water today. Your liver will thank me."

She peeks one of her red-rimmed blue eyes through her fingers, and reaches for the cookie package with a pained moan. "Are you heading to the diner?" She questions with a mouthful of cookies.

"Yup, gotta leave soon, or I'll be late." I take a few more sips of my coffee, hoping that it will wake my tired ass up, for the long day of waitressing at the diner down the road, before I head for my bartending shift at the club later with Daisy. "I'm going to be tight with rent as it is, girl. I might need to bum some money off you for rent for a week until I can get caught up."

"You know I'll give it to you, but you wouldn't need to work so many hours if you just stripped, or came with me to *'the hole'*. You'd make rent in a few days, instead of busting your ass all month at both places and barely scraping by." She gives me a sheepish look, and I roll my eyes. We've had this discussion before, multiple times, in fact. There is no way I'm stripping at the club, I can barely stand bartending there.

A shiver races down my body at the thought of taking off all my clothes, and doing what she does at *'the hole'*. If I thought the strip club was seedy, *'the hole'* is a whole other level. The name is a pretty accurate description. Even though from the outside, it looks like an adult toy store, and inside, hidden in the back, is a completely different story. Various booths can be accessed for a fee by willing clients, where they can use the glory hole drilled in the wall to fuck Daisy, and the few other sex workers that work there. She swears that she is safe while doing it, and that the thrill, spontaneity, and anonymity of a faceless fuck, turns her on as well as pays her well for her tasks.

The images that rise in my head anytime I think about being used by a faceless stranger, having them fill my pussy, ass, or mouth with their cocks and fucking me, all while I have no idea who it is, causes my core to clench and my panties to dampen. I would never admit it to Daisy or anyone else, but it turns me on, and secretly, I know I have fantasies that would probably shock my outgoing and fearless friend.

"I... I have to go shower, or I'll be late," I stammer, as I place my empty cup in the sink and rush out of the kitchen to get ready, without meeting Daisy's eyes. Damnit, now I need a quick cold shower before I head to the diner. I rush into the bathroom, locking the door, and turn on the hot water, with the images still playing in my mind. The vision of large, veiny hands grabbing onto my hips and forcing me to stay still, as a hard, thick cock pounds into my pussy without mercy, causes a throaty moan to escape my lips. A faceless man using me in any way he desires, while I am forced to take it, and have all my holes filled with his cum. He would call me his slut, and a whore, and tell me how he was going to fill me up and rip me apart. Fuck, now for sure, I have to make myself cum before I leave the house.

As I strip off my pajamas, I get a good look at myself in the mirror above the sink. My eyes are wide, my dark pupils blown, and a pink flush is rising across my cheeks, neck, and chest. I look like I'm high on lust, the thought makes me want to giggle at how insane I am. Shit, who needs porn? I get off on my own imagination. My nipples stand erect, painfully waiting for someone to suck and play with them, even though there is no way that will happen unless it's my own touch. I slide my hand down my neck, using my fingers to grip and tighten on the column, as I picture rougher, longer digits committing the act instead of mine. My core clenches, spasming and reminding me that I'm so empty. I need something to fill me up, but I have no desire to trek back into my room to get my B.O.B.

My gaze lands on my roller brush on the counter, and I bite down on my lip as I contemplate the thick, round wooden handle. After a peek at the door to ensure I engaged the lock, I wrap my fingers around the cool handle and slowly allow it to trail down my chest, encircling first my right nipple and then my left, causing a shiver to race up my spine, before I push it down my abdomen, and use it to apply subtle pressure to my throbbing clit. I run the cool surface through my drenched pussy lips, coating it in my slick moisture before bringing it back up to my clit, and tapping lightly against the throbbing surface. Fuck, it feels good, but I need more. I need the sensation to be harder, rougher. I push the end of the handle to my tight hole, pressing just the tip inside of me before pulling it back out, as a moan escapes my lips. My head tips back with pleasure, my loose auburn hair cascading down my back, the sensation of the silky tendrils against my hot flesh adding another level of stimulation.

I push the handle further inside of myself, thrusting forcefully and quickly, until it's buried as deep as it can go. My wetness coats its surface, and I'm forced to wrap my hand around the bristles to keep it from sliding back out. The bite of their hard, prickly surface on my fingers and palm makes me want to feel it slapping against my wet pussy lips. I need a slice of pain with my pleasure, to experience all the sensations wrapped into one. I drive the bristles against my swollen flesh, the bite of pain ripping another moan from my lips, and forcing me to bite down hard on the inside of my cheek to contain it. My rhythm picks up, thrusting roughly and urgently inside of my cunt, as a shiver causes my limbs to tighten, and a blast of heat starts at the nape of my neck and makes its way down my limbs. My legs shake as the orgasm rises, causing me to have to grasp onto the sink with my other hand, and keep myself upright.

My mind conjures up a large man in shadowed darkness, his face hidden behind an ominous mask, covered in blood, with huge, menacing fangs. Only his hazel eyes are visible, and filled with molten heat. His large hand circles my throat, stopping all my air from flowing into my lungs, while his other hand clutches a sharp blade at my breast, and nicks my soft, creamy skin over and over, and rivulets of blood slide down my hot flesh. His cock pounds into my pussy at a punishing tempo, not trying to pleasure me, but instead to punish me for being a disobedient brat. The sound of skin slapping against skin, and his manly, gruff, grunts fill the air. "Come for me, whore," he demands near my face, as he drives himself hard one last time inside of my throbbing pussy, and my orgasm explodes over me, in wave after incredible wave of euphoria. I cum, soaking the hairbrush, my fingers, and the sides of my thighs, my breaths coming too quickly, as I try desperately to gulp in air and calm my racing heart.

An incessant pounding on the bathroom door brings me back to my reality, and with a grimace, I pull the hairbrush handle from inside of my sensitive pussy, and then throw it in the sink. The water is still running in the shower, and it is no doubt cold now that I've lost myself for so long. Fuck, I drag my hands down my face, my musky smell reaching my nostrils. I reach forward and shut off the water, annoyance filling me at how I just allowed the fantasy to overwhelm me.

"What?" I yell through the door, as I stare at my flushed appearance in the mirror.

"You better get out here now! Toothless just vomited up parts of your comforter that he decided to chew on! Oh, Jesus, not my shoes, Toothless!" Daisy screams, and I hear her footsteps rushing away from the door, and my dog barking like a psycho.

I turn on the sink and wash my hands and the brush, looking longingly at the reflection of the shower in the mirror, and knowing that I no longer have time to take a shower before I have to leave for the diner. I stare at my appearance, and I don't like what I glimpse. *Get it together, Chrissy. You don't have time for shadowed men and great fucks, you have to worry about keeping yourself alive.*

I push away from the sink, wrap my ratty, old robe tightly around myself, and prepare to fight a massive cane corso over the last blanket I had left. How did my life get here? This certainly wasn't where I thought I would be at twenty-seven.

"CHRISSY! He's got my shoe in his mouth! Come get him!" Daisy's high-pitched scream almost shatters my eardrums, as I race out of the bathroom door and forget all about my shadowed man.

Chapter 5

Santa

After rifling through their dirty recycling bins before I escaped undetected last night, which was not exactly one of my finest moments, I managed to grab items with Chrissy's full name, and that of her roommate, on them before I gave up on my night of stalking, and returned home, filled with frustration that I didn't get to satisfy my craving for her death at my hands.

I've barely slept more than three hours, the anticipation and excitement of a new hunt, and capturing my delectable prey, keeping me wired. I tap along my keyboard at rapid speed, doing a deep dive into everything Chrissy Cranbrook. My eyes focus on the information appearing, and painting a less-than-inspiring picture of the woman who caught my unhinged interest, by getting me thrown out of the bar.

She's twenty-seven, according to her driver's license, and a Boston native. She spent most of her formative years being shuffled from one house to another in the foster care system. A brief mention of her mother, in a sealed document I hacked, provided information on her one and only parent, who seems to have taken her own life when Chrissy was three years old. Despite what must have been a challenging youth, she excelled academically and in sports, and seemed to stay out of trouble. *Go figure, with a mouth on her like she has, I'm surprised.* Her multiple achievements materialize before my eager eyes, and they all appear to end with her high school graduation. The bitch even won a national spelling competition in the eighth grade, and was homecoming queen two years in a row. Why didn't she go on to college? I can't imagine a school not wanting to accept her, based on her grades alone, and give her a free ride.

More and more questions arise in my mind at the puzzle before me. I check her bank account records next, and observe that she's almost constantly in the red, despite seeing two different paycheck sources being deposited. Her credit cards are all maxed out, and she doesn't seem to be using them to buy frivolous things for herself. Instead, I see payments for mundane things like her phone bill, groceries, and pet store charges. A recent charge for a thousand-dollar vet clinic catches my eye. That must be for the damn beast that could have eaten me last night.

Her social media accounts are nothing but pictures of her, her roommate, and a huge black dog who has to outweigh her by more than fifty pounds, yet she treats it like a baby. Nothing indicates that she has a significant other, or many friends aside from the one named Daisy. She has videos and pictures of different park settings, all within the city and all featuring her hellhound. *This chick is boring as fuck, and I would be doing her a kindness, ending her existence.*

A few more clicks of my fingers bring up any possible interactions with law enforcement. More boring shit, years ago, she got a few speeding tickets and one drunken, disorderly citation at nineteen. I keep looking; there has to be more on this woman, something I can use to lure her to me, wrap my chains around her neck, and rip her beating heart out of her chest. My cravings for destruction and mayhem are rising to unmanageable levels. Soon, I will lose control, and then it will be a bloodbath.

What's this? The police have a sealed file? I break open the file with no issues, my skills unmatched for their flimsy attempts at keeping me out, and my eyebrows rise to my hairline. It seems *Miss Perfect* had battery and assault charges against her when she was seventeen. She did community service instead of time, for assaulting her ex-boyfriend with a crowbar, after he attacked and beat her and her best friend, and tried to rape them. *Interesting.* The pictures of the condition she left him in make me feel all warm and tingly inside, or as close to that as possible, since I usually feel nothing at all. It seems there's rage buried under all that creamy skin. *Delicious, I can't wait to experience it, and mar its perfection.*

I quickly take note of his name and current address, so I can pay him a visit and release my current frustrations on him. Not because I give a shit what he did to Chrissy. I don't have the capacity for most human emotions, having been diagnosed years ago with antisocial personality disorder. The broad spectrum of petty things, like remorse or kindness, don't interest or move me. My sociopathic and psychopathic tendencies usually lead me to focus only on satisfying my own needs. Right now, I need to see blood splattered across various walls, and hear the screams of someone begging me for their worthless life. The fact that Mark Fisherville hurt Chrissy once upon a time means nothing to me. He's a means to assuage my fury at losing my prey last night.

I take note of the time on my computer screen. I wonder if she's working at the diner listed as her other source of employment right now. My cock jerks in my sweatpants at the thought of seeing her. It could be amusing to have her serve me, without realizing that I'm the same guy from last night. There is no way she would be able to correlate me with the male she had thrown out of the bar without the Santa costume. I wonder if I could charm her, make her fall for me, and then use that as a way to get her alone. I could drug her and take her to my cabin, far from the bustle of the city, and do whatever I want to her.

Fuck, now I'm hard, as I picture her tied naked and spread eagle against the rough, wooden St. Andrews cross I made. Her body would be covered in lashes from my leather whip, and bite marks from my teeth. She would look so beautiful with tears sliding down that perfect face. Her mouth filled with one of my ball gags, and a collar around her throat, restricting her airflow. All that creamy alabaster skin just waiting for my wicked ministrations, and that rich, soft, auburn hair wrapped around my fist, as I force her neck to arch for me.

My phone vibrates on the desk next to me as I palm my aching, hard cock, the images flooding my brain causing me intense pleasure. It stops and starts again, the annoying person pissing me off, and breaking my concentration on my depraved daydream. I wonder if her cunt is as pretty as her face, and if she'll scream and plead for her life, while I fuck her pussy with my cock, while shoving one of my blades in her ass. "What?" I shout, as I place the call on speaker and pull my cock out, fisting it, and giving it deep, hard strokes.

"Is that any way to greet your father, Nicholas?" A deep, annoyed, cultured voice questions. "I'm positive your mother is rolling in her grave, thanks to your deplorable manners."

I squeeze the pierced tip of my engorged cock firmly, swallowing a moan, and yank on one of my testicles, the hit of pain making my cock even harder. "Pretty sure she's also rolling in there after watching the rotating line of young whores you continuously stick your cock into, *Dad. You* know, the ones young enough to be your daughter or granddaughter." I bite down hard on my bottom lip, the taste of blood adding further enticement to my aroused state as I pick up speed, my fingers tightening around the metal piercings in my shaft, as I stroke myself rapidly toward completion.

"You don't get to judge me, boy." His bitterness makes the corners of my lips quirk upwards, fuck, I love winding him up. The truth is I couldn't care less who he sticks his dick inside of. "No, only the taxpayers whose money you spend, so your whores spread their legs wide for you can judge you, but they don't, do they? 'Cause I make sure to wipe clean all your sins before they can get wind of them." A grunt leaves my lips as I cum all over my hand and lap, the warm sticky fluid giving me momentary relief from all my aggravation, at having to deal with this asshole. I raise my fingers to my mouth and lick them clean, the salty, bitter taste of my cum hitting my tongue, and making me want to explode all over again. The truth is, if I could contort my body so I could suck my own cock, I'd probably never leave the damn house again. Alas, I can't, so I need my victims to help slake my thirst.

"I have something I need you to take care of. Where are you now? I'll send your brother to you." I wipe the remaining cum on my pants and shake my head in vexation. This asshole only calls me when he gets himself buried in shit. Otherwise, he's happy to ignore his oldest son just fine. "I'm heading out in a bit. Whatever it is will have to wait, something else already has my attention."

"Table it, Nicholas, whatever it is, it's not important. Christmas is in four days, I can't have this shit spilling into the news," he argues, and I can hear the fear he's trying to hide in his tone.

"What did you do?" I get up, grab my phone, and head towards the bathroom to shower. I wonder if I can make him beg me for my help. It might make me feel better, even if I know nothing he does is ever sincere. If I'm a psychopath, it's because he was my example and role model growing up. A huge, frustrated sigh sounds down the line, and I hear the distinct sound of his office door slamming. Shit, this must be really bad if he's actually in his office, and not out schmoozing with lobbyists and fucking prostitutes. "Your idiot brother was involved in a hit-and-run last night. He was driving high as a kite on coke, and a hooker was giving him a blow job, when it happened."

A deep, rumbling laugh escapes me at the picture he paints with his words. I laugh so hard at the image of my eager-to-please, shiny, and perfect younger brother getting himself into such a damaging situation. "It's not funny, Nicholas. This could crucify me in the polls. He killed someone, and left them there bleeding in the middle of the street."

As much as I want to keep laughing, he's right. This is not funny, and my brother is an idiot. Knowing him, there is no way he took care of the hooker who witnessed what he did, or covered his tracks with the body. "Where is the body?" I question as I strip down and palm my cock again with sadness, knowing full well I'm not likely to get another round in now.

"At the city morgue, listed as a hit and run. It will only be a matter of time before they start going back through the traffic cams, and the local CCTV. They'll see it was him, because he was driving his own car." The sound of something shattering, on his side of the line, gives me a good indication of how worked up he is already. Great, my father is an asshole on a good day. A little fear of losing everything he's got will make him bloody unbearable, and I don't look forward to having to be in his malignant presence. "I'll take care of it. Have him meet me at the Scrambled Fork in forty minutes, and Dad, you'll fucking owe me for this shit. No more playing Santa at your events."

I hang up the phone on him before he can get another word out, and turn the water to the highest setting. It sluices down my hard, rigid body, causing my muscles to relax, and my tattooed skin to redden. Thoughts of what I want to do to Chrissy re-enter my mind, and I fuck my palm hard and fast, until my cum paints the tiled wall of my shower.

Stalking Christmas

    I hope she's as much fun in real life as she is in my imagination. I guess we're about to find out.

Chapter 6
The Gift

The morning rush has finally died down, and I can finally catch my breath. I'm just about to grab some much-needed food, and head to the back for my break, when the diner door opens, and in walks a large, dark-haired man, with a black leather backpack thrown over one of his shoulders. He has to duck his head as he enters the doorway, and he pushes the wood and glass diner door wide to accommodate his sizable form. My eyes survey his huge, muscled physique, taking in his expensive-looking, open, charcoal gray wool jacket, and the burnt orange knit sweater below, right down to his dark denim jeans and the black combat boots on his feet. His head's tipped low, so I can't get a good look at his face. However, I'm guessing he's a looker based on the rest of him.

"Chrissy, that one's yours, I'm going on my break now," Dolores groans as she quickly walks to the kitchen, and avoids my glaring look. Dammit, I was next to take a break, my feet are killing me, even in my *Converse*. With a giant sigh, I walk over to the table where he's getting settled, the one furthest from the door and kitchen, which will mean extra steps for me. *Asshole*. I drop the menu on the table in front of him and pull out my notebook. When my eyes finally glimpse his face, my breath chokes me, and I end up gasping and coughing like a fool.

"You alright?" His deep, husky voice questions, as he slips off his jacket and meets my surprised gaze. I lift a few fingers, indicating he should hold on while I die, or cough up one of my lungs in front of him. When I finally have myself under control, and I can feel the heat of mortification rising all along my neck and face, I croak and wince, "Fine. I'm just fine."

Intense dark gray eyes, that remind me of molten silver, narrow as they meet mine, the corners crinkled. His forehead furrows, causing a line to appear between his dark, thick brows. My gaze slides lower to his straight Greek nose, and descends to his full, pink lips, the top one slightly plumper than the bottom. His face has a dark shadow of a day or two's facial growth, with a few hints of gray hiding within the dark, giving him a further air of intrigue. *Damn, this guy is seriously gorgeous.*

His mouth twitches as if he can read my lustful thoughts, obviously trying to disguise a smile at my expense. I roll my eyes at him, and ensure my fictitious armor is back in place. Men, no matter how they look, don't impress me; underneath, they are all the same, *animals.*

"I'll give you a minute to look over the menu. Can I get you something to drink in the meantime?" I question, as the desire to get as far away from him as possible causes my body to tense up. I wonder if I can bribe Dolores to come back out and take this table. Maybe if I offer to scrape all the gum from below the tables alone on Sunday, she'll do me this solid.

"Coffee, black, and I have someone joining me, so leave a second menu," he dismisses me with an abrupt tone that somehow pisses me off immediately. I give him my back, going to get the coffee pot and gripping it tightly, even though the unreasonable need to pour it in his lap is trying to convince me to do just that. Fuck, get your shit together, Chrissy, we need this job, and can't afford to get fired, because of someone like this. I place another menu down across from him and head back behind the counter without another word.

He doesn't even bother to look over the sticky menu. He just pulls out his shiny laptop and starts keying away, oblivious to my gaze. What is someone like him doing in this neighborhood, and eating at this hole-in-the-wall? He doesn't look like he belongs here, and I'm positive I've never seen him in here before. My curiosity instantly annoys me, and I force myself to go about my business, checking on the other two tables I still have to finish up, and attempting to ignore his presence.

After a few minutes, the door opens again, and another large male enters the diner. This one's slimmer than the first, but their similar features immediately hint at the fact that they must be related. He scans the restaurant until he lays eyes on the first guy, and makes his way over. If the original guy stuck out like a sore thumb in here, this one's even worse. This guy's wearing a three-piece navy blue checkered suit, with a dark overcoat thrown on top, and shiny loafers. A snort escapes me before I can contain it, at his appearance, and it causes the first man to raise his gaze my way. His eyes scan over the guy rapidly approaching him, and a scowl crosses his features.

I watch from a distance as the clean-cut guy removes his expensive coat and takes a seat, and they begin a conversation in hushed tones, both leaning forward in their seats, so their conversation can't be overheard. I wonder if these two are developers or something. Maybe they're scoping out the neighborhood with the intention of buying up all the homes, and kicking everyone out, so they can gentrify the area. My anger begins to simmer just below the boiling point at the possibility. I can already barely afford to live in the crappy rundown house I share with Daisy and Toothless. If the area starts getting bought out, where the hell are we going to go?

I walk over with the coffee pot, hoping to catch their conversation and confirm my suspicions. The minute I get close, the two of them stop speaking and lean back in their seats. The newcomer glares at the larger man, and never bothers to look my way as I pour coffee into a cup and place it in front of him. "You know what you want to order?" I question with a snarky tone bordering on hostility. The slender guy pries his eyes from his companion and finally looks in my direction. The glance he gives me is all heat; he sits up and turns his whole body my way as he gives me a full body perusal, starting at my red *Converse*, over my ripped black skinny jeans, and up to my *Aerosmith* band tee that has seen better days. I notice he's cataloging all my exposed flesh, and my few visible tattoos. The look is so intense that it causes a shiver to race down my spine. He's looking at me like I'm a tasty treat he wants to consume.

"Ow, what the fuck, Nic?" He jumps back, pushing his slender suited form into the bright blue vinyl banquet seating, a vicious scowl on his face, directed at the man across from him. *Did he just kick him for staring at me?* My glance moves back and forth between them, and there's a furious, predatory look coming from the larger man. His lips are downturned into a grimace, and his eyes glare daggers, that resemble pieces of flint, at the slender man. "Keep your eyes to yourself, or I'll do more than kick you, Micah."

Nic and Micah, I file that information away in my mind in case I need it. "Are you two ready to order, or are you just going to take up a table all day?" The one named Nic looks around the diner with an amused expression. "I can see how busy you are in here. The place is swarmed with patrons. I guess you'll be needing the table straight away, right?" *What a douche.*

"That's irrelevant. This is a business. Order something or leave." I fold my arms across my chest, and his eyes track the movement, causing the hair on my arms to stand on end. Everything about this guy is making red flags wave vigorously in my mind. He's a walking trigger warning, and my stupid lady parts are not heeding the warning.

"Pretty lady, let me apologize for my brother's rudeness. I'll take whatever your breakfast special is, with a side of taking you out later on a date." *Jesus, what a corn dog.* My eyes glance at Micah, and I compare his features against those of his brother. He has the same gray eyes, but his are lighter and filled with mischief. His nose is the same, but his face is more slender and clean-shaven, compared to his brother's more rugged masculine look. He has a cupid's bow on his pouty lips, and he flashes me his pearly whites in a teasing grin. Where his brother is muscled, with a thick neck, this guy is built more like a swimmer, lean and slim.

"Does shit like that ever work for you?" I reply, my voice and expression filled with disdain.

Micah jerks back as if I've slapped him, and Nic releases a loud, throaty, and manly chuckle that has my core tightening. "I'm sorry, what?" Micah asks with incredulity, as if he can't wrap his head around the fact that a woman wouldn't fall for his shitty charm, and cheesy pickup line. I lean forward until my lower body is pressed against the diner table, and I'm staring right into his widening eyes. "You're not as hot, or as slick, as you think you are." Amusement fills me as his jaw drops open, before I pull away from him and stand back up. "Order something, or get the hell out."

Micah sniffs, his arms folding across his chest, and his mouth set in a hard line as if I've offended him. He yanks his gaze away from me, staring across the table at Nic. "Two of the specials, don't fucking spit in them, none of your attitude, and a refill on the coffee," Nic growls, and easily dismisses me with a look of arrogance.

My lips purse as I glance his way, and the look he returns is filled with animosity, as he wrinkles his nose as if I smell like shit, and am disturbing him. Well, fucking fine then. No way I'm not hawking up spit in this fucker's food now. I slap my hand down on the tabletop, and snatch away the menus with a spite-filled look. "Coming right up, and the attitude is on the house," I sneer, as I walk away to place their order and avoid their table.

I'm successful for a while with ignoring them, and despite Nic's insistent motions to refill their coffees, I just ignore them. When their food order is up, I let it sit for a bit at the pickup window in their view while I scroll my socials, and ensure they'll eat their food cold. A text message pops up on my phone from an unknown number, and causes my eyebrows to shoot up.

You look beautiful when you're being a brat. I'd love nothing more than to smack my hand into that fine ass of yours.

Who the fuck is this? Is this some kind of sick joke? My eyes search across everyone in the diner, and I even glance out the windows, but no one is looking at me or showing me the slightest interest. Could this be my douche ex playing games with me? I swear I'll break his damn nose if he keeps this creepy-ass shit up. I press call on the number, ready to give him a piece of my mind, only to have the operator tell me this number cannot receive incoming calls. I promptly delete the message and slip my phone back inside my pocket, but the hair on the back of my neck is standing on end, and it feels like insects are crawling along my skin.

I grab their plates, turn my back to the tables, and spit in each of their food, right over the greasy homestyle hash browns. With a devilish grin across my face, I finally bring their food to the table and place it in front of them, walking away before they can ask me for anything. I successfully ignore them for the next hour, as they eat, chat, and go over something on Nic's laptop. I know I'm being unprofessional and petty, and there was no real harm done with Micah's attempt at flirting, but I can't force myself to be nice. I deal with slimy assholes like him every single night at the strip club, and my bullshit tolerance has reached its max.

I print out their tab when I notice them putting on their jackets, and Nic packing up his laptop. I walk over and place it down on the table, and without a word of thanks for their patronage, I walk away. I know the likelihood of getting a tip from that table is probably going to be nonexistent, and I desperately need the money, but I can't make myself act pleasant. I'm all out of fucks. They both walk towards the door, Micah exiting first without a look back, but Nic stops, his sexy eyes meeting mine before his lip quirks, he winks at me, and then he's gone.

Shit, did they just stiff me on the bill? I wouldn't put it past two assholes like that. I rush over to the table, and the tab is sitting there face down, and below it is a stack of bills. I count the money underneath, and my legs threaten to give out. I recount it, in case I'm imagining shit. He left me a three hundred dollar tip, on a thirty-dollar tab of food that I spit in. *What the fuck?*

My eyes search out the large, dirty diner windows to see if I can spot him, but he's long gone. I pocket the money, a moment of regret filling me at my salty behavior. This money will help towards what I'm short on rent, and there's no way I would have made this much in tips today. I bite down on my lip, as I contemplate whether I'll ever see either of them again.

Probably not, although if I'm honest, I wouldn't mind laying eyes on Nic again. I would even try to be friendly, well, maybe.

Chapter 7
Santa

The shadows hide my form as I disable all of the security measures for the morgue. I'd already digitally broken into the police mainframe, and made sure to erase any trace of the hit-and-run victim, not to mention I spent a miserable morning destroying evidence in the police lockup, and bribing officers with lots of dark secrets to hide. The prostitute who had the misfortune to suck my brother's cock is now lying in pieces in the Quabbin Reservoir. To be perfectly safe, and ensure my idiot brother isn't going to end up behind bars, and as someone's cum rag, here I am, slipping into the morgue after dosing the medical examiner, and his morgue technician, with a sleeping agent in their shitty coffee. Honestly, they deserve it for just willingly consuming that crap, not that I'm one to talk, since I drank that coal-tasting shit from Chrissy's diner.

My body is here, completing my tasks that'll get my malignant father off my back, but my mind is with the auburn beauty who had the audacity to tell me and my brother off this morning. A small smile breaks across my face, as I remember her *'fuck around and find out'* attitude. My cock stirs in my black pants, at the thought of forcing her to her knees before me. Would she still hiss venom out of that sweet mouth of hers? There is so much anger inside of her, and it calls to me, like a moth to a flame.

I can't wait to see her again, to allow my eyes to feast on her features, and marvel at how soft her skin looks. I bet it'll mark so prettily once I start using my favorite toys. Will she beg me for mercy? Somehow, after witnessing her once again in action today, I doubt it. If I can just get this shit done, and out of here, I might still be able to make it to the strip club before she's done her shift, and watch her from the shadows for a bit before I dare to capture her.

Stalking Christmas

A part of me doesn't want this game of cat and mouse to end too soon, I'm enjoying playing with my food, and I just know she's going to taste like the rarest delicacy, once I get my teeth into her.

I approach the temperature-controlled containers, and locate cabinet 2C, the one with my brother's unfortunate victim. I pull out the drawer, and on its metal surface lies the still and cold body of a forty-three-year-old, naked white male, who was on his way home to his new wife, and crossed my brother's drugged-out path. If I was able to feel any emotions, I would probably feel sorry for the sap right now. Fate is a fickle thing, and it looks like this guy just didn't have any luck. Fortunately, none of this actually moves me. The only thing I feel is pressed for time, and the urgent need to get out of here, so I can move on to more enjoyable things. Specifically one Chrissy Cranbrook.

The problem is that my dark desires also beckon; they lure me to commit heinous and unspeakable acts. The sickness in my veins beats a deep tempo, one not unlike the human heart, as it forces blood to rush through my veins. That tempo is a delight to someone like me, and I'm finding it harder and harder to resist it, even though I know it will lead me down a perilous road, one I may not find a way out from.

I pull back the sheet and look down at the damage my brother's Mercedes caused. There are visible bruises and lacerations over the torso, where the largest part of the impact took place. I'm lucky the medical examiner hadn't commenced any type of autopsy yet, and the body is still intact. My eyes trace over the slack face before me, the skin already appearing gray and dull, lifeless, an empty vessel. My gloved finger skates over his bloodless lips, then across the bridge of his hooked nose, and over the closed eyelids that hide the windows to the souls, or so they say. I press my thumb firmly against the lid, and feel the squishy eyeball below. With a little more force, I rupture it, and it makes a popping noise that has my cock twitching in my pants. I repeat my actions to the other one, and dark brownish blood squishes out from below the caved-in lashes, and coats his upper cheeks.

I wipe the surface of my gloves against his hollowed-out cheekbone. Leaning forward, I pull down my mask, press my head against his, and take a deep breath of his decaying scent. I draw back, my head tilting as I look at him from all angles. My work isn't inspiring me, at least not yet. He could be so beautifully tragic. A work of art, really, but my brother did an amateur job of sending him to his maker. I'll have to remedy that. I reach into the pocket of my dark pants and pull out a scalpel, the sharp metal glinting in the muted light. How I wish I had more time with him, and, at the same time, I wish I was never here. It's no fun when they're already dead. You can't make the dead scream, and I long for the sounds of misery.

A spark of uncontrollable rage rises within me, like a flicker from an electrical current. My arm slashes forward, the blade slicing through dead tissue, cells, and nerves, until a deep gash opens on his cheek. It doesn't bleed like it should. There's no spray of crimson to coat me, no rich metallic scent to soothe my lust. There are no tears and words for mercy, just silence.

GODDAMMIT! I slice again, this time cutting through one side of his mouth, and then repeating the action on the other side, until he looks like some grotesque silent version of the *Joker*. Still, it's not enough; I could slice every part of him up one section at a time, and I know with certainty that it would bring me no joy. My cock deflates, not getting what it needs to push me over the edge of my depravity, and the feeling of numbness overtakes me. I resign myself to just getting this over with, so I can find some living prey to assuage my wrath.

I pull out the bottle of acid from the backpack over my shoulder, and tip his head back further on the little stand that cradles his neck, before forcing his jaw to lower and his mouth to open. I attach the angled nozzle to the bottle, and push past his teeth and down his throat, before squeezing. "There you go, buddy, deep-throating like an expensive whore. Bet you never thought this would be your end, *huh?*"

I squeeze the bottle until the contents shoot inside and down his throat, burning its way through his tissue. When that part is done, I use my scalpel to puncture a hole in his chest cavity, and produce another bottle, repeating the process. When I'm convinced that the damage to his internal organs is complete, I pull back and stare down at him. "Sorry, fucker, but they're going to want a closed casket for you once I'm done with my work." I bring out a mixture of acid that has a thicker consistency and pour it across his face, abdomen, pelvic area, and thighs, essentially tarnishing any possible evidence. "Guess you were a grower, huh? Well, let's hope your wife doesn't miss that part of you too much. Maybe I'll send her a dildo, just in case. Wouldn't want her to get too lonely."

When I'm done with the mess, the intoxicating scent of chemicals is making its way through the room, and my facemask itches on my jaw, I pull the sheet back up and close the drawer. The next person to open this is going to pass out from the smell and the goo. Damn, I should have set up a camera, so I could watch their horrified expression. Maybe I can still tap into the camera system here; that way, I can get at least a little enjoyment out of all this effort. "See you in hell, bud." I tap the closed drawer once in a farewell and make my exit, using the same stealth as I made my entrance. No one will ever know I was here, just the way I like it.

When I reach my car, parked three blocks away in a dark alley with no camera angles, I strip out of my external clothing and throw it into a metal dumpster. I light a cigarette and, after a few tokes, throw it inside. I'll be long gone before the contents start burning. It's time to enjoy my night and go hunting for my pretty prey. I hope she's ready to play with me, 'cause I know I have a lot of energy to burn off.

Chapter 8
Santa

I pull into the parking lot down the street from the strip club. The soft classic rock song I was listening to ends, and the radio personality returns with a solemn voice that I don't believe for a second. I sit back, my whole body attuned to the words they utter.

"The public is urged to come forward with any information regarding the last whereabouts of a man found in his burning vehicle off of route twenty-five-B, in the early morning hours of yesterday. The victim has now been identified as Fredric Dryden of Boston Proper, a fifty-two-year-old used auto parts salesman. The victim is believed to have known his attacker, and allowed that person to drive him to the location where his body and vehicle were found and set aflame. As of yet, there are no leads in the case; Boston PD requests anyone with any information to contact them directly. At this time, there is no mention of a reward for information."

Reward? Are they fucking kidding me? I did them a public service by ending that piece of shit's life. If anyone deserves a reward, it's me for having to put up with his ass in the strip club, and risking contracting some deadly disease in that vehicle. As for leads, good luck. This is not amateur hour; I'm a seasoned killer, and I know how to hide my tracks. No one will come forward with any information, and no one will mourn that piece of shit's death. I would've had to screw up royally for them to catch me, and that's not in my nature. I'm at my prime, an apex predator, and I don't leave things to chance. Those that get sloppy and complacent, get caught.

I slide out of the car, and stalk slowly through the shadows provided by the nearby buildings. I didn't think it wise to park my car in the club lot two nights in a row, in case someone recognized it. I've decided not to attempt to approach the club from the front, but instead, to slip in through the side door

I witnessed the women leaving through the night before. I'm hoping that the little security they have is focused on the inside of the club area, and the front door, and they ignore where the staff come and go from.

After waiting patiently for a few moments, behind a stack of old pallets near the side entrance, I slip inside, and I'm immediately accosted by the loud sounds of holiday music blaring through the speakers. *Ugh, not this shit again.* My eyes trail over the landscape before me, as the ripe smell of sweat and alcohol accosts my nose. The neon lights flare all around the club, highlighting naked dancing women, but never doing much to brighten all the dark, seedy corners. I slip behind a deep burgundy velvet curtain that leads you toward the VIP area, and the sounds of grunting catch my ears. I keep myself hidden as I search for the source of the noise, as irrational anger rises inside of me, at the thought that it could be Chrissy with some low life.

A hint of bright blonde hair meets my gaze, as it travels over exposed tanned flesh to the woman on her knees, in a barely there Mrs. Claus costume, and I release the pent-up breath I was holding. Her silly hat bobs precariously back and forth with the momentum of her head, as she deepthroats the guy she's sucking off, as he leans against a column with his head tipped back and his legs widely spread. After another minute or two of watching, he cums down her throat with a guttural noise, and she rises to her feet, wiping at her red lips with a devious smirk.

"That's fifty." She holds out her hand in expectation, as the guy does up his pants and pulls out his wallet. I release a sigh of relief that it wasn't Chrissy, and I don't need to go on a killing spree, and irritation fills me. I shouldn't care; she's nothing to me, but a way to soothe my bloodlust. She's a prize I want to win, torture, and then dispatch. I don't have attachments with women, never have, and I'm not about to start now. I also can't stand the thought of anyone else's skin touching hers, and her down on her knees for some random asshole. *Fuck, what the hell is the matter with me?*

I creep along through the shadows, searching for my target, and ignoring all the debauchery around me. When I get closer to the bar, I don't spot her, and a hint of unease rises within me that I immediately force down. My eyes search all the sections of the club, and I finally glimpse her hair, highlighted by the streams of bright lights, and that tiny uniform, over by the main stage. She's holding a tray filled with various drinks, and serving a group of rowdy men, who are cheering on the two strippers dressed as reindeer on stage. I observe one of the men sliding his meaty paw up the back of her bare leg, as she leans forward to hand one of his friends a beer. She instantly straightens, swats away his hand, and gives him a death glare, but the useless fucker just laughs at her ire. A flare of rage simmers in my veins, and I know that before the night is over, that asshole will be missing that hand. No one touches what is mine, and right now, until I'm painted in Chrissy's pretty blood, she belongs to me.

She finishes handing off the drinks, and winds her way back through the various tables to the bar area, her sexy, full ass swaying in the tiny shorts, and her legs looking impossibly long with those transparent, sky-high stripper heels. My cock swells in my pants, and my mouth waters with the need to take a bite out of the ripe, round globes of her asscheeks. She's delectable, a wet fucking dream that my mind has conjured up. The only thing possibly missing from her perfection, is her crimson blood pouring from her various orifices, and the sound of her screams for my mercy.

My eyes catch a few men staring at her, one of them going as far as to palm his cock as he sits there, and his eyes drill holes into my girl's ass. I grind my teeth and fist my hands, to prevent myself from marching over there and slamming his head into the sticky table in front of him. He gets up after a few moments of zeroing in on Chrissy's movements, and heads towards the men's washrooms, and I follow, keeping to the shadows. I enter the empty room and don't find him at the urinals. One of the stalls is closed, and I can hear soft panting and the sound of a hand whacking off.

Motherfucker is in there, jerking off to images of my prize right now. *That just won't do. No one gets to picture her naked but me.* I quickly lock the door to the washroom before backing up and shoving my foot against the stall door, forcing it to slam open and reveal the shocked fucker, sitting on the toilet with his pants around his ankles, and his hard cock enclosed in his fist.

He doesn't get a word out before my fist is flying at his face, and making contact with his nose. His head slams back against the dirty tiled wall with a cry and a thud. He tries to rise off of the toilet, but I slam my heavy booted foot down on his lower abdomen, getting his deflating cock in the process, and a high-pitched screech leaves his mouth. My hand thrusts out, and I grab a fistful of his greasy hair, holding it taut before punching him again and again in the face, until my knuckles are split and his blood coats most of my hand, and the walls of the stall. I have to force myself to take deep breaths and try to calm myself down, before I kill this asshole here without any way of getting him out of the club and disposing of his body. *Risks*, I'm exposing myself to too many risks. What the fuck is the matter with me?

I reach into his pants and grab his wallet, opening it, pulling out his driver's license, and waving it in front of his disoriented eyes. "Joey Bastion, if you report what happened here to anyone, I'll be paying you a visit at your home, and I'll just bet you have a wife that would like my attention. Do we understand each other, *Joey?*" His terrified glance meets mine as he nods his head over and over like a broken doll. "Oh, and Joey, don't look at any of the waitstaff, or the next time, I might not be so kind, and instead slit your throat."

I wash my hands in the sink, refusing to look at my reflection in the mirror. I don't want to analyze why I just completely lost my shit, over a guy daydreaming about a woman I plan to murder. I slip back into the strip club and notice the asshole that touched Chrissy earlier, staggering drunkenly for the front door. The need to maim and destroy fills me, the beating I gave Joey not pacifying me in the slightest. One more couldn't hurt; I'll just teach him a lesson about keeping his hands to himself by cutting them off.

Chapter 9

Santa

Okay, the first step is to admit you have a problem, and I can do that. I can admit I have a fucking problem, I think, as I wipe off my bloody hands, after disposing of the body of the man who touched Chrissy at the strip club. My problem is I seem to have lost my damn mind. While I've never suffered from something as silly as remorse before, and thoroughly enjoyed cutting off his hands before slitting his throat, I know I shouldn't have. I'm allowing my irrational part to take over more and more, and I blame *her*. She's the cause of my reckless actions in the last couple of days. I'm usually so careful and methodical about my stalking and my kills. I never just murder anyone randomly, and without a prior plan in place to dispose of them.

I watch as the lifeless body of *'Jerry'*, who swore up and down that he was really sorry he touched my Chrissy, disappears under all the dirt I shoveled on top of him, in the wooded area I dragged him to, after pretending to be his scheduled pickup driver. Humans really have no self-preservation, taking others at their word, without even checking. A quick glance at his phone would have prevented him from getting in my car and ending up where he did, but the loser couldn't even be bothered. My intentions were just to cut off his hands, and teach him a lesson about not touching what doesn't belong to him, but then my mind kept supplying the image of him laughing up at Chrissy's furious face. Before I knew it, I had not only cut off his hands, but slit his throat from ear to ear and then ripped open his abdomen, allowing all of his guts to spill out. He died calling for my mercy, something I have always lacked.

Now, I'm standing in the woods, covered in sweat, blood, and dirt, thoroughly annoyed with myself, and realizing that the chances of me kidnapping Chrissy tonight are slim. *Fuck, I'm a mess.* I reach down and grab the hands I cut off of Jerry, that are wrapped in his shirt, and trudge through the thick crop of Evergreen trees, back toward where I left my vehicle. I'm going to have to do a deep clean inside of it to ensure that none of that asshole's DNA is left behind. I look down at the bloody bundle in my hands. *Why the fuck did I even keep these?* I don't usually do mementos of my kills, I'm not deranged.

Maybe I should gift them to Chrissy as a peace offering between us? I, of course, couldn't let her know they were from me, but maybe they would bring her some satisfaction, that there was one less grabby asshole wandering around that she would have to deal with. Would she look at them with admiration for my hard work, or with disgust? The logical part of me is yelling inside of my thick skull that no one gifts women bloody hands, but the psychotic part of me is telling that one to shut the fuck up.

Ugh, I'll figure out what to do with them later. Firstly I need to head home and clean all this shit off me, and make sure I have my alibi of where I was nicely wrapped up tight. My dad is going to have to play along, unless he wants another one of his sons to end up on the news. Tonight has been a bit too messy, and I'm less than satisfied with the outcome. I place the bundled hands down on the passenger floorboard with an aggravated sigh, and look at the time on the dashboard as I start up my Mustang. Chrissy's long gone from the club now, and probably back behind the walls of her home where the beast is protecting her. There's no way for me to grab her from there tonight. Jesus, between the morgue, Joey from the toilet stall, and now this Jerry cunt, I've wasted my whole night, and I'm no closer to getting to her.

I need a plan, and in order to do that, I need more information on her. I know where she works and her financial situation, but I need eyes on her at all times. The diner she works at should be closed for the next few hours. If I can get home, get cleaned up, and over there, I can install some cameras, so I can watch her while she's there. Then maybe, while she and her roommate are out, I can dose the hellhound and slip into her house, and install cameras there, too. Yeah, that will work; that's more than reasonable, and will be productive.

I head home with a plan firmly in place on what to do about my pretty prize, even though the shouting in my brain is getting louder that I'm losing myself to this unstable need for this woman. It's a good thing I'm able to ignore anything that doesn't suit my needs.

Chapter 10

Santa

Done. The last microscopic camera is in place inside the diner. It was far too easy to gain access to the space, after I disabled their pathetic alarm. I wander into the back room where the employee lockers are kept, and my hand trails over the one marked 'Chrissy'. I pry it open and pull out her dark blue apron, and the notepad she uses to write orders down, allowing my fingers to skim over the indentations of her loopy writing on the blank page. Like the creeper I'm becoming, I lift the apron to my nose to see if I can get a hint of her smell, but it instantly disappoints me. I throw it back into the locker, pull out an extra shirt she keeps inside, lift it to my nose, and am rewarded with the faint hint of laundry detergent, and a distinct floral scent. I slip the shirt into my backpack for later, so I can wrap it around my cock and dream of the breasts it belongs on.

 I place everything else gently inside the locker, ensuring nothing looks out of place, before leaving the diner the same way I got inside. The sun is starting to crest over the fading night sky, and with it comes the crisp, clean smell of another day. My tired body protests that we're not heading home and to my opulent bed, but instead creeping back towards the direction of Chrissy's house. I left the Mustang back at my home, ready for a deep clean, and instead took a nondescript beige sedan, that I occasionally use when I'm stalking my prey, so I don't garner unwanted attention. It fits in better with her neighborhood, and won't be immediately questioned if it's found closer to her house.

 I wonder if she's an early riser like I am? Does she like to have hot coffee while staring out the window at the sky of a new day? My brain is filled with jumbled thoughts and curiosities about her, and it's starting to stress me out. Why do I care if she likes coffee in the morning? Soon enough, she'll have her throat slit and her blood coating my hands and cock, and what she likes to drink and do won't matter. I drag my hands down my tired face, and attempt to shake off this unknown, and unwelcome, feeling that is inhabiting me. *She doesn't matter. She's fucking prey. She's a means to satisfy an itch, that's all.*

I slide into my vehicle down the street from Chrissy's house, where I can monitor her movements. The radio plays Christmas music in the background, as I check through my phone for any mention of my brother's hit-and-run. I pull up an article, with my father and brother featured in the accompanying photograph, and roll my eyes at the title.

"Governor Brantford and his youngest son, Micah, giving back to the community."

If I thought the title was a cheesy joke, the article itself is even worse. Someone actually gets paid to write this crap?

The Governor, and his youngest son, took part in a Christmas toy drive for underprivileged youth at the Burnside Center. The event raised over four hundred toys for local youth, and featured a real-life Santa they could take pictures with, and tell their Christmas wish lists to, while sitting on his lap, as well as offering a complimentary buffet dinner. The Governor has always championed the more impoverished neighborhoods in Boston, and has stated that we should all be extending hands of assistance to our neighbors with less. He truly is a man for the people.

Yeah, right, he's a real man for the people, like he didn't have one of his staff suck his cock on the way to the event, that he showed up to in a stretch limo, while his sons watched. *Real fucking hero, that guy.* I shouldn't even be surprised that I didn't get any credit, as the unfortunate soul who was forced to play *'Santa'*. I did all the fucking work, while he and my brother smiled for the cameras. Nothing new there, I guess.

I search for a few more minutes, but don't find any mention of the accident, or the condition I left the morgue in last night. Hmm, I wonder if they haven't discovered what I did yet. I pull my laptop from the back seat and break into the morgue cameras, without them having any idea I'm in their system, taxpayer's dollars at their best. A chuckle leaves my lips at the shocked faces of the morgue technician, and the two police officers, overseeing the state of the corpse's remains. The metal drawer is pulled out, and thick goo is sliding off the edge of the surface, and pooling on the floor below.

Stalking Christmas

The sheet has been pulled back, and melted flesh greets my eyes. There's no sound available, but based on how the two officers are looking green, and one has his mouth and nose covered with his arm, I'm guessing they're not enjoying the holiday gift I left them. Pity. If I had more time, I would have made it even better. You can't rush a work of art.

Movement on the street catches my eye, and I slam my laptop closed and scrunch down in my seat. Coming out of the house a few doors up from my precarious position, is none other than the object of my current insanity. She has her rich, auburn hair thrown up into a messy bun, and her face is clear of makeup. The thick jacket hides the rest of her from the cold temperatures, and I only get a glimpse of her legging-covered legs, and red *Converse* shoes, as she walks with purpose down the street in the direction of the diner.

One down, one to go. Now to check my work on the hellhound. I had already left him a little peanut butter-covered gift in their backyard. If he ate it a little while ago, there's a good chance that he's having a much-needed nap time. I leave my car, after confirming no one on the street has eyes on me, and make my way to the side of their house. The window I had pried open last time is my best way inside. I slip a small metal crowbar out of my side pocket, and use it to force the window open. I halt, waiting to see if the demon canine will hear the noise, and come running to accost me. After a minute or two, and no sign of it and its ferocious mouth, I force the window higher, and pull my body up and through the opening, landing in a crouched position, and once again waiting to see if my presence has been noticed.

My eyes adjust to the darkened interior of the messy bedroom. Clothes are haphazardly thrown everywhere, and surfaces are littered with makeup, gizmos, and half-drunk water cups. A feeling of revulsion rises up my body at the state of her room, and my OCD demands that we immediately leave this space or, better yet, set fire to it. How does she live like this? I don't know how you would ever be able to find anything in this state. A snoring noise coming from the direction of the double-sized bed has me stalking toward it, the crowbar still clutched in my hand and ready to strike out. Fuck, I never thought I would be the type to hurt an animal. People, yes, animals, no, but unease spirals through me. This thing will rip me to pieces if given the chance.

I pull back a holey, deflated-looking comforter, and underneath lies a massive monstrous furball, outstretched against the surface of the mattress, his large paws spread out, half under a lumpy pillow, and his face is turned to the side with his long tongue slobbering outside of his mouth, and his sharp teeth on display. Jesus fuck, this thing looks like a mythical creature of death. I use the end of the crowbar to lightly poke one of its muscled hind legs and hold my breath, knowing my life will flash before my eyes if this thing is awake. Other than one of his paws and ears twitching, he remains snoring away. Fuck, I guess the tranquilizer worked. Thank fuck.

I release the tense breath I was holding, and continue looking through the mess that coats every surface in Chrissy's room. A bright pink piece of fabric on the messy floor catches my sight, and I bend down to grab it, as I keep watch on the beast from the corner of my eye. It would just be my luck if this fucker suddenly woke up and took a bite out of my ass. I raise the pink contraption only to groan. Fuck, it's her thong. I clutch it in my hand and bring it up to my nose, and the musky smell of her pussy scent lingers, and causes my balls to tighten and my cock to throb. My tongue slips out, and I lick at the cotton crotch of her panties, the hint of her taste still left on the fabric. The urge to pull my cock out right now, and fuck the scrap of cloth, almost overwhelms me, but lucky, the snoring furball reminds me about my perilous position in this house.

I tuck the panties into my front pocket, and proceed to quietly set up a few cameras in her room. Honestly, I doubt she would even notice if I left them out in the open with all this mess. I'm just about to install the last of them, when a noise out in the hallway has me tucking myself into Chrissy's overcrammed closet, as the bedroom door swings open. "Toothless! Where are you, boy? Do you need to potty before I leave?"

I watch as Daisy walks into the room, her hands on her hips, and face filled with annoyance. "I swear if he wasn't a big teddy bear, I would ignore his ass and let him suffer having to hold it, 'til his momma comes back from work." Ah, fuck, this chick is going to try to wake that beast, and then I'm going to die. I should have tranquilized her ass too. "Toothless, you goof, wake up. Don't you want to go potty, *pretty boy?*"

She leans down and puts her face near the beast's snout while shaking him. I hold my breath, counting down the last seconds of my life. After shaking him more than once and the dog not budging, she straightens and rolls her eyes. "Fine, you better not pee anywhere, and stay away from my damn shoes. I mean it, Toothless," Daisy groans as she leaves the room, the bedroom door remaining wide open, and I release a huge sigh of relief.

Once I hear the front door slam shut, I quickly make my way out of the closet and get to work placing the remainder of my cameras around their house. I hesitate at the other bedroom door, presumably Daisy's room. I should put a camera or two inside there just in case, yet I can't make myself open the door. I don't understand the feeling that is slamming into me; I've never felt it before, and I sure as fuck don't like it. With a groan, I move away from the door and back towards Chrissy's room.

Her laptop catches my eye in the corner, thrown on top of a bunch of dirty laundry, and curiosity gets the better of me, even though I know I'm strapped for time. Toothless could wake up at any moment, or Daisy could decide to return. I quickly open the laptop, and snort at her lack of password. This girl is too much. Her background screen is a photo of the beast snoring away, wearing a colorful sombrero. I get to work installing my spyware, so that I can hack into all her files, and watch what sites she visits. Before I crawl back out the window, I quickly pull out my phone and test all the cameras, ensuring all of them are sending back an image. I give a snoring *'Toothless'* the finger, climb back out of the window, and make it back to my car without incident. *Toothless - 0, Stalker - 1.*

Before I leave her back yard, I slip up onto the back porch and discreetly pull out a package from my backpack, wrapped in thick black wrapping paper with a bright red bow, and leave it on the patio table littered with an ashtray filled with cigarette butts, and forgotten beer bottles. Once I'm in my car, I pull out the pink thong, rubbing it against my hardening crotch, and before I get on the road, I pull out my stiff cock and wrap the fabric around it tightly, until it almost hurts. This is going to be a long fucking drive home.

Chapter 11

The Gift

My eyes keep glancing at the diner door every time it opens, not because I'm worried we'll suddenly have a rush of customers, but because I'm looking for one specific customer to come back through the door, even though I know, the likelihood of that happening is probably slim. He and his brother didn't belong here, and stuck out like a Catholic nun at a Black Sabbath concert. Still, there is a part of me that wants to ask him why he left me that outrageous tip after the way I treated him, and if I'm being honest with myself, I found Nic incredibly hot. So hot, in fact, that I might have cum with his name on my lips, and his image blazing a hole in my mind, this morning in the shower.

The reality is that I'll probably never see either of those pretentious fools again, and that's arguably a good thing. I don't need to be getting myself hot and bothered over anyone. I have so much other shit to worry about, like how I'm going to come up with the missing amount of rent for this month and next. January is usually slow at the diner, and I'm guessing it will be the same at the strip club. A surge of disappointment runs through me, knowing there is no way I'm going to be able to afford the social worker courses I want to start taking at the local community college in the spring.

Once again, I'm reminded of all my shitty choices. I could have gone to college on a full-ride, straight out of high school. Instead, I allowed something that happened to me, through my own trusting naivety, to derail my life and lead me down a further path of struggling. It seems like I'm doomed to make one mistake after the other in this life, with no refuge in sight.

Daisy tried to talk reason into me this morning, telling me to just do one day at *'the hole'*. I didn't immediately shut her down like I usually do; if things continue to go to shit on me, soon enough, I won't have much of a choice. Can

I really allow some random stranger to fuck me, without ever seeing their face, for money? A shudder races down my spine at the thought, and unfortunately for me, it's not filled with revulsion.

As I'm contemplating how far I'll stray from my moral compass, and berate myself for being an uptight bitch about sex, my phone vibrates in the waistband of my leggings. I pull out the phone that has seen better days, with its cracked screen held together by transparent tape, and all my hopes and prayers, and see that it's a text message from an unknown number.

Sweet little temptation, what if I wrapped my hand around your neck and pulled you forcibly into a dark corner, taking your ability to scream away? Would you fight me, or would your pretty cunt flood with juices?

Shall I remove all your options, including the one to breathe, and see what happens? I have a theory, and I'd like to be proven right.

What the fuck, who the hell is this? My eyes almost pop out of my skull at the perverse words on my screen, and I find myself scrutinizing the patrons within the diner, to see if anyone in here is playing a joke on me. When no one stands out as suspicious, I decide to reply.

Listen here, freak. You come near me, and I'll gut you like a pig at the slaughterhouse. Stop fucking messaging me, you coward.

I delete the messages and block the number, rage filtering through my bloodstream, and making me hot all over. Who is this sicko that's messaging me? Could it be one of the bouncers or regulars at the club? Maybe it's the slimy neighbor on the corner, who stares at me whenever I head to work at the diner. How did they even get my number? More importantly, how would they know that being kidnapped and restrained, with no ability to fight back, is a fantasy of mine?

"Hey, *Princess*, can you stop daydreaming for a bit, and get that order over to table five, or shall I do everything around here, while you stand around and look pretty?" Dolores's raspy, smoker's voice startles me out of my thoughts.

I grab the food from the service window and drop it off at the table, my mind still on the text messages and who they could be from. "Will you look at this?" Dolores gets my attention and points up the television screen we have in the corner, flashing the news. On the screen, there are a bunch of people coming and going from a gray brick building, in full, bright yellow hazmat suits. I read the banner below that states they've had a chemical breach at the local morgue. Dolores reaches for the remote and takes it off mute, the diners around us forgotten.

"The breach is believed to be the work of local gangs, wanting to destroy incriminating evidence. The coroner's office has indicated that all precautions are being taken to assure the safety of workers, and that the remains are being handled respectfully. The chief of Boston PD released a statement indicating they're committed to finding and arresting the culprits, and keeping the community safe. More on this story as it develops."

"Lord have mercy, you can't even die in peace now, without someone desecrating your body. What is this world coming to?" She huffs as she gets back to work, and mutes the television once again. With one last look at the screen, I get back to work, hoping to make enough tips to grab Toothless another bag of kibble, before all the stores are shut down for Christmas.

At least one of us will be having Christmas dinner.

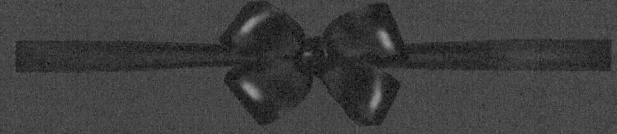

My feet are wet, frozen, and killing me, as I walk up to the front door of my house, trudging through the dirty slush that litters the concrete walkway. The rest of the day dragged on at the diner, and I'm dead tired. I have a few hours left before my shift at the strip club, Toothless still needs his walk, and other than three cups of coffee and some burnt pancakes, I haven't eaten much today. Not that there's considerable hope for a lavish meal at home, but I'm pretty sure there is still a can of tomato soup, and some stale crackers in the pantry.

There's a bright yellow ticket taped to the glass of the front door, and with a discouraged sigh, I rip it down, already knowing that it's a collection notice from the electrical company, warning that they're going to shut off our service. *Dammit, I thought Daisy said she took care of this.* I shift the large bag of kibble from one arm to the other to insert my key, and my head tilts, as I realize that I don't hear Toothless pawing at the door like usual when I get home. I hope he hasn't gotten out again, or Daisy hasn't forgotten him outside all day, and he's frozen.

Shit. I push the door open, rushing through the hallway in my wet shoes, and calling out for Toothless, as my heart bangs rapidly in my chest. "Baby, where are you? Toothless, come to momma, right now!" I can hear how frantic and shrill my voice is, and I'm seconds away from having a full panic attack. That dog and Daisy are my only family and I can't lose either of them. I throw the bag of dog food down on the kitchen table, and race from one room to the other, searching for him, but I see no sign of his large black body.

I reach my room, and a massive lump below my comforter has my breath catching in my throat. *Please don't be dead, fuck, please. I won't be able to handle it if you are.* I approach the bed slowly, my legs trembling as my breathing increases, and terror claws at me. I grab the edge of the worn comforter and push it back, until a large head is revealed with two dark hazel eyes staring back at me lazily, and a tongue wagging out of his mouth. "*Jesus, Toothless*, you almost gave me a heart attack!" His ears twitch, and his stubby tail moves the remainder of the comforter in happiness to see me. "Why didn't you come to greet me at the door, *lazy bones?*" I wrap my arms around his ample neck and squeeze, burying my nose into his warm fur with relief. He lets out a gruff of annoyance at how tight I'm holding him, and squirms on the bed with a groan. "Come on, boy, let's go potty."

I release him and walk out of the room, chastising myself for almost having a mental breakdown. Toothless follows behind me, looking a little dopey as if he's still fighting sleep, but heads out to the backyard when I let him out. I turn to search for the can of soup, my stomach rumbling loudly, and decide to heat it while he's doing his business. Then I can feed him and take him for a walk, even though everything in me protests, and says I should take a nap instead. I reach the bookcase that acts as our pantry, and dismay hits me like a ton of bricks. The can's gone, and so are the crackers. Other than a few cans of carrots and peas, and a random can of pasta sauce, the shelves are bare. "Fuck, I guess I'm going hungry today."

I pour Toothless his kibble and make myself a cup of instant coffee, to ward off the hunger in my belly, while I consider eating the can of peas and carrots. I head back to the door with a towel, ready to bring him inside and wipe his wet paws, but he catches my eye out on the porch. He's climbed up on the dirty patio table, and is busy sniffing something that I can't see. *Shit, is he eating cigarette butts again?* Fuck, I told Daisy to get rid of that shit. I can't afford another vet bill, because Toothless ingests stuff he shouldn't.

I race out onto the wet patio in just my socks, and try to grab him by the collar, to haul him back and away from whatever he's intent on. "No, Toothless, don't eat any of that!" I attempt to wrestle with the beast that outweighs me by over fifty pounds, and finally manage to push him away, but not before he tears into whatever he's trying to get to. He whines and barks, trying to get around my body, as I yank him off the table. *What the fuck is that?*

On the patio table littered with old discarded, empty beer bottles and half-smoked butts, is a torn package wrapped in black wrapping paper, and a red bow lies lopsided and damaged next to it. There's a chunk out of the side of the box, and Toothless's distinct teeth marks gracing it. *Shit, what is that?* Could it be poison from that idiot neighbor two doors down, who is constantly calling animal control on Toothless? "No, boy, you can't have that. It could be bad. It's not a treat!" I grapple with the giant beast, and finally manage to get him back inside the house, before returning and lifting the package.

"Hey, Chris, you home?" Daisy's voice calls from within, and I turn to look at her through the patio door, while still holding the package in my hands. She opens the door wide and steps outside, her loopy smile letting me know she's smoked a blunt, and is high. "Hey, what's that?" She approaches me and tries to take the box from my hands, but I pull back and prevent her from reaching for it. "Don't know. It was out here on the patio table, and Toothless tried to rip it apart. I'm guessing it's probably fucking rat poison or some shit, from the guy two doors down."

"Hmmm, whatever it is, it's dripping, Chrissy." Daisy points at my hands and down at the red-stained slush at my feet. A feeling of revulsion fills me. *Did this asshole send us a dead animal to scare us? Fuck, what is wrong with people?* I place the box back down on the table and rip it open, fully prepared to march down to his house with whatever dead animal is in there, and shove it down his unstable and vengeful throat. When the package is wide open, bile races up the back of my throat, and I have to lurch to the edge of the patio, to release the meager contents of my stomach. I can hear Daisy's screams, but they seem to be coming through in a fog. My eyes trail back to the destroyed package on the table, and disbelief and fear fill me.

"Is that... what... what I think it... is?" Daisy questions through a sob. I can't take my eyes off the red mess in front of me to stare at her and try to reassure her.

"It's two hands, severed hands. Male... male, if I were to guess." Jesus fuck, someone left severed hands on our back porch for our dog to find.

"Does... does that mean... whoever they... belong to is... dead?" Daisy questions, and she grabs onto my bicep and pulls me closer to her, burrowing her tiny body at my side, as the sound of Toothless's excited pawing at the door is heard.

"I don't know... but I hope not," I exclaim, unsure of what to do. "We have to call the cops."

"Are you nuts, Chris? We can't call the cops. I still have a warrant out for my arrest, for forging bad cheques. They'll take me in." Daisy shrieks, and releases her hold on me. I go to drag my hands down my face in frustration, and realize that they are covered in blood, and Toothless's slobber. "What do you suggest we do with them, Daisy? Someone sent us severed hands, for fuck's sake. That's not sane!"

"I... I don't know... we get rid of them... maybe at the club. I can't go to jail, Chrissy. It's the holidays!" This can't be my life; any moment now, I'm going to wake up, and all of this will be nothing but a bad nightmare. *Please fucking wake up now.* I blink my eyes a couple of times, hoping that the mess will disappear, but unfortunately, this is my reality and not some sick dream.

"Get me a couple garbage bags and the small shovel," I instruct, and Daisy scrambles off to do my bidding. She comes panting back and hands me the bags. *Shit, I forgot to ask her for some gloves, not that I think we even have any.* "Hold the bag open wide." I grab the bloody box and throw it, and its contents, into the black garbage bag, tying it off and putting it in another one. "What are you going to do, Chris?" Daisy questions with a pale face.

"Bury it. What else can we do?" I set to work in my soaked socks, digging a hole into the frigid ground of one of our disheveled flower beds, with the shovel that I swear we must have stolen from a kid. By the time I'm done, I can't feel my fingers or my toes, my chest and face hurt from the cold air, and I'm positive I'm losing my mind.

Why would someone send us two male hands? Who the hell would be deranged enough to do that?

Chapter 12

The Gift

"Seriously, Ron? I'm back on the floor again tonight? You promised me I'd be behind the bar." I scowl with annoyance at the ruddy face of the owner of the strip club. He gives me a lascivious look, from my stupid heels over the barely-there uniform to my breasts, that are hanging on for dear life in this non-existent bra. "You'll make more money on the floor. Didn't you say you needed to earn more over the holidays?"

I roll my eyes, knowing full well I'm getting nowhere with him, and as much as I hate to admit it, he's right. I'll make more money serving the floor, rather than behind the bar tonight. I'll also get hit on and touched a lot more, too. "Just pretend they're ants you can crush under the soles of your shoes, *Sugar*. Grin and bear it, and you'll make double the tips from the bar tonight; it's a full house," Sasha, one of the other servers, whispers to me while grinning at a customer who is blowing her kisses.

I straighten my shoulders, grab my metal tray off the bar, and head towards my assigned area for the night. There's a group of six construction workers, still with their neon safety vests on, being loud and rowdy, and enjoying themselves after a shift. Here's hoping they're generous tippers. "Evening, gentlemen. What can I get ya?" I cock a hip and force myself to smile, while jutting out my precariously strapped tits. Six pairs of eyes immediately center on them, and my skin crawls with the sensation. *Just breathe, you can do this, we need the money.*

"Hey, pretty lady. Aren't you a sight for tired eyes? What's your name?" A dark-haired, older man questions. I force myself to continue smiling, even though I would love nothing more than to roll my eyes and walk away. *Think groceries and rent money, bitch.* "Chrissy," I croak out.

"Chrissy, I think you might be the prettiest girl in this place tonight. Are you dancing too?" One of the others exclaims, his eyes locked in on my breasts, as he runs his tongue over his lips.

Fucking gross. "Nope, just serving. What can I get you all to drink?" They start throwing out their orders, and I make a mental note of them, before heading back to the bar to grab the drinks. Goosebumps rise along my exposed skin, with the feeling of eyes on me. I discreetly look over my shoulder, and catch men from different tables ogling my ass, and have to bite down on my bottom lip to contain the swear words that want to escape. My eyes rise to the center stage, and I watch as Daisy contorts her body around a pole, in nothing but a sparkly red thong, her face entirely at peace as a fucked-up version of *'Oh Holy Night'* plays. I wish I had her confidence and *'give no fucks'* attitude, I'd probably be a happier person. Maybe I should down a shot of tequila; it seems to help her get through the night.

After delivering the drinks to that table and pocketing the tips, I turn around and see a man in a dark coat sitting at one of the smaller tables, farther away from the stage in my area. A kernel of excitement fills me, at the prospect of making enough to completely cover rent tonight. Maybe Sasha is right; picture all of them as something I can crush, and keep going. I make my way over to the table, sashaying my hips and plastering a fake smile on my lips. "Hey, what can I get ya," I question, and the smile falls off my face as I get a good look at who's sitting at the table. *Nic. What. The. Fuck.* Oh my fucking god, this day just keeps throwing me curve balls over and over again.

His gray eyes slide over all my exposed skin, with a nonchalant, unimpressed look, before he returns his glance back up to the stage. "She's really something, ain't she?" He motions with his chin at Daisy, who's now doing the splits in mid-air, and only gripping the pole with one hand. A flare of jealousy accosts me, and I have to tamp it down immediately before I embarrass myself. What do I care if he finds my roommate hot? He doesn't belong to me, even if I saw him first. I remind myself I was a total dick to him the last time I served him, which really he didn't deserve, and he still tipped me well. "Yeah, she's amazing. She used to want to be part of Cirque or something when she was younger. Can I get you a drink?"

My eyes move over his tall frame, taking in his dark hair, five o'clock shadow dipped with silver, and the thick muscles across his chest, in the snug-fitting shirt he's wearing, as he removes his jacket, hangs it off the chair next to him, and sprawls with wide open legs, on the chair that's far too small to accommodate his large frame. Dark, molten silver eyes meet mine, and the corner of his pink lips lifts. "Are you going to spit in it? 'Cause I'd rather you didn't."

Heat rises on my face with embarrassment; *shit,* did he see me spit in his food at the diner? "I'll try not to, no promises though," I reply as my lips twist into a mischievous smirk. He returns to watching my roommate up on stage, his hands folded on the sticky tabletop, and I catch a glimpse of a black tattoo peeking from below the sleeve of his navy shirt. My mouth waters at the thought of more of them across his golden skin. *Get it together, weirdo. He's obviously not interested in you, and has Daisy in his sights.* The thought that he might hit on her, and take her home for the night, has my fingers tightening on the edge of my tray, and the desire to bash it in his face, riling me up. I force myself to take deep, cleansing breaths before I do something guaranteed to get me fired.

"Scotch, neat, no spit, and top shelf." He dismisses me with a raised dark eyebrow, and I find myself stomping away like a petulant child who has had her toy taken away. Honestly, I'm a mess; what the hell is the matter with me? It's not like I want the guy for myself. Out of the corner of my eye, I watch him stand up, walk over to the stage, and throw some bills at Daisy, who is now rolling her hips sensually on the stage. She winks back at him and blows him a kiss, as she shakes her ass in his direction. I've never wanted to murder my friend before, but right now, I do, and that makes me come to a stop. I can't be behaving this way. I need to focus on making enough tips to survive the holidays, and not worry about some random guy, regardless of if the fucker is the hottest male I have ever seen, and I want to climb his tall length like a damn tree.

With my internal pep-talk complete, I return to his table with his scotch, sans spit, and place it in front of him. "That'll be twenty." I wait as he pulls out a fifty from his wallet and hands it to me. "Keep the change."

I pocket it quickly, and move on to the next patron trying to get my attention. Soon, I'm running back and forth to the bar, as the club fills up to capacity with men out celebrating the holidays. One of the construction workers snakes his arm around my waist as I'm going by, and tries to pull me into his lap, but I manage to dodge the hold without breaking his jaw. I roll my eyes at his flirty words, promising me a huge tip if I sit on his lap, and elbow him in the chest. My phone vibrates in the pocket of my tiny uniform shorts, and I pull it out to take a look. It's another text message from an unknown number.

Sweet little temptation, you always look good enough to eat, and I'm positively starving for a taste of you. How about you let me take a bite?

My eyes scan the crowd of men around me, to see if I can spot anyone with their phones out or looking in my direction. This is getting creepier and creepier. The crowd is too thick, and numerous people are holding phones and recording the stage, even though that's clearly not allowed here. I quickly reply, block the number, and shove the phone back into my shorts, ignoring whoever this stalker wannabe is.

How about I take a blade to your eye socket if you try? Stop fucking messaging me, psycho.

After a while, I head back to Nic's table, and find one of the blonde strippers sitting across from him in an absurd snowman costume. *Who the fuck picks this shit?* Her tits look like two snowballs about to explode from the fabric, a sparkly carrot is imprinted on her crotch, and she has a mini black top hat strapped to her hair. I observe as she unabashedly flirts with him, and I release a relieved breath, realizing that it isn't Daisy. "Hey, doll, can you get me a shot of tequila on his tab?" Terri smirks and winks in my direction. I'm sure she thinks she's found her meal ticket for the night, but the look of boredom on Nic's face indicates her assumption is wrong. I don't want to look too closely at why that makes me unreasonably happy. I wait for a nod, and his motion to bring two of them, before heading to grab them. When I return, he gives me another fifty dollar bill and takes the shot with Terri, who's now made her way to perch on his knee.

Well, shit, I guess I was wrong. He doesn't seem to be minding her attention after all. "Hey, Chrissy, table four needs another round," Sasha calls, as she stops next to me and admires the sight before her with a sigh. "Word of advice, girlie. Stay far away from the ones that are destined to hurt you." She juts out her chin in Nic's direction before moving away. I take her words to heart and go about my business, serving the rest of my customers, and ignoring what's happening at Nic's table. Obviously, he has a thing for blondes, and right now, I'm kind of glad I'm not one.

I'm taking a quick break at the side of the bar, trying to stretch my tired legs and get blood flowing into my aching toes. I do a quick search of my area, releasing a groan at how busy it still is. Nic's table is now vacant, the empty glasses left abandoned, and no sight of Terri either. I wonder if she took him to the back area for a private lap dance, or something else. Disappointment and misery war within me, and irritate me because I should know better than to think any guy would choose me over someone sexier, and willing to give it up. Has my nightmarish past not taught me anything? I am never any man's first choice.

A thought pops into my head and has me instantly stilling. How come Nic didn't seem surprised to see me working here? Nothing from his demeanor, or the way he interacted with me, gave me reason to believe that he was surprised to see the waitress from the diner also at a strip club ten blocks away. "Hey, Chrissy, the guy from table two said to give this to you before he took off." Sasha hands me two hundred dollars and gives me a radiant smile. "Guess he was a big spender. Congrats, girlie."

I pocket the money, even more confused, and put the mystery of why Nic wasn't surprised to see me here on the back burner. All the money I've already earned tonight guarantees I have at least my portion of the rent now. Anything I make from this point forward will go towards groceries, so at least Daisy, Toothless, and I will have food for the holidays. "Hey, Sasha, did he leave with Terri?" I hate the vulnerable tone in my voice, as I bite the inside of my cheek and avoid her eye contact.

"Naw, she's next up on the stage, he left alone." *He left alone.* That shouldn't please me the way it does, but I can't help it. He wasn't interested in Terri, and he left me a huge tip. Who is this guy?

Chapter 13

Santa

Breathe. We can't be killing anyone here tonight; too many people witnessed us inside the strip club, including Chrissy. I try to talk myself down from my murderous rage, after watching men stare at *my little temptation* with lust all night. The fucker who tried to force her into his lap is lucky I didn't decapitate him, right there in the middle of the packed club. My restraint held on by the thinnest thread, as I watched her deal with him and continue to force the smile she was wearing all night. *Oh, my pretty girl, how I long to take you and make you only mine.*

The only thing that brought me even the slightest hint of pleasure, other than watching her sexy ass sway and her perky tits bounce, was the evidence of her jealousy that she tried so hard to hide, when I complimented her roommate's performance, and when that bleach-blonde bimbo was sitting on my leg. *Which reminds me, I need to burn these pants now.* I honestly thought she might bash her face in, with the tray she was holding so tightly. It seems my girl has a bit of the green monster inside of her. She doesn't need to worry, though; I only have eyes for her now.

I stroll over to the dark green pickup in the lot, my head lowered into the collar of my jacket, and my knit cap pulled low to disguise my features. I check over my shoulder to make sure no one is watching me as I approach the vehicle. I watched, as that douche that wrapped his arm around Chrissy came over, and grabbed his phone from inside of it a while ago. If I can't risk murdering him for daring to touch what's mine, the next best thing is to destroy something he values. I slide the sharp blade out of the sleeve of my jacket and puncture the first tire, then methodically move on to the rest. Once I'm satisfied this asshole won't be going anywhere tonight, I pull out my tools and break into the passenger side of his vehicle, ensuring that I'm staying in the shadows provided by the thick trees that surround the parking lot. I reach into the glove compartment and pull out his registration, taking a picture of his name and address.

Simon Blakely, you've been a real *bad boy*, and are on Santa's naughty list. Forget the lump of coal. You'll be lucky if you're still breathing for the new year. I put everything back and make my way to my vehicle, this time a black pickup truck with fake plates.

As I sit there, defrosting myself with the heat blaring, I go over today's activities. I watched from my home through the hidden cameras, while stroking my hard cock, as my sweet Chrissy found the little present I had left her. She didn't react exactly how I thought she would. I'd expected the police to be all over her door, but my girl surprised me by throwing the severed hands into a garbage bag, and instead spent the next hour digging a hole in the frozen ground with a kiddy beach shovel.

Now, why would she do that? Why wouldn't she have reported it to law enforcement? Only one possible reason comes to mind, and I decide to pull up her roommate's information on my phone, and start a preliminary search on her, checking her background, and whether she has any priors. *Here we go:* Daisy Santos has a warrant out for her arrest for forgery. So my girl was protecting her friend. *Silly girl, doesn't she know that no one else matters but herself?*

A smirk catches my lips as I reread her response to my last text message. She'd like to put a blade through my eye socket; a shiver races through me at the possibility of that type of foreplay. I should give her an actual blade once I take her, and see what she can accomplish with it. I bet she's going to put up a good fight. Lust fills me at the thought of her filled with rage, spitting mad, and covered in blood, as I pound into her ass while I force her to submit to me. My cock stirs in my pants, and I squeeze it, wishing I could pull it out and jerk myself off here.

Just as I'm considering giving in to my needs, my phone pings with the confirmation of my delivery to Chrissy's door. When I was there, I noticed that she barely had any food in the house, just some random cans of beans and carrots, and spoiled milk in the fridge. I know she's tight on money, so I made sure to tip her heavily tonight, and even threw a couple of hundred bills at her roommate. I can't wait to watch her reaction when she pulls up to her house tonight, and sees the various containers filled with groceries that I had sent. Just to make sure nothing gets stolen off her porch in her shitty neighborhood, I paid the delivery guy extra to sit in his car, and babysit the groceries all night. Will she refuse to take them because of her pride, or will the reality of her situation force her hand? My money's on her being spiteful, but caving when hunger sets in.

The things I do for this chick are entirely out of character for me. I reason with myself that it's no fun if she's too weak from hunger to fight back when I finally take her, and I will take her. I've already decided that Chrissy won't be heading home tomorrow after her shift from the club. Instead, she's going to be going away with me for the holidays. Whether she'll be alive at the end of them, is highly unlikely.

My phone buzzes again in my hand, and I release a huge, aggravated sigh. I swear to God, if this fucker has gotten himself in more shit, I'm going to ensure that I'm an only child. "What?" I growl.

"Hello to you too, brother. I was just thinking that I might go back to that diner tomorrow for breakfast. The food was pretty decent, and the staff was great to look at," he laughs, and I hear the sound of quiet murmuring in the background. My eyes check the time on my dashboard: quarter to midnight. He's probably at one of my dad's stupid clubs, helping him wheel and deal donors to the cause of the great Governor of Massachusetts, destined to fuck all your daughters, granddaughters, and maybe your wives too.

"I'll break every bone in your body, Micah, and then I'll cut off your cock, and make you choke on the tiny thing," I sneer, as my hands tighten furiously on the steering wheel, imagining it's my little brother's neck instead.

"So you're calling dibs then?" Micah chortles through the phone, and I immediately want to slam my fist into his stupid face. "We're not ten, Micah; you don't call dibs on a human being. What the fuck is the matter with you? Don't you ever grow up?"

"You're so uptight, Nic. Every once in a while, you should take the massive stick out of your ass. You might even enjoy life a little." The bloody nerve of this asshole, talking to me like that after I spent the night in the morgue, destroying evidence that could have gotten him ten to twenty in the state pen, not to mention my father booted out of office. "We can't all live carefree lives like you, Micah. Some of us have to clean up after the mess others leave behind. Was there a point to this call, or did you just want to ruin what was left of my night, with the sound of your whiny voice?"

"Dad wants to see you first thing in the morning. He says there is something you missed, and he needs it taken care of right away," Micah says, in a bored tone that immediately sends my blood pressure skyrocketing. "I don't miss shit, Micah." I gruff as I place my vehicle in drive and head out of the parking lot, with a smirk in the direction of the pickup with the four slashed tires. Hopefully, the fucker learns to keep his hands to himself, even though a part of me hopes he doesn't learn, so I can come back and gut him.

"Don't know, but he was furious about whatever it is. Might have called you a few choice words. Anyway, the message has been delivered, and my date is waiting to deep-throat my cock. See ya, asshole." The call disconnects, and I'm left with the silence of the truck cab, my mind rapidly going over what my father thinks I might have missed, and the temptation to commit patricide first and foremost on my mind.

Maybe I should kidnap Chrissy tonight and take her out of state. I have more than enough money stashed to live a very comfortable life somewhere else, far away from the constant demands of my father. As I jump on the interstate in the direction of my home, a jarring thought has my breath stalling in my chest, and I almost crash into the vehicle in front of me.

I was thinking about a future with Chrissy, far from Boston and my family, and in that future, she would still be alive and with me. Am I considering not murdering her like the rest of my victims? When did my needs change from ending her pretty life to having her be a part of mine?

Chapter 14

Santa

I watch with humor, through the camera I placed on the porch across the street, as Chrissy throws a fit on her front porch at three in the morning, when she sees the stacked containers filled with food I've left her. The delivery guy peeled out the minute she arrived, before she could question him. *Smart fucker.* Her roommate, Daisy, jumps around like a little kid, opening presents on Christmas day, as she rifles through the various plastic crates, and shoves an apple comically in her mouth. Daisy starts dragging them inside, despite Chrissy yelling at her not to. *Come on, sweet little temptation, take them.* I find myself willing her to give in to my desire to see her not starve. *What the fuck is wrong with me? Where the hell are thoughts like that even coming from?*

After arguing with Daisy for a few moments, and watching their massive hound dance around them, banging into everything like a giant ogre, Chrissy relents, carries the containers into the minuscule kitchen area, and starts investigating what I sent. Most of it is packaged goods; I figured she would trust those more than anything fresh. I observe, with silent judgment, as she opens the pricey container of organic peanut butter, and rather than feed herself, she shoves a spoon inside and lets the demon beast lick at it. I find myself rolling my eyes and chuckling at her antics, despite the late hour, and the annoying frustration that gnaws at me.

I pry my eyes away from the screen that displays all sixteen of the cameras on a grid that I've placed inside their small house. I know it's overkill, but I wanted to make sure I caught every moment of what she was doing. They've become my raunchy reality television, and Chrissy has quickly evolved into more than an obsession for me. I can't seem to focus on anything or anyone else other than her. It didn't help that when I went through her laptop

history, I found a ton of porn sites she had recently visited, plus searches on glory holes. I've spent the last couple of hours retracing her viewing history, and have already jerked off twice.

It seems my little temptation has dark and depraved fantasies, ones I wholeheartedly approve of. Fantasies where she's restrained, gagged, and forced to take cocks in various holes, without the ability to stop anyone from committing any action they desire with her sexy body. I especially enjoyed the videos that featured BDSM, and had the female stretched, gagged, choked, and flogged, awaiting her master's pleasure. The thoughts of doing that to Chrissy, and so much more, run through my mind on a loop, and keep me perpetually hard. Fuck, at this point, my cock is going to be chafed before I even get to be inside of her.

I pull out my burner phone and decide to mess with her before she goes off to sleep. There is something about Chrissy, and her reactions, that elicits a morbid fascination and causes my blood to heat with constant desire, not only for her blood and death at my hands, but for her life. For the way that she gets those little lines between her eyebrows when she focuses, or the tightening of her jaw when she's frustrated. I enjoy watching all her micro-expressions, and I can safely say I've never had that happen with anyone that I've stalked before.

Would you enjoy it if I tied you down, stretched all your limbs, and blindfolded you, while I spent my time filling all your holes with my thick cum? Would you whimper and beg for me, my sweet little temptation?

Would you cum like my own personal slut, while I filled your pretty pussy, and stretched your ass?

She pulls her phone from the pocket of her black oversized sweatpants, and stares at it with surprise. The thought that those pants might have belonged to some asshole she was previously with causes rage to sizzle through me, and the irrational desire to get in my vehicle, drive over there and rip them off her, is almost blinding. My breathing becomes ragged, as I forcefully tighten my hands on the armrests of my gamer chair, until a cracking sound permeates the air. I can feel my nostrils flaring, and one of my eyes is twitching, as my brain provides images of some random cunt touching what's mine, making her moan and beg for his cock. I'll painfully destroy anyone who tries. She's fucking mine now; no one else can have any part of her.

Her deep chocolate eyes narrow, as a frown rises across the perfection of her alabaster skin, and she gives the phone a dirty look, her beautiful face contorting with fury and disgust. Her expression is so comical it causes my lips to quirk up. I want to commit such dark, perverse, and unspeakable acts on her. I want to listen to her scream and plead with me for mercy. I covet her eyes, meeting mine, and knowing that I hold her death and her life in the palms of my hands, and which one I choose is utterly dependent on how she pleases me. My breath stills in my chest as I wait for her to respond to me, but instead, she slips the phone back into her pants and ignores my message.

NO! That just won't do. I spring up from my chair before I can stop myself, and start throwing clothes on. The feeling of raw, sharp anger springs through me, rising like a hurricane attempting to make landfall, one that is prepared to destroy everything in its path. I know my reaction is unjustified and unreasonable, but I can't seem to reel myself in. A part of me wishes I could see inside her mind, to the truths and lies she tells herself. Does she think that I'm some prankster sending her messages, rather than the dangerous predator that I am? *Time to change that.*

My little temptation needs an early morning visit from me, and she's going to get one. I head towards where I have my tranquilizer gun stored, knowing full well I will have to incapacitate that giant furball, before I can have my wicked way with her, and I have limited time before the sun rises. On second thought, I should also tranq her roommate. I wouldn't want her walking in on my fun and calling the cops or, worse, shoving something as mundane as a kitchen knife in my flesh.

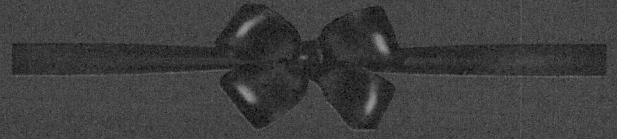

I quickly tweak the lock on their back door with my kit, my motions quiet, practiced, and careful, despite the thundering of my heart in my chest, and the sound of my blood whooshing in my ears. I raise the tranq gun and hold it steady, as I make my way inside their small kitchen area, prepared to take down Toothless when he undoubtedly comes charging at me. I don't have long to wait, as I hear the sound of paws and scratching nails against the ceramic tile. A low, deep growl rents the air, and I don't hesitate to fire, as I meet his amber-glowing eyes. The little whimper he releases, as the tranq dart imbeds in his fur, almost has a foreign emotion that suspiciously feels like remorse rising. I shake it off; there is no room inside of me for any of that.

I survey as he goes down to a sitting position, a snarl still across his black lips and his sharp, vicious teeth on display, ready to rip me to pieces if only given a chance. *Come on, asshole, go to sleep.* After another few seconds, he's down on his side, his large pink tongue hanging outside of his mouth, and snores escaping his nose. *That's it, buddy, night night.*

I release a relieved breath behind the dark mask covering my face. *One down, two to go.* Before I left my home, I made the decision that I would incapacitate Chrissy too, but not entirely. Just enough that she thinks she's in a hedonistic dream. I want her to be aware someone is with her, and I plan to leave her with evidence of my visit. A ghost of a smile spreads across my disguised face, at the thought of her waking up covered in my cum and not comprehending where it came from, or better yet, feeling sore 'cause I fucked her pussy raw while she was slumbering. My cock twitches inside my black cargo pants with the possibilities of what I will do to her.

I make my way silently down the hallway to her roommate's room, and notice the door is ajar a crack. I push it wider, and get a glimpse of Daisy in just a pair of neon green panties, spread eagle across her rumpled bed, face down and snoring louder than the hellhound I left passed out in the kitchen. I pull out a syringe filled with a sedative and stalk forward, until I am right beside her while she's utterly unaware. The state of her vulnerability should call to the monster that lives inside of me, that craves death and destruction, but nothing about this woman moves me in the slightest. She's just a pretty body waiting to die, and unless she gets in my way, I won't be the one to take her life. I plunge the sedative into the exposed vein on the side of her neck, and she twitches for a mere second then continues snoring.

Now, off to enjoy my time with my sweet little temptation. I remove the syringe, with a mixture of a paralytic drug, and a light sedative I plan to dose Chrissy with, out of my back pocket. I don't want her to be able to fight me off, but I do want her to be semi-conscious, and partially aware that someone is with her. Not just someone, the monster stalking her. The one she so carelessly dismissed earlier, that has deemed her his prey.

Adrenaline pours through my veins, heightening my senses as I approach her door. The dog must have pushed it wide open, as he left to investigate who was in the house. I get my first live glimpse of my girl in her own surroundings, as she sleeps curled up and wrapped in her comforter on her bed, oblivious to how much danger she is truly in. A hint of moonlight breaks through the broken blinds, and makes parts of her auburn hair glow in the dim light. She's stunning, and resembles something otherworldly. My own personal goddess, ready for me to prostrate myself at her altar, like the deviant sinner that I am.

I approach the bed, unable to take my eyes off her, as an intense hunger fills every part of me and demands that I take my fill of her. She whines in her sleep, her head moving side to side across her pillow, and a look of distress mars her stunning features. *What does she dream of? Who is causing her distress in her dream state?* An unquenchable need ascends within me, to fight off the demons that plague her, even though I know I'm about to become one.

I lean forward, inhaling deeply of her floral, soft, and resplendent scent. *Mine.* My fingers itch to feel the softness of her hair, and the delicateness of her skin. They want to grasp her, and tighten, until every single digit is imprinted along the surface, so that she wears me like a second skin. So that anyone who dares glance her way knows immediately who she belongs to. *My pretty, sweet little temptation.*

I blow warm air towards her face, and she burrows her chin further into her covers, like a child trying to hide from the boogeyman under her bed. Too bad that there is no escaping me, and I am much worse than anything she's ever feared. I hold the syringe in my hand and thrust forward, grabbing a fistful of her hair as I plunge it into her neck. She wakes with a start, a scream on her lips, and her chocolate eyes wide with terror, as her body attempts to thrash off the covers. I witness the moment when she gets a terrified glance at me in my all-black attire, with the skull mask hiding all of my features, excluding my eyes, which I've donned black contacts to disguise. I know that I resemble a fearsome demon right now. As much as I want her to realize that it's me, it's too soon. When she finally does put the pieces together, I want the two of us to be secluded, and far away from anyone who could rescue her from my grasp.

"Hello, *sweet little temptation.* Are you happy to see me?"

Chapter 15

Santa

Her scream gets choked in her throat, the rich, gasping sound of her terror forcing a husky groan to leave my lips. I hold her firmly in my grip, as her limbs try to shake free of the comforter to liberate herself from my grasp, but it's no use. I witness the moment the drug cocktail begins to take effect, leaving her weak, and her body languid for my use. Her lips go motionless, a frozen look of terror across her features, but her eyes, those pretty pools of dark, rich chocolate, they continue to stare into mine with a heady alarm. My blood rushes in my veins at a galloping speed just gazing at her. My perfect sweet temptation is now mine to do with as I please, and no one can stop me, not her, her atrocious beast, or her roommate; she is utterly at my mercy.

I release my grip on her hair, her head falling back against the rumpled pillow, as I allow my fingers to stroke over her forehead, and trace the arch of her brow. I slide my finger down the bridge of her nose, skimming over her high cheekbones and freckles, until I reach the destination of her pouty mouth. I slip my forefinger inside her parted lips, into the warm, wet heat of her mouth, coating it on her tongue and wishing desperately that it was my cock. "So pretty and yet so very fragile. With one snap of my hands, I could end your short life, *sweet little temptation*," I growl, leaning forward until my face is mere centimeters away from hers, and I can look deep into the irises of her panicked eyes. I pull back my finger, tracing the wetness across her plump lips, before moving it down to her jaw and then her throat. My fingers strum against the delicate flesh as if I were playing a guitar, and she was my desired instrument.

Even in the dim light provided by the waning moon, I can see how rapidly her pulse beats in her neck, and it calls to me to make it race even quicker. I want her so frightened that she will give me all of herself when the time comes. I am the hungry wolf who has come knocking at her door, and she is the foolish red riding hood that didn't do enough to stop me, filled with the utter falsity of her safety.

No doors or windows can prevent me from getting to her; she can run and even attempt to hide, but I will always find her. My fingers tighten on her neck, causing the sound of her breathing to become ragged and tense. Tears slide from those all-too-often defiant eyes, and skate down her creamy skin until they disappear, much like my sanity. "I know what you crave in the dark, when you think you're alone." I tighten my grip until I'm sure no air is making its way inside her lungs, and her face starts to turn an attractive shade of red. "I know you want to be ravished and used, to have all of your choices taken away from you. You want to be my pet, and my slut; well, here I am, ready to grant you your wish, my beauty."

I release my hold, and air screeches back inside her lungs, her chest rising and falling rapidly, the only movement the cocktail will allow her. My hand continues on its path, making its way above her t-shirt, down the valley between her breasts. I push back the comforter, revealing every inch of her to my waiting eyes, and I'm not disappointed. The sleep shirt has ridden up and is pooled on her stomach, leaving her pelvis, panty-covered pussy, and legs bare. I slide the palm of my hand over the dark cotton panties she's wearing, using the meaty part of my palm to apply pressure to her clit, while my other hand forces her legs further apart. My fingers long to slip deep inside of her cunt, but I hesitate, allowing the fear and tension to build between us. I stroke her above her panties with my fingers, pushing the thin fabric between her pussy lips, and using my thumb to rub circles across her needy clit. I can feel the material dampening, and the heat coming off her body in waves.

My little temptation is terrified, but she's also turned on. My other hand pushes the shirt above her breasts, and it pools around her neck. The need to suck on her perky, pink nipples tears through me, and I can't bear to deny myself a taste of every part of her. I grab the shirt and drape it over her face, using the fabric as a barrier between us, so that I can lift my mask to my forehead and take her stiffened tip into my mouth. My tongue laves at the surface, and her skin pebbles. I pull my mouth away, sucking in some of the soft flesh of her globe before biting down on the surface, and repeating the action on the other breast, so that she'll have matching imprints of my teeth, before returning to sucking each of her nipples hard, and scraping my teeth along their engorged tips. Each movement causes her chest to rise in a frantic tempo, and I can see she's struggling to breathe. Death is beautiful, but so is passion, but a mix of both, that's my fucking drug of choice, and I'm a willing addict.

My hand glides down her abdomen and below the edge of her panties, until my fingers are touching her silky skin, and rubbing against the trimmed pussy hair above her mound. *Fuck*, I need to see how pretty her cunt is, and get a taste of her core. I force myself away from her breast, and use both my hands to grip the panties on either side of her hips, slowly pushing them to slide down her legs, until the panties puddle at one of her trim ankles. She looks like a sex doll, all pliable and ready for me to do with what I want. My own personal doll, that I can fill with cum, and rip apart, only to put her back together again.

I pull out a small switchblade from my pocket, and graze the sharp knife along the surface of her upper thighs, careful not to give her anything more than a few shallow cuts, at least for now. I don't want her to bleed out here, only where I can bathe in her blood. "You're so pretty, my sweet slut; your skin is so soft and perfect for my blade." I trail the handle of the blade between her slick pussy lips, coating it in her essence, before slipping the handle into my mouth and getting my first taste of her. Her sweet and musky flavor explodes in my mouth, overwhelming my taste buds, and causing a growl to rise from my throat. "Fuck, you're *delicious*."

I discard the blade next to her on the bed, as I lean forwards and slip my tongue along the surface of her flesh, licking one pussy lip, and then the other, before my fingers spread her open for me so that I can feast. My tongue snakes out, licking at her clit, and then down to her entrance before I thrust it inside of her. I fuck her with my tongue, pushing as far as I can inside of her tight, warm heat while my thumb strokes her hard, little nub in time with my thrusts. I pull away from her cunt with a moan, and sink my hands below her thick asscheeks, until I can tilt her pelvis upwards so I can reach every part of her, as my tongue licks and sucks her from her clit down to her puckered hole. A gargled noise escapes her, and brings a vicious smile to my lips. She's enjoying my touch and the way I'm eating her cunt. I wonder what sweet noises she would make if I stabbed her with my blade, while I shoved my cock down her throat. Fuck, that sounds like heaven.

My fingers spread her cheeks open, allowing me to thrust my tongue inside of her asshole, and I simultaneously plunge my middle finger inside her pussy. Her core grips my digit as her asshole tightens around my tongue. Her heady taste fills my mouth, and her smell drives my nose crazy. The feel of her soft skin under my grasp overstimulates me, until my cock is dripping steady drops of precum inside the constraint of my pants. I switch my hold, pulling my finger from inside of her pussy and plunging two inside of her ass, as my tongue thrusts in and out of her cunt with abandonment. I can't get enough, she's the sweetest dessert I've ever consumed.

Her whole body tightens, the muscles in her core compressing and bearing down on my fingers and tongue, as a gush of her cum fills my mouth and soaks the bed below her. Her breathing is harsh to my ears, and the sound promises me fond memories of tonight. The first of many nights I will have her to myself. I withdraw my fingers from her ass and pull back, pushing my mask back down over my face. The smell and taste of her pussy instantly covers the interior of the mask, and quickly becomes my favorite scent. I rise so that I can stare at her expression, forcing her shirt back down on her chest, as I push the fingers that were inside of her ass into her mouth, and coat her tongue in her taste. "My *little temptation*, you cum so beautifully. Taste yourself, taste how fucking amazing your sexy ass is. I can't wait until you take my cock inside that tight hole." I force my fingers to the back of her throat until she makes a choking sound, and I pull back as saliva coats her mouth and chin, and more tears slide from her pretty eyes. "We'll have to work on training your throat; my cock is substantially larger than my fingers, and you will have to take me down your tight throat, my beauty."

I get a glimpse of the fading darkness through her broken blinds. I'm rapidly running out of night, and I hate that my time with her will be so short, but in just a few hours, if everything goes according to plan, I will have her forever. My personal sex slave, to do what I wish, when I wish. When I get tired of her, I'll just dispose of her like I have all the others. A part of my mind calls me a liar. There is something different about Chrissy; she's not, and will never be, like the others. The thought of not having her makes my stomach clench, and a bout of nausea rise, but I push all of those thoughts down.

I stand up, unbuttoning my pants and pulling down my zipper, as her eyes dart to the side to watch me pull out my cock. I wonder how terrified she is right now. I have a feeling that if she wasn't sedated, she would be fighting me with everything she has, and I would be immensely enjoying her bloodying me. "I have no way of tying you down on this shitty bed that doesn't even have a headboard, so this was the closest I could come to fulfilling your fantasy for the moment, my *sweet little temptation*, but soon I'll give you everything you dream about." My cock bobs in front of me, long, thick, and painfully engorged, despite how many times I've already fucked my hand to thoughts of her tonight. "You want to be ravished, used, and taken against your will; that's what you dream about. Those are the thoughts you fuck your fingers and your dildo to, right here in this bed, isn't that right?"

I reach over, slide open her bedside drawer, and pull out the large, bright pink rabbit vibrator she has. I hit the button, and the mechanical vibrations are the only other sound in the room besides our breathing. "As much as I want inside of you, my pretty girl, this will have to do for now. When I have you, and I will have you, Chrissy, I want to spend hours buried deep inside of you, and take my time stretching all your holes while you scream for me."

My hand with the vibrator moves over her breasts, then down her stomach, until I press it against her clit. I use her wetness to lube the rounded end before thrusting it inside her tight hole, ensuring the protruding part sits snugly against her nub. Once I have it buried as far as it will go, I release my hold, forcing her legs to close tightly and then flip her over, until her asscheeks are meeting my hungry eyes. I force my eyes away from her creamy flesh and glance at her face, adjusting her so that she can still breathe, and her hair isn't blocking her view. I climb up on the bed, the light catching the glint of metal on my Jacob's ladder as I straddle the back of her legs, adding weight down on top of her, as the vibrator forces her body to endure the pleasure, and the torture, all at once.

My eyes catch sight of the abandoned blade, and a smirk lifts the corners of my mouth. I wrap my fingers around the handle, that is covered in her scent, and trail the blade down one asscheek and then the other, leaving behind the presence of shallow cuts, and beads of crimson in my wake. Her blood is stunning, as it runs in tiny rivulets down the round globes of her cheeks, and paints a macabre abstract painting along her skin, only to meet her light sheets. "Soon, my sweet, I will carve my name into your flesh as a reminder to you, and anyone who dares look at you, exactly who you belong to. You want that, don't you, my naughty girl? You want to belong to me." The lack of an answer frustrates me; I want to hear her voice pleading with me. I want to hear the timber of terror in her screams.

 I drop the blade at her side, as my hand raises the mask just enough that my mouth is uncovered as my hands grip her asscheeks, pulling them apart, and I hawk up some spit and let it fall into her crack. I do it again, observing as it slides over her puckered hole, and pools where her pussy meets the dildo. I slip my cock between her asscheeks and clench them firmly together, so they encase my hard dick in their heat. I start thrusting, dragging my throbbing cock back and forth, through the tight channel I've made of her globes, and begin a punishing rhythm, all while digging my fingers into her ass, and the fresh cuts I made, to leave my fingerprints behind on her flesh. "One day soon, I'll fuck this tight ass, my sweet, and bury my cock deep inside of you."

 My breathing picks up with my momentum, pants and growls leaving my lips, as the shitty mattress bounces with our combined movement, and the sensation of the vibrator adds another element to how good she feels. I feel my balls tightening and electricity rising up my spine with a zing. I push my upper body against her back, crushing her into the mattress and breathing down her neck. Her mouth is open as if she's just dying to scream, but nothing but silence greets me. Pity, I bet she sounds lovely when she does.

 I watch as all the emotions and sensations overload her system; her eyes widen as her body convulses, and her eyelids flutter, those gorgeous, thick lashes shutting away the windows to her soul. The one I crave to own just as much as I do her body. With a subtle wheeze, her eyes roll back completely, and finally, she succumbs to all the overwhelming emotions. Her body goes deathly still, but I know she can still hear me and see me. It's a gift she's giving me, allowing me to watch as her body betrays her.

As my fingers, cock, and mouth wrench pleasure after pleasure from her without her permission.

Her large brown eyes reopen, and are filled with a mixture of fear and desire; her nose flares, and I feel her body tighten again as she once again orgasms, this time due to the toy deep inside of her. With a grunt and a final thrust, I explode, ropes of cum painting her lower back, and my stomach, and pressing the hot, sticky mixture into both of our skins. "Fuck, I can't wait to do that inside of you, pretty girl," I rasp into the side of her face, my tongue licking a line from her neck to her ear, before I bite down on her lobe.

I pull back, not bothering to clean any of the mess off of me, before I tuck myself away inside my pants. My eyes survey my work of her lower back, and a grin breaks across my lips. She looks beautiful, lying there used, filthy with my cum, and her blood, and sated. I push my mask back over my chin, and bend down on the side of the bed, until we are once again face to face. "I know what you're thinking, *sweet temptation*. You believe the minute this wears off that you'll go to the cops and report me, but here's the thing, pretty girl, you won't. We both know that you enjoyed that. That it's what you want, deep inside in the secret places you hide from the rest of the world, because you fear others will judge you, if they only knew how depraved you are."

I allow my fingers to slide through the silky strands of her hair. "I will never judge you for any of those needs, my sweet. You belong to me now, and I protect what is *mine*. You can't escape me, Chrissy, and if you try, I will murder your friend Daisy, and anyone else you care about, including that fucking beast, Toothless." I lean forward, pressing my masked forehead against hers, our eyes close together, until I can clearly see all of the amber flecks reflected back at me. "I will never let you go, and you won't want me to, soon enough. I am what your heart desires, the monster you call out to, and beg to come and save you. I am as much a part of you as you are of me."

I stand up and pull the comforter back over her mostly undressed body, leaving the vibrator still deep inside of her. I wonder how many more times she'll cum before it finally runs out of juice. With a final stroke to her hair, I turn and leave the same way I came in. The beast's ears twitch as I walk by, and for a moment, I consider just slicing its belly wide open and allowing it to bleed all over the floor, so I don't have to deal with him stopping me from getting to Chrissy again. In a moment of clarity, I realize that it would cause her pain and distress. She loves and treats the massive lump of drool like one is supposed to a child. Can I do that to her, and would she forgive me?

The unusual thought has me stilling at the back door, I've never cared about anyone's feelings before, not even my brother's, and he's the only person I allow close to me. What the fuck is happening to me? Am I genuinely losing my mind over this girl? Maybe I should have just killed her tonight; no good can come from feeling any emotions for her.

I let myself out of the house, ensuring to relock the door, and make my way silently under the quickly disappearing darkness of night, that is ready to welcome the morning light, to my car, all the while pondering this new change in me. One thing is for sure, I don't fucking like it.

Chapter 16

The Gift

I feel Toothless' wet tongue against my still face, and it has me swatting at him from below the cumbersome covers, as he whines loudly to be let out to pee. For a moment, I freeze, a thought entering my mind like a lightning bolt. I can move; nothing is restraining me. I wiggle my toes and rotate my ankles, all of them moving in time with my mind's command.

Was it all a nightmare? Did any of that truly happen? It's not possible. I'm just slowly losing my mind. I blame all the hours I've been working, and all the stress of constantly trying to figure out how I am going to survive. I push my hair away from my face and rub my tired eyes. I feel like I've been up all night, and the horrifying dream I had didn't help. *Jesus fuck, get it together, Chrissy! We have to be up soon and at the diner shortly.*

I shift my body, a feeling of soreness, and fullness, in my core causing a gasp to vacate my lips. *Did I masturbate in my inebriated state last night?* The sound must frighten Toothless, because the fearsome giant hound slides back and barks at me, as if I might be a threat to him. I'm just about to force my body out of bed when something shiny catches the corner of my eye, and has all the breath stalling inside of my chest. *What the fuck is that? Is that a blade?* Panic settles inside of me and has me darting from the bed with a screech, and when I do, my pink vibrator drops from between my legs to my bedroom floor with a heavy thud. Toothless darts forward towards it, and I have to dive for the bloody thing to keep him away from it, and from thinking it's something he can chew on. "No, Toothless, *yuck*. Don't lick that!"

I grab the warm vibrator and stare at it, with not only awe, but foreboding. All of that was real; everything that happened to me last night actually really occurred? I thought I was tripping on Daisy's weed, and the half a bottle of wine from the anonymous crates I guzzled before I went to bed. I search through my room, racing to the window and yanking up the old blinds to check the window. The glaring sunlight hurts my eyes, and I squint at the frame that is firmly shut. I spin around, pulling back the comforter, and stare at the stain on my sheets, realizing parts of it are still damp. My legs tremble, and threaten to have me collapsing to my bedroom floor, as I grasp onto my dresser for support, and get entangled in all the clothes I have haphazardly everywhere.

"No, no, no, no, this can't be happening," I whisper, as my hands shake with the forgotten vibrator still clutched tightly in my grip.

Toothless' barking and whining pulls me from my disbelieving thoughts. I drop the vibrator back on my bed as if the pink phallus burnt me, and race across the room, needing to get far away from the space where something unquestionable, and inconceivable, happened to me last night. Is it possible I hallucinated the whole thing, or did it all to myself? I've been watching too much unhinged porn. How do I explain the blade though? As I race from the room, cold sweat erupts all over my body, and my ass stings. I come to a thundering halt in the hallway, and lift the back of my nightshirt and get a glimpse of my ass, covered in small cuts, and dried blood. *Jesus fuck, not a dream.* There is no way I did that to myself.

I don't have time to think clearly. I can hear Toothless barking at the back door, demanding to be let outside. As I cross to head into the kitchen, I almost collide with a half-asleep Daisy, coming out of the bathroom in nothing but a pair of green panties. "Daisy, fuck, put some damn clothes on, before one of the neighbors gets a glimpse of you through the windows."

"Ugh, they're just titties, Chris. No big deal, and if they want a closer look, they can come check me out any night of the week at the club," she yawns and pushes past me to the fridge.

I roll my eyes at her antics and release a frantic Toothless into the yard, before he leaves a puddle on our kitchen floor, or breaks through the door. "Did you hear any noises last night? Anything suspicious happen in the middle of the night?" I bite my bottom lip, fear racing through my veins as I wait for her to respond, and shuffle side to side uncomfortably as my sore core clenches, and my full bladder demands relief. Surely, if all of that happened, she would have heard something, right? What about

Toothless? If a strange man had broken into our home and came to accost me, there is no way that he wouldn't have attacked him. He's completely loyal, and protective of both Daisy and me.

"Girl, I have never had a better night's sleep. I slept like a damn log." She pulls our newly gifted eggs and bread out of the fridge, and gets to work on making breakfast. I begin to really consider that I have lost my ever-loving mind until she goes to pull her hair up into a messy bun, and I get a glimpse of her neck. There's a small bruise forming right where her pulse throbs, and I shift forward, grab her jaw and force her to tilt her head to the side, so I can get a better look, as she releases a surprised gasp. In the bright daylight streaming through the window, I can see a faint prick mark right in the center of the bruise. Shit, someone drugged her, probably the same asshole that drugged me. Did he touch her too? How did he get past Toothless? Did he drug my dog too? Oh my God, what kind of psycho drugs a dog? Somehow, the thought of him drugging Toothless enrages me more than him doing it to me or Daisy.

"I'm going to ask you something messed up right now, and I know I'm about to sound like I have lost my damn mind, but I need you to answer me truthfully. *Please*, Daisy, it's important."

"Shit, girl, you are scaring me. What the hell is going on?" Her blue eyes stare into mine with concern, the food forgotten, as I contemplate how to phrase what I need to ask her without sounding like a complete basket case.

"Did you wake up feeling like someone had touched you, especially your vagina? Was anything inside of you when you got up this morning?" I raise my hand at her look of stupefaction. "I know I sound insane right now, but I'm positive someone was in our house last night and drugged us. I... I woke up with my dildo inside of me, and I wasn't the one to put it in there. Plus, I have cuts on my ass, and a blade was on the bed next to me. I didn't cut myself, Daisy."

She blinks a couple of times, like she's not quite seeing me, or able to process the unhinged words leaving my lips. Her mouth opens and closes, then opens again. "How much of my weed did you smoke last night? Girl, I think you went on a bad trip. I'm going to kill Tyler if he laced that shit with something."

Frustration courses through me, and battles with the fear that is snaking up each of my limbs. She doesn't believe me, but I know I'm not wrong about this. Someone was here last night; they did something to me to ensure I couldn't move, couldn't fight them off, and used me for their pleasure. Maybe it's best if she doesn't remember; what if he hurt her too? I shrug my shoulder and step away from her. "Yeah, maybe it was the weed or the wine. I must be trippin'." I go to open the door for Toothless, and an image of black eyes and a skull mask enters my mind. It's so vivid and realistic that it has my breath catching, causing me to choke, and forcing me into a coughing fit.

I force myself to make coffee, and all the while, images from last night race through my mind. I relive every moment, every touch, every depraved word that he uttered to me, as if it was happening in technicolor in my mind. It plays out like some fucked up porn movie that I starred unwittingly in. All the while, this psychotic asshole played with my mind, and my body, and made me orgasm again and again under his ministrations. Just as I'm about to argue with Daisy, taking back my words about the drugs, and instead insist that we both head to the hospital to get tested, or file a police report, his words come back to me.

"I know what you're thinking, sweet temptation. You believe the minute this wears off that you'll go to the cops and report me, but here's the thing, pretty girl, you won't. We both know that you enjoyed that. That it's what you want, deep inside in the secret places you hide from the rest of the world, because you fear others will judge you, if they only knew how depraved you are."

I can feel the ghost-like sensation of his cum on my lower back, the warm stickiness, coupled with the harsh stinging from the combination of his sweat and mine, on my ass against the cuts he made with his blade. The same blade that is still in my room. The sensation of his thick, long fingers stroking my hair as his intense black eyes, and the frightening skull mask, stare back at me as I lay there, unable to move or speak. My core clenches again, and I feel wetness dripping out of me. *What the hell is wrong with me?*

"I will never judge you for any of those needs, my sweet temptation. You belong to me now, and I protect what is mine. You can't escape me, Chrissy, and if you try, I will murder your friend Daisy, and anyone else you care about, including that fucking beast, Toothless."

Oh my God, he threatened to murder Daisy and Toothless. This psychopath believes I belong to him. What the hell am I going to do? I have no idea who this could be. He could be anyone, and we are all in danger.

"I will never let you go, and you won't want me to, soon enough. I am what your heart desires, the monster you call out to, and beg to come and save you. I am as much a part of you as you are of me."

His final words have my legs finally caving, and I have to grip the rickety kitchen table to prevent myself from falling to the ground. Toothless comes over and licks at my hand, a whine leaving his lips as he senses my distressed state. Daisy looks over at me with concern and brings me a glass of water. She thinks I'm still on a bad trip; she doesn't realize how close we both came to dying last night in our beds. What's to stop him from doing it again tonight?

What's to stop him from fucking me and carving me into little pieces? A part of me wants to run screaming from this house with Daisy and Toothless. The need to run is visceral, but so is the dark desire that is pooling in my stomach, and running through my veins. His words keep replaying over and over in my head.

"I am what your heart desires, the monster you call out to and beg to come and save you. I am as much a part of you as you are of me."

Is it possible that he's right? I do have a bunch of dark and depraved fantasies, ones I hide from everyone but myself. Did I summon this man into my life with all my dark cravings? Is it possible that he's just living out the fabrications my perverse mind has conjured up? Do I really want to stop him from coming back?

All these thoughts race through my mind as I try to reassure Daisy that I'm fine, and as I get ready for my shift at the diner. Only one thought keeps relentlessly circling through my mind: Do I know him? My mystery man, who went to extremes last night to recreate one of my recurring fantasies. The mask he wore ensured that he could be anyone, and I wouldn't be able to tell if he was right next to me in public.

This can't be a stranger; it has to be someone I know. Someone with intimate knowledge about my darkest desires, the question is who?

Chapter 17

The Gift

My head is a muddled mess as I walk down the street towards the diner. I'm replaying every action and word that I heard last night. All of it now seems so fresh in my mind, as if a door has been ripped open, leaving me standing in horror in the aftermath. I burrow further into my coat, both from the frigid weather around me, and from the chill that has overtaken my bones, at the thought of enjoying a masked madman using me, and leaving me covered in his cum and my blood.

My phone vibrates in my jacket, and I pull it out, expecting a message from Dolores from the diner, as I'm already late for my shift. What I see has me stopping dead in my tracks. The person behind me slams into me and swears at me, before moving swiftly around me. I don't dare take my eyes off the screen though.

You tasted delicious this morning; I can't wait to taste you again, my little temptation.

What. The. Fuck. I'm so distracted that I don't realize I've stopped in the middle of an intersection, until the blaring of car horns, and the yells of drivers, snap me out of my state. My startled eyes rise with panic as I rush to make it onto the curb, before someone runs me over. My eyes search out every male pedestrian to see if anyone is watching me, but everyone is going about their lives, and some of them are giving my crazy ass a wide berth. As I keep walking, dread rises in the pit of my stomach; what if this asshole means to murder me or, worse, hold me hostage as some sort of sex slave?

My eyes dart to every parked car, scouring for anyone that could be sitting there, laying in wait to shove me inside a vehicle, and take me away. By the time I manage to make it to the diner's front door, I'm a shaking mess filled with chaotic thoughts. My breathing is exiting me in labored pants, and I'm no longer cold, but a sweaty mess under my jacket, and the desire to crawl right out of my skin is overwhelming me. *Get it together, Chrissy. This fucker is a creep.* I pull out my phone and decide to message him back.

Listen, sicko, you come near me again, and I'll rip your balls off, and feed them to you.

I rip open the door of the diner with more force than necessary and stomp inside, a furious scowl across my face. I refuse to allow this psycho to intimidate me. All my life, people have tried to scare me, to force me to cower before them, and every single time I've fought back, so now won't be any different. I refuse to play the victim, or be the prey this jackass seems to think that I am.

My eyes meet an aggravated Dolores, who rolls her eyes at me from behind the counter, as she pours coffee for one of our regulars, Chuck. I start stripping off my jacket, knowing she's going to chew me out for leaving her to handle all the patrons alone. *I've got bigger problems than serving coffee to the masses, Dolores, like someone has their unhinged sights set on me.* I quickly scan how many tables are occupied, and my eyes land on a large figure wearing dark clothing, sitting in a booth in my usual section. Seeing him there causes me to stall mid-motion in removing my jacket, and I feel my jaw dropping. *Nic.*

What the hell are the odds this asshole is back again? My breath attempts to choke me, and I break out into a fit of rancorous coughing, that has various patrons staring at me with horror, but he never even looks my way. He's so engrossed in whatever he's looking at on his laptop that I bet if a bomb went off, it wouldn't even faze him. "Missy, you gonna work today, or just stand there and look pretty?" Dolores's croaky voice questions.

Shit! What is the matter with me? Who cares that he's here again? Maybe he likes eating shitty food people spit in, and getting food poisoning. I rush to the back and throw all my stuff in my locker, before strapping on my apron and getting to work. "Table five is yours, girly; he hasn't ordered anything but coffee yet. The other two tables are waiting for food to be up, so get to work."

I straighten my shoulders, and force myself to mask my emotions, as I approach his booth and stand there waiting for his acknowledgment. I have to clear my throat twice before he pries his eyes away from the screen in front of him, and turns to acknowledge me. Dark, tempestuous gray eyes bore into mine with intensity, and have me taking an unconscious step back. "Back again? Didn't get enough of the shitty food the last time?"

The questions I really want to ask him run through my mind in rapid succession, but I don't voice them. *Does he live around here? Is he planning on bulldozing my neighborhood? Does he have someone to ride that wide lap of his?* Instead, I cock a hip and pull out my notepad, ready to take his order.

"Apparently not. It must be the great service." A smirk lifts the corners of his mouth, and my heart rate speeds up. This guy is stupidly hot, like the cover of a magazine, would spend my last dollar to buy it hot. It irritates me that he's getting this kind of reaction out of me. "The blonde from last night on the stage, is she a friend of yours?"

My eyebrow rises with his question, and I feel my grip tightening on my notepad. "*Daisy*, her name is Daisy, and yeah, she's a friend and my roommate. What about her?"

He pushes his laptop away, and places both of his elbows on the top of the table. The sleeves of his tight-fitting knit top are pulled back to the elbow, and I get a glimpse of all the delectable ink he has, and how muscular his forearms are. Shit, I hope I'm not drooling like some prepubescent teenager. That's all I need to top this miserable fucking day with, acting a fool in front of a hot as fuck guy.

"She seeing anyone?" His question slams into me like a slap, and I can feel the heat on my neck and cheeks rising. Oh my fucking God, he's into her and not me; how embarrassing! It feels like a boulder the size of the state of Texas has just crushed me. For a moment, I want to tell him that she's involved with someone, just to see if his interest will sway my way, because of how devastated I feel, but then anger blazes within me. Who the fuck cares if he's not into me? He's not the last man on the planet, and he's probably an entitled rich prick.

I'm furious with myself for placing myself in a situation where I now feel less than. Yes, I'm attracted to him, and he's incredibly drool-worthy, but I refuse to act a fool for any man, and I'm no one's second choice, fuck that shit. He's not interested in me, his loss. "Not to my knowledge, but you'll have to ask her yourself. What can I get you to eat?"

"Just the special, and I will. She working at the club again tonight?" He questions, leaning his large frame back against the booth seat, and crossing his arms over his broad chest. My eyes follow all of the movements, and when I meet his eyes again, the bastard smiles at me, showing me perfect white teeth. "More coffee too. Don't spit in my food, *Chrissy.*" He leans forward and reads my name off my tag with exaggeration, and I'm irrationally irritated by the way it sounds coming across his lips.

Does the stinging from my cuts on your perfect ass turn you on every time you move, sweet little temptation? We both know you like the pain.

The phone almost slips from my hand as my head pivots up, and my eyes search the diner for males with their phones in their hands, or glancing in my direction. Other than old Frank, who's a hundred years old and only has one working leg, no one is even looking at me. *Jesus fuck, this guy is super creepy. Is he watching me right now?* My eyes return to Nic, who is consumed with his laptop, with no phone in sight. *Could it be him? Could he be my masked stalker?* I discard the thought almost immediately, because he's not interested in me; Daisy is the one who has caught his eye. If it were him, he would have been in her room last night, not mine.

The fact of the matter is, there is some deranged, creepy, mask-wearing fucker out there, who knows a bunch of very intimate details about me, and what I fantasize about, and they know that I enjoyed what they did to me. If I'm being truthful with myself, I would allow him to ravish me again in the same way, or worse. I enjoyed the depravity, the inability to fight back, and to have all my choices taken from me. I'd never admit that out loud, but inside my head, where it's safe, I can't lie to myself.

When I bring Nic his food, he mutters, *"thanks,"* in a deep voice, without looking up at me, his fingers flying across the keyboard of his laptop. When I endeavor to get a peek at what he's working on, he shifts the laptop away from my eyesight, and grunts like a fucking Neanderthal at me. I should have spit in his food again; the thought rips through me with annoyance. God, this guy couldn't be less into me. There's definitely a better chance that old Frank is the masked stalker than this guy.

Do you want to play a game, my sweet temptation?

Is this asshole for real? Does he think this is all a game? I start typing out a message, telling him where he can go and shove himself, but before I can hit send, I change my mind. Maybe I can get some answers into who this psycho is, and how dangerous he is.

You want me to play along with your sick games, I need answers to my questions, otherwise, go fuck yourself.

I peek in Nic's direction from below my lashes, hopeful that I'll see him with his phone out, only to be crushed, when the fucker is typing away and no phone is in sight. A message immediately pops up in response to mine.

You're not really in a position to bargain with me, little temptation. Shall I remind you that I can get to you wherever and whenever I want? I'll humor you, though, and give you two questions if you play along. Choose wisely, but first, you humor me.

Touch yourself over your clothes behind the counter. Rub that sweet little pussy and make yourself drip while everyone else is having breakfast and only wishing they could taste you.

How do I know you'll answer my questions if I play along? For all I know, you could refuse after I've done what you've asked.

Take a risk and find out. You're a brave girl.

I quickly glance around, checking if anyone is watching me, and position myself further behind the counter, bending my knees so I can obscure what my fingers are doing, as I rub them in circles over my jeans against my needy clit. His words and demands have already got me dripping, and soaking my panties. I know this is brazen and wanton of me, but a part of me wants to see how far he'll go with it. After a few seconds, I'm already frustrated, the material of my jeans is too thick and cumbersome, and I can't seem to apply enough pressure to my throbbing clit. I dart another glance around the diner to see if anyone is watching me, and how close Dolores is, before slipping my fingers down the front of my pants below my apron, and underneath the band of my panties, and use them against my needy clit until a shudder runs through me. Fuck, it won't take long for me to explode, this all has me worked up. Am I really going to make myself cum right here, with all these people eating not more than a few feet away? The phone vibrates in my hand, and I stare at it as I apply more pressure to my clit, my breath becoming raspy, and my fingers being soaked in my arousal.

Naughty little temptation. Ask your question.

I typed one-handed, not quite ready to stop, as I bring myself closer and closer to release.

Who are you? What do you want from me, and are you going to kill me?

You only get two questions, little temptation. If you want more, you have to earn them, like a good girl.

I'm an admirer, fixated on you. A predator hunting his pretty prey. As for what I want, that's simple: you. I want every part of you, from your beating heart to that sexy ass and that pretty pussy. I want to consume you.

I read his words, and rather than terrifying me, they push me over the edge, and I have to bite down on the inside of my cheek to stifle the sound of my orgasm, as it rushes through my body like electricity zapping through a live wire. *Who says shit like that, that they want to consume you?* Some part of my rational mind knows this is a dangerous game that I'm playing, along with someone who is more than a few apples short of a bushel, but the other part of me doesn't seem to care.

How do I earn more questions?

Head to 'the hole' after your shift at the diner is done. Go to the last booth at the end in the back. It will be marked with an 'x' on the door. Strip naked, put on the silk blindfold, and press your sexy ass into the hole. If you obey and please me, I'll give you two more questions, my sweet little temptation.

How will I know it's you and not some other man? Anyone could be there and touch me.

No one will touch you but me, little temptation. The last man that did, you currently have his severed hands buried in your backyard.

Holy shit! It was him that sent the severed hands that I painstakingly froze my ass off to bury in the backyard. Who was the last man to touch me? Whose hands did this fucker cut off? I'm utterly terrified, and yet also turned on at how murderous and insane he is. I remove my cum-soaked fingers from my pants and wipe them on my apron, my whole body feeling flushed and languid, now that I have orgasmed.

Just remember, little temptation, you're now an accomplice to the crime I committed. You buried the hands, rather than reporting them. Tick tock, I'll be waiting.

I look away from my phone, and with visceral disappointment, I notice that Nic is long gone. I walk over to his table, and see that he's left two hundred dollars to cover his tab, which can't equal more than twenty bucks. Fuck, I really hoped that it was him that was stalking me. I know that I shouldn't dare go and meet this disturbed psycho anywhere, never mind at *'the hole'*, but instead of feeling terror, all I feel is excitement, and I can't wait for my shift to be over. *Fuck, there is something seriously wrong with me.*

Chapter 18

Santa

I watch her get increasingly flustered, as I inquire about her roommate; she doesn't hide her jealousy well. My little temptation doesn't want me to be attracted to Daisy or anyone else. She wants me for herself, but she's too stubborn to acknowledge that, or make a move. I'm enjoying the spider and fly game we're playing. Slowly and surely, I'm weaving my web tighter and tighter around her, ensuring that she will never be able to escape me. She's my tasty morsel, and I find that I'm ravenous for her now, after having a taste of her pretty pussy.

An idea pops into my mind to mess with her some more; I love how irate she gets, and how her smooth skin flushes red with her wrath, causing her adorable freckles to become more pronounced. I know earlier, she was questioning what happened to her, and if it was real. I watched through my hidden cameras, as she came to the terrifying realization that it wasn't all in her head, when she saw the small injection site on Daisy's neck in her kitchen. I heard her pose her questions to her roommate to find out if I had touched her too. It was a stunning sight, the fear reflected across her expressive face, and the way her body went rigid and on the defense, as if I could still harm her from a distance. Technically, I could, but I don't want to. Not yet, I want to be close enough to smell her fear, and watch all her microexpressions in real time. I know I'm sick and deranged, but that's never bothered me. I am unapologetic about the monster that I am.

I send her a text about her ass stinging, because I can see her grimace every time she shifts; the cuts I left her with must be rubbing against the fabric of her panties. I force myself to hide the satisfied grin that wants to cross my face, at the memory of how prettily she bled. She'll shed so much more of the bright crimson before I'm done with her.

She doesn't disappoint me, as a scowl mars her face, and she scans the room for a man watching her, or on his phone. *Silly little temptation* doesn't realize there's a way around all of that if you have the technical skills, which I have in spades. I avoid looking in her direction, pretending to be completely engrossed in work. Little does she know that right now, capturing her is my only priority.

She ignores my text and pushes the phone back into her pocket, going off to serve other patrons and avoiding me, as if I have the fucking plague. That won't do; I need to hear her voice, and the snark behind all her words, as she executes her venom in my direction. I wonder if she'll spew that angry malice once I have her tied up, naked, and in my bed? I picture her lying against my dark silk sheets, all that soft skin on display, and red hair spread across my pillows. In my mind, she's wearing one of my steel collars, a leash trailing down her neck ready for me to wrap in my wrist, a ball gag shoved inside of her mouth, and nipple clamps clipped to her pretty rose tips, as her arms and legs are spread and bound to the hooks I have built into the four corners of my bed frame. I need to make that a reality as soon as possible. My cock throbs inside the confines of my pants, at the provocative images playing inside my mind.

I send her another text, hoping to get her attention. Her body stiffens for a moment as she feels the vibration of the phone in her pocket, but she resists reading my message. Instead, she heads behind the counter and wipes it down. *Naughty girl, you can't avoid me for long.* If she doesn't respond to me soon, I might have to do something drastic she won't like at all. Something that will have a whole bunch of people bleeding on this tacky diner floor, starting with her rude coworker, Dolores.

Maybe she'll pay attention if I slam my blade into Dolores' throat, and watch as her blood cascades down her stained blue uniform, or perhaps I'll stab out the eye of the old fucker at the counter, that keeps watching my temptation's ass sway every time she moves. The need for blood and violence spreads through me, and I have to clench my hands into fists, to resist the urge to put my fantasies into action.

She finally pulls out her phone and reads my message. Her eyebrow rises, and the corner of her lips tilts downwards with disapproval. She begins to type something back to me. I watch my screen from the corner of my eye, as words appear with her keystrokes, and then disappear again. She has no idea that I've cloned her phone and can see everything she's doing. The message pops up with her response, and I have to use my fist to disguise my laugh, and pretend to cough.

You want me to play along with your sick games, I need answers to my questions, otherwise, go fuck yourself.

She's such a hot-blooded spitfire; maybe that is what attracts me to her. She refuses to cower, even when she knows she's outmatched.

You're not really in a position to bargain with me, little temptation. Shall I remind you that I can get to you wherever and whenever I want? I'll humor you, though, and give you two questions if you play along. Choose wisely, but first, you humor me.

She has no idea that my words are true. There is nowhere that she could hide from me, that I won't be able to get to her. Chrissy Cranbrook is *mine* in every way until she takes her last breath, and I have no intention of allowing that to happen until I've had my fill of her. Even then, I might keep her in a cage like a favorite pet.

Touch yourself over your clothes behind the counter. Rub that sweet little pussy and make yourself drip while everyone else is having breakfast and only wishing they could taste you.

The little minx searches the crowd again, as if whoever is demanding such depraved actions from her is just going to make themselves apparent. Her eyes land in my direction once again, but I bring the cup of shitty coffee to my lips, and continue typing away on my laptop, one-handed. Is that a frown of disappointment across those sultry lips? Does she hope that it's me who is behind the requests? *Soon*, my sweet temptation, you will realize that it has always been me.

How do I know you'll answer my questions if I play along? For all I know, you could refuse after I've done what you've asked.

She's right; I could, I'm not really an honorable, standup guy. After all, I get my kicks murdering people, and she will be no exception when I eventually lose interest in her. A niggling thought in the back of my mind tells me that isn't likely to happen with her. I've never felt obsession and infatuation like this for anything or anyone. All these new feelings and emotions are starting to really worry me. I don't have any use for them in my life.

Take a risk and find out. You're a brave girl.

She scrunches down lower behind the counter, to disguise her actions from the patrons not more than a few feet away from her, and oblivious to my obscene request. After just a few quick moments, a look of frustration furrows her forehead, and causes lines between her brows. She's not getting the friction she needs over the thick material of her pants, is my guess. My cock goes rock hard and pushes against my zipper, as I watch her through the camera closest to the counter, as she slips her hand down the front of her jeans, below the fabric of her apron, and plays with herself. I force myself to swallow the growl that wants to loudly announce how attracted I am to her.

Fuck, I may cum in my pants like a schoolboy, without even touching myself. She's so deliciously naughty, perfect for me in every way, my *sweet little temptation*. I can't wait to slip inside of her, and bury myself to the hilt in her tight warmth. The memory of how wet and perfect she was, just a few hours ago, as I fucked her pussy and ass with my fingers, and then the vibrator, has been playing nonstop inside of my mind. Will she moan and cry out as I thrust inside of her ruthlessly? Will she beg me for mercy, as I use my blade across the perfection of her porcelain skin? *Fuck, I hope so.*

Naughty little temptation. Ask your question.

I observe with humor as she types one-handed, refusing to stop her attempt to make herself orgasm now that she's turned on. Her neck and cheeks are tinted in a pink blush, and her deep brown eyes sparkle with mischief. She knows full well that what she's doing is wrong by polite society standards, but it doesn't stop her from seeking what she wants. *She's fucking perfect.*

Who are you? What do you want from me, and are you going to kill me?

Sneaky little brat, that's three questions, and just cause she tries to roll them into two doesn't mean I'm not paying attention, although I will admit, I am more than ready to pull out my hard, throbbing cock and cum all over this sticky diner table. In my opinion, my cum would be an improvement to the aesthetic of this place.

You only get two questions, little temptation. If you want more, you have to earn them, like a good girl.

Fuck, I hope she wants to continue to play along, and she's more than curious about me. I want to see how far she's willing to go to get what she wants. I know that there is no stopping me from obtaining my goals once I have set them. Right now, all of them revolve around the pretty redhead about to cum all over her fingers in a diner filled with people.

I'm an admirer, fixated on you. A predator hunting his pretty prey. As for what I want, that's simple: you. I want every part of you, from your beating heart to that sexy ass and that pretty pussy. I want to consume you.

I watch with unhinged glee as she cums, her body going rigid as she forces her face to remain neutral, and avoid giving away what she's doing to herself. I have to get out of here and release my cock from its tight confines. I'm so close to embarrassing myself right here, and then I will give away that it's me, or at least make her think that I'm some deviant. I am, but I don't want her to know that just yet. I start to pack up my items, pulling out a couple of hundred dollar bills and dropping them on the table, to cover the mostly untouched food. As I'm heading for the door, her text comes through, and I know I'm not making it to the car before I cum.

How do I earn more questions?

I rush towards my parked Mustang, throwing my laptop bag inside on the passenger seat, and yanking my zipper down, to free my engorged cock that's dripping with precum. I savagely stroke myself right here in broad daylight, in a parking lot filled with other vehicles, and pedestrians walking on a sidewalk, not even six feet from my car. It doesn't take me more than a few tight strokes before I'm cumming all over my hand, and lap. Fuck, fuck, fuck.

Head to 'the hole' after your shift at the diner is done. Go to the last booth at the end in the back. It will be marked with an 'x' on the door. Strip naked, put on the silk blindfold, and press your sexy ass into the hole. If you obey and please me, I'll give you two more questions, my sweet little temptation.

I throw my head back against the backrest of my seat, and try to calm my racing heart, while my cock sits at half-mast, entirely exposed to anyone daring to look closely inside. My windows are mostly tinted, but you can still see through the front windshield, and right now, I'm indecent.

How will I know it's you and not some other man? Anyone could be there and touch me.

Her question instantly infuriates me, with images of other men daring to touch what's mine. I would mercilessly murder anyone who even lays eyes on her naked flesh. She's mine, and I don't fucking share. The last man that touched her lost his hands for doing so, and the other fucker is only still breathing because I couldn't get my hands on him at that moment, but I have plans for him, and much like his vehicle, he'll be filled with holes soon enough.

No one will touch you but me, little temptation. The last man that did, you currently have his severed hands buried in your backyard.

I can picture her reaction to my confession. She'll be terrified now that she realizes I sent those to her, and that I've had access to her all along.

Just remember, little temptation, you're now an accomplice to the crime I committed. You buried the hands, rather than reporting them. Tick tock, I'll be waiting.

I lick the palm of my hand, getting a taste of my salty cum, and instantly missing the taste of Chrissy's sweet pussy. *Soon.* Soon, I will be covered in her juices as I fill up all her holes. I put the car into drive, heading off to put my plan into motion; it's only a few short hours before I'll have her in my grasp. It's time to move up my plan and take what's mine.

Merry fucking Christmas to me.

Chapter 19

The Gift

The rest of my shift moves slower than the glaciers melting in the Arctic, and I'm ready to crawl out of my skin with anxiety. You would think, with the orgasm that I gave myself, I would be relaxed, but instead the opposite has happened. It feels like my skin is on fire, and every move my body makes, makes me highly aware of how sensitive and sore my pussy is. Even my nipples seem to be chafing against the fabric of my bra. My body is wired tight in anticipation of what will transpire at *'the hole'* in a few short hours, with a masked man who could very well try to end my life.

Has common sense tried to prevail uselessly, where I've attempted to reason with myself about how bad of an idea this is? *Yes.* Do I plan to listen to any of that reasoning? *Not a fucking chance.* The thrill is what's igniting an out-of-control inferno within me. I've never felt like this before, never wanted to risk everything for a moment of excitement. Lately I've been feeling like my life was dull, lacking purpose, and filled with constant struggle. While this madman doesn't really change the latter two, he does give me something to look forward to, other than going back and forth between my two shitty jobs, just to be able to barely survive.

The danger speaks to me; it whispers sweet, enticing words of seduction, calling to the parts of me that I keep hidden, deep inside, from the world. The ones that hunger for the touch of a masked stranger, doing inexplicably naughty and depraved things to me. "Girlie, what is up with you today? You've gone from being snappy like a gator, to antsy, and jumping around like a damn meerkat with a bladder infection. Give it a rest, will ya? You're giving me a headache." Dolores walks by as I'm clearing the last of my tables before my shift is over, and debating on whether I should heed common sense, and self-preservation, and head home, lock my doors, and pray he doesn't come to find me. *He will. The doors were all locked last night, and that didn't stop him. Toothless, a giant one hundred and fifty pound cane corso wasn't even the slightest deterrent.*

"Whatcha got a hot date or something?" She croaks in her deep, smoker's voice with sarcasm. Her question has me stilling in my motions, and I end up choking on my own saliva, much to her horror. She races over, and pats me hard on the back with one of her veiny hands, and knocks the wind out of me. "Was it a bug? I'll bet it was, just like the one I saw this morning. *Huge, I tell ya!* I told that cheapskate Carl to call the bug people, but he keeps telling me I'm seeing things."

Fucking gross, I really have to stop working here, and I shouldn't consume anything Carl cooks, ever. "Nope, air just went down the wrong way. I'm good, thanks." I put space between our bodies, grab my discarded rag, and head to throw it in the bin to be washed. I have never been comfortable around others crowding my personal space. I know it stems from my childhood trauma, and my time in the foster care system. I should work on it, but right now, I have too many other things on my mind.

I grab my tips for the day, including the hefty one that Nic once again left me. What is a guy with that kind of money doing in a place like this, not once, but twice, within the same week? If he's not out here scoping out the neighborhood to bulldoze it, then what's he accomplishing? His confirmation that he's going to see Daisy at the club tonight, almost makes me want to call in sick to my shift, so that I don't have to experience the soul-crushing emotions of being rejected, while being forced to watch that shit go down. *You'll probably be murdered at 'the hole', so no worries about having to watch your roommate get asked out by the rich guy you're lusting over.* She's about to get her *Pretty Woman* moment, and I'll be lucky if I don't end up looking like a character from the *Scream* franchise. Some bitches have all the luck, I guess.

I guess that's one silver lining, but seriously, I hope this guy isn't psycho-psycho, like not *Dahmer* eat me, psycho. I can handle a little masked, rough kink play, but I'd like to still be breathing at the end of it. My phone buzzes in my pocket, and I yank it out but don't look at it, as I throw my apron in my locker and start shoving on my jacket. I stare back at the apron that I wiped my arousal-wet fingers on. I should probably take that home and wash it; it has to be some kind of health violation or something. After another second of debating, I close my locker, leave it behind, and head for the front door. Fuck it, it matches the rest of the nasty place, plus we don't have any laundry detergent at home.

"Hey, Dolores, that guy who was in here earlier, the prissy big one. Have you ever seen him before the last time I served him and his brother in here?" I don't know what prompts me to ask her that question. I should be worrying about meeting up with a masked stalker, and not the large, hot dude who wants nothing to do with me. My phone buzzes again in my grip as I hold the door open, and Frank slips through, muttering his thanks, while trying to get a close-up glimpse of my tits through the opening of my jacket. *Dirty old perv.* I shake my head at his antics, and return my attention to Dolores, who's also giving him the stink eye.

"Never, girlie, but if he comes in again, I'm taking his table. I saw what he tipped ya, big spender, that one."

Fucking great, I'll lose the guy to Daisy, and the future tips to Dolores; it pretty much sums up my life, nothing but bullshit all around. "See ya tomorrow, Dolores!" I holler as I walk out the door, and finally take a look at my phone.

Don't bother to run home instead of here, all you'll do is piss me off, and I'll end up fucking you harder and leaving more marks on your skin.

The second text is just a GIF of a clock ticking. Jesus fuck, this unhinged bastard is impatient to get his hands on me. The defiant part of me wants to do precisely the opposite of what he's instructing me. If I had the money for a motel, that wasn't infested with bed bugs and cockroaches, I would go hide out with a bottle of cheap Merlot, but I don't, and I can't risk him taking his anger out on Daisy if I do.

So, instead of doing that, I send him back a photo of me giving him the finger. I know I'm just tempting fate at this point. They can write that in my obituary. *'Here lies Chrissy Cranbrook, an ornery bitch who tempted fate one too many times, and lost her life as a result.'*

I burrow into my jacket, the biting cold wind pushing against my body, as I make my way down to the bus stop. Some part of me knows this is beyond fucked up. I'm about to take a city bus to a place where a man I don't know, who broke into my house yesterday, and drugged me and my roommate, can fuck me, in hopes that I can get some answers about who he is. *Yup, my sanity is all up there for sure.*

Here goes nothing; I hope I'm still alive at the end of this day. If not, I hope Daisy adopts Toothless. Fuck, I should send her a message now, telling her she's Toothless' backup momma.

Somebody better play *'Songbird'* at my fucking funeral, or I'm coming back to haunt everyone.

Chapter 20

The Gift

I walk into *'the hole'*, and a chill plunges down my back. The interior looks just like an adult toy shop. Dildos in every color and shape line the walls, and ball gags, leashes, provocative clothing, and anal plugs are everywhere. I get distracted by a giant green dildo that I swear looks like *'Godzilla'*. Brings new meaning to the term *'being fucked by a monster'*, I guess.

The sales guy looks up, his bright green and blue mohawk so sharp that I'm afraid he could take my eye out, even at a distance. God, look at how pretty his eyeshadow is; why can't I manage my makeup like him? Instant jealousy fills me at how flawless his makeup looks. "That's one of our best sellers, really does the job, ya know." I nod in agreement, but fuck if I know what the peacock, with the best contour I've ever seen, is talking about. I like my appendages bright pink, and of reasonable male species size; call me fucking boring. I shift uncomfortably, not knowing how to ask about how to get to the back rooms. Does one just say, *'Hey, I'm here to get fucked through a glory hole?'* or is there a more polite and civilized way to ask for something like that?

I keep looking around in desperation, touching things I have no business touching, like a massive heart-shaped butt plug, that suspiciously looks like a bookend Daisy has on her shelf in her room. *Grow some lady balls, Chrissy. Just walk right up to the counter, and tell the nice peacock that you're here to meet a masked man, and probably die in his back room.*

A thought races through my mind: oh my God, what if Daisy is working today? I didn't even ask her before I left for the diner. Shit, I don't want her involved in any of this, and I also don't want her to think that I want to do this for cash. "Hey, is Daisy working today?" I question as I approach the counter, and a new layer of terror lands on my shoulders. At this point, I'll have a nervous breakdown before I make it out of the butt plug section. He gives me an appraising look, from the soles of my dirty fake Ugg boots to my puffy jacket. "You a friend of Daisy's?"

"Something like that. I'm... I'm here to meet... someone in the back." I swallow the lump in my throat, square my shoulders, and try to give off the vibe that I belong here, instead of I should be running for the hills. "She's not working today. Which room?" He questions with suspicion, and I release the breath I was holding. Thank fuck, at least one thing is going right today.

Oh my God, what room did that psycho say? My mind draws a blank, and I have to pull out my phone to search for our message. When I find it, I flash the screen at him like a terrified virgin. I swear if a crater suddenly opened in the ground, I would dive right into it, and pray that it swallowed me up. "Back one," I whisper. A lascivious grin crosses his face, and he cocks a pierced eyebrow at me. *Gawd, why is he so pretty? Just look at that perfectly shaped eyebrow.*

"You're all good to go, he paid extra to make sure all the rooms around you are empty too. *Lucky bitch!*" He nods his head in the direction of a door that's painted to look like a wall. "You and your *daddy* have some safe fun now."

Ew, what the fuck? Nope, that's just not happening; I don't have a daddy kink. No shade to anyone who does, but I'm not walking around calling anyone daddy. I have enough issues with my mental health as it is, and my daddy was a deadbeat who left my momma high and dry, or at least that's what I believe, but no one knows for sure 'cause his name isn't listed anywhere. I slide the door open and walk through, my knees trembling, and my legs threatening to give out on me. He paid extra to make sure that no one else was around. Is that because he plans to murder me, and he doesn't want anyone to hear me scream? *What the hell have I gotten myself into?* Someone is going to find my rotting corpse back here in a few days.

My eyes dart back and forth, in the space that holds various doors on either side of a narrow hallway. I keep going until I'm at the very end, and staring at an off-white door marked with a black 'X' in some sort of tape. There's still time to change my mind and race out of here. I can grab Daisy and Toothless, and make a run for it; he wouldn't know where we are, *right?* Maybe we can go off the grid and live in a hut or something. Toothless can help me hunt for our food. *Who am I kidding?* That lazy ass doesn't even want to go for a walk around the block with me; I'm fucking doomed.

My hand reaches out and turns the knob, the door swings open, and I'm not quite sure what I was expecting, but it really wasn't this. There's basically nothing in the room. There's only a dim glow from a nightlight in the corner. The walls, floor, and ceiling are all painted black, probably to hide the stains; Jesus fuck, I hope no one ever brings an ultraviolet light in here. A low bench covered in black vinyl sits to one side of the room, and that's basically it for furniture. I step inside, the smell of bleach cleaner, mixed with sex, assaulting my nose. The room's small; I could maybe reach both my arms out and touch each of the walls with the tips of my fingers. My eyes glance down at the surface of the bench, and a fluorescent green sticky note lies on top of a piece of silky black fabric.

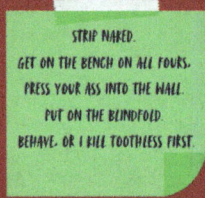

The writing is neat and very masculine. I reread the note several times, trying to decide if I should proceed, despite the threat to my baby. *Would he really kill my furbaby? You have to be a special kind of insane to kill a dog.* My breathing is coming in rapid bursts, and my skin feels all flushed. Despite my apprehension, my panties are soaked, and my mind is racing with possibilities. Will he hurt me? Do I want him to? Will he show me who he is when we're done? Will I still be breathing at the end of this, or will I be a lesson to young women everywhere on what not to do?

My jacket slides off my frame and hits the ground, followed by my shirt, bra, and jeans. When I'm just standing there in my panties, socks, and goosebumps, which have erupted all over my skin, I close my eyes, reaching down and stripping the last layers off. Now that I'm naked and my nipples can cut glass, I realize the room is quite cool, some of the lust is starting to dissipate, and rational thought is beginning to trickle in. *I shouldn't be here. This is crazy, I'm crazy!*

A rustling noise on the other side of the wall catches my attention, followed by the sound of something clicking shut. My heart races in my chest, and all of a sudden, I can't seem to get enough air into my lungs. I grab the handle of the door and try to open it, but it doesn't budge. Holy shit, this psychopath has locked me in here. I bang on the door with the palm of my hand. "Hello! Let me out of here, I don't want to be in here!" I use my bare foot to kick at the door as I feel hysteria rising. "Peacock, let me out! I can't be trapped in here; I have anxiety, fucker!"

Only silence greets me, as the hairs on my arms and on the back of my neck stand on end. My eyes catch a glimpse of the discarded note, that has fallen to the floor on top of my clothing, and I dart from it to the bench and back again. *Toothless, my poor, sweet, gentle giant.* My masked stalker is not going to let me out of here until I comply with his demands. I can do this. I can get through this; I just have to stay calm. *Breathe, bitch, it will be over quickly. Most guys don't last five minutes.*

I climb onto the bench, grabbing the silky blindfold in my tight grip. A thought races through my mind: Where the hell is the hole? This is a glory hole, but I didn't spy any voids in the walls. I frantically search the walls with my eyes, but I don't see any openings. I use my fingers to feel across the surface of the wall, and right where the bench meets the wall, there's a slight gap, as if something slides within the wall itself. Am I really going to go through with this? *What choice do you have? Do you honestly think he will just let you go?* The psycho broke into your house and drugged you last night, so he could get off on touching you, and left you with a vibrator inside your pussy all night.

I reach up and loosely tie the blindfold over my eyes, and take a few huge gulps of air, then I get on all fours on the bench, and press my ass against the wall and wait, as my heart races, and I can hear my blood rushing in my ears. "Bitch, I don't fuck without a condom. I don't care who the fuck you are; put a damn rubber on," I yell with false bravado, even as my arms tremble. It's as if he's watching me, which, added to everything else, just makes this even more super fucking creepy. The minute I'm in position, I hear the section in the wall slide across, and a masculine groan rents the air.

"Hello, *sweet little temptation*. Look at what a beautiful present you are for me."

Chapter 21

Santa

I watch her on my phone, through the hidden cameras I had installed in the shop, as she works up the courage to strip off her clothes. I thought for sure she would tuck tail and run, once she got to the shop and had to question that cunt, Garrett, at the front desk about the glory rooms. I totally enjoyed watching her squirm with embarrassment, and cataloged everything that she found intriguing for later. The pretty heart-shaped butt plug is going to look spectacular against her pale flesh, and that monster dildo, well, I'll look forward to working her in so that one day soon, she can take that.

If I didn't know through my stalking and research that Garrett was gay, and utterly uninterested in Chrissy in a sexual nature, I would have slit his throat as a consequence of the way he looked at her, as if she was a pretty object he coveted, a piece of tasty meat to be consumed. I'm not saying she's not, but that's not the only thing about her. There is such depth and fire to my sweet temptation, such bravery below all the different layers that make her up. Everything about her intrigues and calls to me as an enticement, and I plan to peel back one layer at a time, until I get down to the dirty and rough parts that I know are similar to mine. If she sheds a little blood in the process, so be it.

Her body trembles as she stands there, unsure of what to do next and it's like a shot of adrenaline to my veins. After a moment, she climbs stiffly onto the bench, her eyes too large in her frightened, pale face. She wraps her arms tightly around her chest, cradling herself as if she could self-soothe, and keep the monsters away. *Not a chance, my beauty, I have intentions of consuming you until there is nothing left.* A look of sheer panic crosses her features, and I survey with humor as she searches the walls for the opening of the glory hole. Her breathing is raspy and too quick, as if she's struggling to get enough air, and the sound has my cock throbbing in my pants, begging to be released from his constraint. Here's hoping she doesn't end up having a panic attack and passing out; I would hate to have all my fun ruined. Not that it would stop me from holding her down and fucking her raw.

"Bitch, I don't fuck without a condom. I don't care who the fuck you are; put a damn rubber on." Her demand and defiance amuse me; she thinks she has a say in what will happen here. Oh, sweet delusional temptation, nothing will be coming between me and you, certainly not a fucking condom. Nothing will stop me from filling her pussy and ass with my cum now, the whole world could be erupting in flames, I would still fill her with my cock, until my cum is slipping from her like a faucet, then I'd gladly clean her up with my tongue.

Once she ties the blindfold obediently across her face, I shift behind my side of the wall, unbuttoning my pants and slipping down my zipper, as I pull my hard cock out and squeeze it in my tight grip. I force myself to swallow a groan, as I spread my beads of precum down my length and give myself a harsh stroke, firmly pressing on my Jacob's Ladder piercings. Fuck, that feels so good, but it will feel even better when it's Chrissy's tight pussy strangling my cock. I can't wait any longer. The monster inside of me craves satisfaction, as a dark haze closes over me. I shift the square partition aside, and it disappears inside the wall, leaving a gap that is just under two feet by two feet in the wall, and the sight that greets me has a pained groan escaping me.

She's fucking stunning, her skin glows from the subtle amber light in her part of the section. The perfect round globes of her ass are perched high and ready for my touch, ready to be spanked and branded with my fingerprints. Fuck, speaking of branding, that's next on my list of things to do to her, my name will look so pretty across her pale flesh. The small cuts I made early this morning with my blade stand out against the remainder of her snowy white skin, not disfiguring it, but rather enhancing her exquisiteness even more. She's everything I've ever dreamed of and didn't know that I wanted. *Mine*, Chrissy Cranbrook, is mine; all of her skin is mine to tarnish, all of her breaths are mine to steal, and all of her cries belong to my ears alone.

She will die with my name on her lips, as she begs me to take her life after I'm done destroying every part of her. The thought doesn't bring me as much pleasure as it normally would, and I question whether I truly want to see her breathe her last breath. My chest tightens with the thought of never hearing her voice, or smelling her sweet scent. No, I don't think I can live without her now.

My mouth goes dry as I continue to stare at her, and I have to use my tongue to wet my lips, the ones that I wish I could already press to her glistening pussy lips. Fuck, she's drenched; all of this has turned her on, despite her fear, or maybe in spite of it. Does she get off on being terrified? I can't wait to find out. "Hello, *sweet little temptation*. Look at what a beautiful present you are for me."

Her body jerks forward on the bench on her hands and knees, and a sultry gasp releases from her lips. My hand darts out and roughly grabs her hip through the opening, steadying and preventing her from tumbling off the bench. "Don't you dare move away, Chrissy; this ass is mine to do with as I please." My voice is rough, and muffled by the skull mask I'm wearing. The one I can't wait to remove, so I can have a taste of her sweet cunt.

"Please don't hurt me," she cries out, but her words lack conviction, as she braces herself on all fours.

"We both know that you don't mean that, my sweet temptation," I dig my fingers into her skin, and roughly yank her back toward the opening in the wall; I refuse to allow her to evade me. My sleeve scrapes against the sides of the opening, scratching my skin, and I grit my teeth as the pain adds to my arousal. My palm rises, and I slap her asscheek hard, the sound loud in the enclosed space; her responding scream has my balls tightening painfully, and more precum slipping from my slit. *Jesus, everything about this woman is so fucking sexy.* I slap her other asscheek, before pulling my arm back through the opening, and removing a blade from my pocket, while my other hand jerks my stiff, long cock to the sound of her mewling pants. "I think you need a few more lines to decorate this pretty ass, my temptation. Did you enjoy finding my blade this morning when you woke? Did you put it away as a souvenir of my first visit? Don't worry, there will be many more mornings to come."

I release my cock and shove my mask up on my forehead, wanting nothing to obstruct my senses of her, even though there is a risk she could see me. I slip open the blade, pushing my arm back through the opening, and allowing the sharp metal to slide across the lower part of her asscheek, where it meets her upper thighs. She has these gorgeous dimples on her ass, and faint little white veining stretch marks on her upper thighs, that are a road map of where my blade should go. I dig the blade into her skin, just enough for a few drops of blood to well and drip down her leg. She hisses out a whine, but it quickly turns into a moan, as I caress and squeeze her asscheek with my other hand. My cock bobs in front of me, begging to be allowed to participate and conquer all her tight holes. I carve another line and press my thumb into the cut, smearing her blood along her soft flesh. "Stunning," I groan as I move the sharp metal closer to her soaked center. "Tell me, *sweet temptation*, is it the pain or the danger that turns you on, or maybe it's both?"

"*Both,*" she croaks before she wiggles side to side, trying to force me closer to her pussy. I wonder what she would do if I impaled my blade inside of her, and sliced her open from the inside? Would she scream and cry as she lay there naked, dying for me? Would she beg for sweet mercy as her lifeblood puddled beneath her, and would I grant it? A shudder runs through my body at the thought of my hands, and cock, covered in her blood. The rich smell of iron, her musky scent, and the fear coming off of her are intoxicating, and I want to get high on it. I slip my forefinger between her pussy lips, while my blade leaves another cut closer to her core. "Please," she whines.

"You beg so prettily, please fuck you, hurt you, or both, my sweet temptation? Which is it that you're asking me for?" I lean closer and bring my face toward the opening between us, so I can get nearer to her scent. A drop of blood drips down the back of her leg, and I press closer to lick it up. "Fuck," she moans loudly, a shiver wracking her body.

"Your blood tastes like the most decadent wine. I should drain you and drink you up. You would enjoy that, wouldn't you, my slut? To be bled dry while I fuck you hard and mean." I lick another drop, her taste coating my tongue, but I need more; I need to have her in every way. I remove my finger from her swollen pussy lips, and slip my tongue between her folds to lick her from her clit to her puckered hole. Her breathing gets loud, moans ripping from her lips, as she presses her lower body further into the opening in encouragement. *Atta girl.*

I suck on her pussy lips, rubbing my rough whiskered chin into her delicate flesh, so she's left red and tingling. I nip her swollen clit, and she tries to dash forward, but I'm not having it. My patience to play is quickly coming to an end with my rising need. My eyes observe as I press the hilt of the blade against her puckered hole, and when she inhales a deep shuddering breath, I thrust it inside until nothing but the sharp metal blade protrudes from her asshole, slicing my fingers in the process, and coating her with my blood. *Fucking perfect.*

"FUCK!" Her scream fills my ears, and I can't wait to hear more of them. Her body almost gives in, her arms wavering and trembling beneath her. I pull back from her pussy, the taste of her swirling in my mouth, coating my lips, and her delicious cum sliding down my chin. I allow my saliva to slip from my mouth and land on her puckered hole, mixing with both our blood as I thrust the knife handle in and out of her pretty ass. I want her coated with every part of me, inside, outside, everywhere, until I'm infecting her, like she's doing to me. My hand grabs my cock in a tight fist, and I push through the opening and impale her pussy on my length in one go. "Fuck, so tight and warm. You really are the best fucking present, *temptation*," I growl as I begin thrusting inside of her, and setting a punishing pace. I yank the blade out of her ass, slicing her lower back in the process, and she releases a pained cry, but it quickly turns to the sound of pleasure. I rest the blade on her back as I drag my bloody hand down her exposed skin, leaving a macabre hand print, all of my fingers prominently on display. I reach forward and around her slim body and grab her breast, squeezing, and using my bloody fingers to pull on her nipple. "Ohmygod, ohmygod," she pants in breathless screams.

Her head tips forward on her shoulders, her beautiful hair obstructing my view of her face and I can't have it, I need to see all of her reactions to my depravity. I release her breast and grab the blade in my slippery hand and drag it up her back, leaving shallow cuts in its wake. "Head up, temptation, or I'll slit your pretty fucking throat. I want to see your reactions."

She hesitates for a moment, lost in her arousal, her body tightening around mine. My little temptation needs to learn some manners, when I give her an order, I expect to be obeyed. I run the blade over her shoulder, releasing my hold on her hip, I force my other arm through the opening and grab a fistful of her hair, and yank her head backwards, until her pretty neck is arched and exposed. My other hand moves forward with the blade and I press it against her slim throat, nicking her in the process. "You will do as you are told, temptation, or I'll make sure you don't take another breath. Do you want to die on my cock, slut?"

The added threat of danger just hypes me up even more, and a ripple of pleasure runs down my shoulders and arms. I want to do unspeakable, unhinged things to her that guarantee she's not leaving this room alive. It would be so easy, just a press of my hand and she would die instantly, while I fucked the very last breath out of her. One part of me is urging itself to press the blade in harder, to hurt her until we hear her dying screams, the other is urging me to keep her alive, so I can keep using all her holes for as long as I want. My blood slips from my fingers in rich crimson drops down her neck and chest, leaving little tracks around her lush breasts and my breath stutters with the image. She would be so beautiful, completely covered in blood. If I can't kill her in this very moment, then I'll plan to kill someone else and fuck her in their blood, very soon. I want to see her painted red, until only her defiant, angry, chocolate eyes are left visible and untainted.

"Oh fuck," she moans, as the sound of skin slapping against skin echoes through the small opening. She attempts to pull away from the blade at her throat, but only succeeds in impaling herself harder on my cock. To reward her defiance, I increase my punishing thrusts, and my hand tightens in her hair, digging my fingers into her scalp, knowing that I'm ripping out strands with my cruelty, and hurting her. "Fuck, too much! Too much!" Her cries fill my ears, and wave after wave of pleasure pours down my body, with decadent enjoyment. "You can take it, *temptation*. Your body was meant for mine. This pretty pussy was made for my cock."

I press the blade to her collarbone, allowing the tip to mar her skin, and a scream leaves her lips at the additional hit of pain. There is so much blood, hers and mine mixed together, that I am sure we are a ghastly sight right out of a horror movie. My testicles tighten with the overwhelming need to fill her core with my cum, and the sharp pain from the cuts on my fingers. The pain must trigger her further, and spur her into her own release, as she starts to push back against my tempo, every muscle and limb visibly taut, and her back arches further, allowing the blade to slice her again. A shuddering breath flees her, followed by a scream, as she tenses like a vice and cums around my cock, her wetness dripping down my length, soaking my balls and my upper thighs. She loses all of her strength, her upper body collapsing onto the bench and, on impulse alone, I move the blade, milliseconds before she ends her own life against its sharp surface, as her rapid breaths leave her open mouth. I wish I could see her eyes, and what the euphoria is doing to them, the necessary blindfold removing the possibility. Do they roll into the back of her skull when she cums? Are they large and glazed over with delight? I release my hold on the blade and hear it clatter to the ground, grab her hip violently, and fuck her hard and mean, until my orgasm races with a bolt of electricity up my spine, and my cum pours out of my cock in thick ropes, and fills her up.

The sound of our heaving breaths fills the air, as I start to return to the here and now, and some of the lust dissipates. My eyes trail over the surface of her alabaster skin, and how its perfection is enhanced by our blood, and my depravity. She looks stunning, a demented sexual dream. One I never thought I would crave. This has gone far past the point of vengeance for me, she's become a sickness inside of me, one cell at a time, corrupted. My chest tightens as unwanted sensations slither through me. I come to a sharp realization: I won't be waiting until later to kidnap my sweet temptation, after all. She's never leaving my side again while she still breathes. How long that may end up being is anyone's guess, but right now, one thing is for sure. Chrissy Cranbrook is more than just an obsession for me; she's the fire in my blood, and an addiction I am utterly lost to. She's stirring up emotions I have no business feeling, and because of that, she'll have to remain at my side.

"You just fucked up, sweet little temptation," I whisper, as I pull a syringe from my back pocket, filled with a strong sedative. "I won't be leaving here now without you." I plunge the drug into her thigh as she twitches and goes still.

It's time I took my gift home for the holidays.

Chapter 22

The Gift

I groan as I adjust my sore neck, and a shooting pain sears down my back, as I attempt to pry one of my tired eyes open. Grogginess and unawareness muddle my brain, and I can't seem to get a clear thought to process. The air is cool around me, and my skin prickles with goosebumps. "Ugh," I groan as my hand slides across the mattress, reaching for my comforter to wrap around myself, but I find nothing but silkiness below its touch. *What the fuck, has Toothless stolen all the covers again?* Slowly, a sense of cognizance returns to me, and I realize the mattress below me is too comfortable and soft, lacking my usual hard lumps that dig into my flesh, and no way are these my worn, cheap sheets.

I compel one of my eyes open, and dim light greets me. The color of the wall across from me is the first thing that registers as wrong to my exhausted mind. Why are the walls painted a dark royal blue instead of off-white? I bring my hand up to my eyes and endeavor to rub the sleep from them. *Am I still dreaming, or am I awake?* I propel my body to roll from my back to my side, and when I do, the sound of metal clicking on metal, and something cold and heavy landing on my shoulder, has me gasping and attempting to sit up in a panic. *What the fuck was that?* My uncoordinated hands bat at what's touching my skin, as fear runs like a herd of stallions through me. My fingers grasp the smooth, cold surface and trail up its length until I reach a smooth band around my neck.

WHAT THE FUCK! My body jerks up into a sitting position as a scream leaves my lips, and the clicking gets louder, along with the thundering of my heartbeat in my ears. "What the fuck! No... God no!" I screech as I yank hard on the band around my neck, and end up choking myself. I'm totally awake now; long gone is any of the drowsiness that assures me that I'm finding myself in a true nightmare, and not just one my mind has conjured up.

My eyes search the room, as I attempt to wrap my arms around my naked form. It's a decent size, with a dark oak dresser across the space, and a boxy accent chair in a geometric brown and cream pattern in a corner. There's a large window with wooden blinds partially closed, but through the slats, I can see the faint outline of clouds in the sky and lots of thick trees. I jump off the bed, and realize the clinking sound is coming from a metal-link chain that is attached to the band around my neck. My eyes follow the long length to a bolted hook in the far wall. "No, no, no... *what the fuck? Where am I?*"

Images accost my mind of the last things I remember: the adult toy shop, massive dildos, the pretty peacock with the great contour, and then vivid memories of the back room come to the forefront. The masked man, the one who drugged me in my home, was there. He was touching me, no, more than touching, he was fucking me with his long, thick cock and another blade, and I was allowing it. His words, and the rasp of his voice, slither across my mind in response to me requesting him to hurt me. *Oh my god, I did that; I asked for that.* My core flutters, regardless of the precarious situation that I find myself in. *How could I have allowed that to happen?* I let him slice my skin with that knife, and use me for his depraved needs, and worse yet, I enjoyed it.

Even now, with terror crawling all over my naked skin, I can feel my pussy weeping with the memory of how he felt, deep inside of me. How my pussy had to stretch to accommodate his length and girth, and the feeling of his piercings that graced his cock, as they rubbed across the walls of my core. *Fuck, get it together, Chrissy, we have to get out of here, the fucker has kidnapped us, and taken us somewhere!* I admonish myself, as my terrified eyes search for a way out of this room, and a way to release myself from the chain holding me here.

I run over to the wall with the hook on unsteady legs, my bare feet slapping against the thick carpet with a thudding noise, the cold air forcing a shiver to wrack my body, and my nipples to pucker into tight points. My panicked eyes glance down at my naked flesh, and I can see blooming bruises, in the shape of large fingerprints, forming on the pale skin of my breasts, hips, and thighs. A cold sweat breaks out across my body despite the chilly temperature in the room, and my ass, lower back, and thighs sting from all the cuts he made on my flesh with the blade. My feet sink into thick taupe carpeting, as I brace my legs and try to yank the chain from the wall. After a few fruitless attempts, I realize the damn thing is secure and going nowhere. Tears begin to slide from the corners of my eyes, as I fight with the sobs that are choking me, and I rush to the other side of the room and force the blinds up roughly, turning the latch for the window. Dread sinks to the bottom of my stomach as I get a glimpse of the bars across the glass from the outside. *I'm trapped in here, this is a fucking cage!*

No, this can't be happening to me; this has to be a nightmare that I'm trapped in. I race to one of the two visible doors, throwing it open, only to be presented with an all-white ensuite bathroom featuring a toilet, a small vanity with various packages on the counter, and a standup corner shower. There's no window in the space, and as far as I can tell, the only things I can use to defend myself are neatly stacked towels on a shelf, and a packaged toothbrush, and hairbrush. I rip one of the towels down from the stack, causing all of them to cascade to the floor, and wrap it around my naked body. One look in the mirror shows me that my eyes are horrifically wide, my skin's deathly pale, and I look like a frightened little girl, running from the boogeyman under the bed. Except my monster is *real*, and he's taken me somewhere and chained me like a beast. I lean forward and get a glimpse of the metal around my neck; it's a thick silver metal collar, and as far as I can see, there is no clasp or seam. The chain that trails from it is linked to an 'O ring' in the center that looks fabricated on. The chain is long enough to span all of the room, and allow me to use the bathroom. I scrutinize it for weaknesses in the links I can see, but it's hopeless; they look well-made and firm.

We are going to die, my mind whispers to me with hysteria. I can't get enough air inside my lungs, my chest is so tight and constricted, as I brace myself against the vanity counter. My mouth fills with sour bile, and has me gagging over the sink until I spew the meager contents of my stomach, as tears and snot slide down my face. How long have I been here? Where is here? How did this fucker kidnap me out of *'the hole'* without anyone noticing? *Oh my god*, was the peacock in on it? He had to be. Rage fills me at being played, and I vow if I ever get the hell out of here, I'm going to bust that idiot's pretty face.

Who is this psychopath, and what does he intend to do with me? All these thoughts race through my mind in rapid succession, causing further anxiety to rise, and before I know it, I'm down on my knees, trembling and gasping for air. I wrap my fingers around the collar, trying to pull it away from my skin as my head spins, and I have a full-blown panic attack. I can't breathe, some deranged fucker has kidnapped me. I clutch at my chest, pain wrenching through it sharply, as my heart pounds frantically. He's going to murder me, and before he does, he's going to make me wish for death. I've watched enough serial killer documentaries to know there is no surviving this, at least not with my mind intact.

The world around me gets dimmer and dimmer as I lose consciousness, and fall to the bathroom floor with a thud. My last thought is that I'll never see Toothless or Daisy ever again. Why was I so damn reckless?

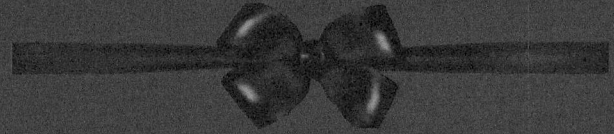

I wake with a start, my body bolting straight up as I clutch my neck, pulling on the weight that feels so heavy around it. I'm back on the bed, this time with a dark beige silk sheet covering my naked body. I kick back the sheet and rise to my feet, racing across the room towards the door I hadn't tried before I passed out. I turn the handle, adrenaline surging through me, but the door doesn't budge, and defeat slithers through me, falling into the pit of my stomach like a ball of lead. *Locked.* Of course, the fucking door is locked, Chrissy! The fucker has abducted you and chained you to a damn wall! There are bars on the windows, for fuck's sake!

How did I get back on the bed? Was he in here again with me while I was passed out? Oh my God, did he touch me again? I turn round and round in the small space, fear causing all my thoughts to mesh together, and my chest tightening painfully again with another impending panic attack. There has to be something I can use to protect myself; I have to do something, not remain here like a lamb awaiting the slaughter.

"Think, Chrissy!" I admonish myself, my hands tightening into fists, ready to pummel him if he pops out of hiding.

    The metal chain drags along the floor, the links clicking together obscenely, and grating on my frazzled nerves. I get tangled in the length, trip, and fall to the ground, the carpet burning against my knees. "FUCK! Let me out of here, you fucking psycho!" I rise and scream, as I charge at the door, and use my fists and feet to bang on it. Other than the sound of my wheezing and labored breath, no other sound greets me. The place beyond the door seems quiet and still, as if no one is out there, but that can't be; someone put me back on that bed.

    My anger ascends at the predicament I find myself in. The one I am to blame for, because I went to that glory hole and allowed him to touch me. I should have followed my first instinct, grabbed Toothless and Daisy, and ran. Now look at me, trapped like an animal in a cage, waiting for a masked villain to do whatever he wants with me. The rage continues to mount inside of me, and I dash to the dresser, pulling on the drawers, but some mechanism keeps them from completely being removed. I can't control myself; I'm so furious that I yank the accent chair, and it topples on its side. Next goes the dresser; I pull it until it falls forward, the drawers all opening and hitting the carpet with a rancorous thud. I race to the blinds and wrench them down from the window, until muted light pours through, and causes menacing shadows from the bars across the walls. I grip the sheets from the bed and throw them to the ground, grabbing the corner of the mattress and upending it on its side, against the window that won't allow my escape. My breathing is hoarse and coming too rapidly. I'm starting to feel lightheaded again, and I'm out of steam. I fall to the floor and crawl to a corner, bringing my knees up to my chest and wrapping my arms around them, to make myself as small as possible, as my body shakes with fear and cold. The chain reminds me of my status, a captive, an unwilling victim of whatever fucked up monster has taken me.

    Tears fall down my face as hopelessness begins to set in. I thought what I had already survived in my life was horrible. All the foster homes I lived in, where I never felt safe and didn't know if I would be beaten, abused, or raped, somehow seemed to be less frightening than my current situation. I think the difference was that I could have run away back then, even though living on the streets as a child would have been difficult and terrifying, but now I don't have that option. This maniac has taken all of my avenues of escape away, and I am stuck awaiting a fate that I don't know if I can survive.

A part of me already wishes for death, knowing it will be a mercy compared to what he could do to me. I know this man is not mentally well; who in their right mind kidnaps someone, after drugging and assaulting them in their home? Who the hell gifts a woman the severed hands of a man who touched her? I still don't even remember whose hands they could be. No, death would be preferable to whatever he's going to do to me.

"Just kill me now, asshole! I will murder you if I get the chance!" I yell into the silence, but not a single sound is heard in response. *Fuck, I am going to die.*

Chapter 23
Santa

I watch her through the cameras as she exhausts herself once again, throws a tantrum like a brat, and destroys the room I placed her in. My eyes roll at her antics; my sweet little temptation is so dramatic, but also filled with a vicious temper, one I long to explore. The words she yells into the silent space amuse me. She wants me to kill her? Does she think that I will give her the opportunity to murder me? *Foolish girl.*

No, she'll remain where she is, and I will do whatever I want with her, regardless of her wishes, for as long as I see fit, and she entertains me. My phone buzzes on the table next to my keyboard, and a grimace crosses my face when I get a look at the screen. What does this asshole want right now? I'm fucking busy, but he thinks I'm always at his beck and call. I've never seriously considered patricide before, but more and more, it's becoming a necessary option. "What?" I question, as I answer and put him on speakerphone.

"Is that any way to answer the phone to your father, you ungrateful asshole? I've been trying to reach you!" His furious voice blares back at me, and instantly causes my heckles to rise.

"What exactly do I have to be grateful to you for, *hmm?* It seems I'm the one always getting you out of shifty situations, *Governor*, not the other way around." My eyes watch as Chrissy's head meets her knees, tears still sliding down her beautiful face, as shudders wrack her petite body. She's going to get dehydrated if she keeps crying like that. She hasn't eaten at all since the diner, and I know she vomited the contents of her stomach earlier. I can't let her get sick. That would ruin all my fun.

I get up from my desk, grab the phone, and wander off to check on my provisions. I know I had a saline bag, and a vitamin pack or two here in my reserves. If she refuses to eat or drink anything, then I'll sedate her pretty ass, tie her down and force her to take nourishment through an intravenous; one way or another, she'll stay alive. She doesn't get to fucking leave me until I'm ready for her to. The fact that I've never cared whether any of my other victims stayed hydrated doesn't escape me, but I'm choosing to ignore it, like all the other red flags that are waving brightly at me. "Are you even listening to me, Nicholas?" My father's voice interrupts my thoughts, and I realize that I haven't heard a word he's been blubbering. "Nope, what were you droning on about?"

"*Jesus, boy!* Get your head out of your ass and in the game, this is fucking serious!" He yells, and the instant need to hang up on him causes my thumb to hover over the red circle on my screen. "You left a witness behind to your brother's incident. One that could put his ass in jail, and tie him to the hooker if she's ever found!" *That bitch will never be found, at least not in one recognizable piece.*

"I didn't leave shit behind, you neglected to provide me with that information. Am I supposed to guess that someone, besides the hooker sucking his cock, saw your idiot son committing a felony? I can't do my job if I don't have all the facts, *Dad!*"

"It doesn't matter who's to blame, Nicholas. The fact remains that this other idiot has already gone to his local police station, and made a report claiming that he witnessed a hit-and-run." He releases an annoyed, self-righteous sigh through the phone, and I can hear him pacing back and forth in those stupid pretentious loafers he insists on wearing, that squeak when he walks. "They haven't put all the pieces together *yet*, and we are lucky that I have friends in each of the departments, to provide me with the necessary information to keep us safe."

Us safe? Like the fucker is really worried about anyone but himself and his image. He has moles and lackeys, not friends; my father doesn't trust anyone enough to consider them a friend. Shit, I'm not even sure he trusts me and my brother, and we are his offspring. No, everything with Governor Brantford is a balancing game of what he can use you best for, and my job is always to clean up the manure he and my brother find themselves neck deep in, so that their hands can remain clean. "Just give me the name, and I'll take care of it, and Dad, I'm going to be unavailable after this shit for a while. You'll either have to make sure you and Micah don't fuck anything up over the holidays, maybe longer, or deal with it yourself."

Silence greets my statement, and I can almost see his beet-red face, stiff jaw, and clenched fists on the other end of the line. My father doesn't like to be dictated to, and he doesn't enjoy boundaries. Well, he doesn't enjoy it when anyone sets them against him. The bastard is a narcissistic sociopath, and I guess the apple doesn't fall far from the tree. "What or whom has you occupied, Nicholas? The holidays are a time for family; we should be together," he grits.

I can't contain the gruff laugh that escapes me, is this fucker for real? "*Family? Together?* Is this some kind of joke, *Dad?* Last year you spent Christmas day with your face in a nineteen-year-old escort's pussy, while your dick was deep inside a male hooker's ass, and you were high as a kite on coke. Neither Micah nor I saw you, until you needed a photo to post for your supporters, in front of your fake tree."

"You're an asshole, you know that, Nicholas? Just take care of Ricky Sanders and make him disappear, and Nicholas, whatever you're up to, make sure it doesn't link back to our family, or I'll have someone make *you* disappear." The bastard hangs up the phone, and I'm left fuming. How fucking dare he threaten me? The only reason I'm going to help clean up this mess, is because I would rather not see my baby brother behind bars, even if he is an entitled, spoiled shit. Plus, there is no doubt in my mind that weak fucker would snitch on me to get a lighter sentence. I glare at my screen; I think the new year is going to bring an unfortunate accident to Governor Brantford, and leave his seat wide open for someone else to take.

After confirming that I do, in fact, have a few vitamin packs, I sit behind my computer and start pulling up everything I can find about Ricky Sanders, who decided to be a good citizen and report a crime like a damn psycho. My glance keeps returning to the screen where Chrissy has fallen into an exhausted sleep on the floor, her arms still tightly woven around herself, as if she's warding off a monster. I guess right now, I'm the monster in her tale, rather than a white knight, not that I ever wanted to be her, or anyone's, savior. Fuck that, where's the fun in that?

The sight of her pale flesh calls to me, making my mouth salivate for a taste of her, and my cock hardens with the need to be deep inside of her tight pussy once again. I glance at the time on the phone, and I see that nightfall will be here soon. That'll provide the best opportunity to deal with Ricky Sanders, without having other witnesses involved. I don't really have the time to play with my sweet temptation, but I can't force myself to resist her lure. She's here under my roof, my captive, my perfect gift, and she's finally mine. I would be remiss if I didn't entertain her for a bit, and make her feel welcome.

I get up, don my skull mask, and pull down my sleeves, ensuring I cover all my visible flesh and tattoos, so as not to give my identity away too soon. I want Chrissy to wonder who has taken her, and build up that sense of fear and determination to fight me. I need her strong, fierce, and filled with spite, just like that first night I laid eyes on her, and she dared to have me thrown out of the strip club. That's the woman who caught my interest and has kept it. She caused her own demise that very first evening, and I've looked forward to having my collar around her neck ever since.

I reach for my tranq gun and ready a dart with a mild sedative; I know it's not really fair to keep sedating her, but for what I have in mind, I want her pliable but semi-alert. I grab my blade and slip it into my back pocket, as lust sets a fire blazing in my veins. I wonder how many cuts her body can endure before she goes into shock, or loses too much blood. I have to be cautious and control my urges to see her bleed. If I lose control of myself, it would be so easy to damage her, or end her life prematurely. I have no intention of giving up my holiday gift; she has to make it to the new year at least, then I can reconsider what to do with her, and if keeping her alive is worth the trouble.

I move through my darkened and silent cabin, a place filled with solitude, peace, and comfort. It's far from the bustle of the city and, more importantly, away from my father and his politics. I purchased this cabin years ago with the inheritance my mother left me and Micah, when she passed away, much to my father's ire. He preferred that I remain close by, or in our family home, so that he could keep his eye on me, and his nose firmly in my business. The cabin is deep in a wooded area, over an hour outside of Boston's city limits, and entirely off the grid. There are no records of my home in any city ledgers; I made sure to wipe any possible traces of it, including making the man who helped me build it disappear. As far as the world knows, Ajor Tsuoc is living a very comfortable retired life in Mexico somewhere, but the truth, however, is that his body is decomposing in a metal chemical barrel filled with acid, in a warehouse in Detroit. More importantly, my malignant father doesn't know its location, so he can't just show up here and attempt to demand my obedience.

I reach the locked door to the room where my temptation is residing. I pull up the hidden cameras on my phone, so I can ensure she is still where I last saw her. A pang of some foreign emotion causes my chest to tighten, when I glimpse her still tightly pressed into the corner, her body stiff and on guard, even in slumber. I shake off the feeling that has no place in my world. Mercy and pity are for the weak-minded, and that's never been me. I don't care that she's scared, just that she is now mine.

I unlock the door with the electronic keypad and slide the door open. I have to push my weight against it, since my little temptation has made a fucking mess of her room, and the accent chair becomes an obstacle to my entry. Her body twitches with the soft sounds I make to get within the space, and closer to her. I point the tranquilizer gun at her shoulder and pull the trigger, and her body jerks backward, as the sharp end makes contact with her flesh. Her arms release their tight hold on her legs, and her head jolts upwards until her frightened chestnut brown eyes open, rise, and meet mine.

Chapter 24

Santa

"N OOOO," she screams, and attempts to get to her feet, but the effects of the sedative are already making their way into her bloodstream, causing her to be woozy as she stumbles back into the wall, and crashes against its surface. Her legs give out on her, forcing her to sit at an odd angle, and her head dips forward, causing her chin to rest against her chest. My poor temptation, doesn't she realize that she's a mosquito fighting a war against a lion?

I push forward, shoving upended furniture out of my way, until I'm a mere few feet away from her, and taking in her appearance in the flesh. Her pale complexion causes the freckles on her skin to stand out, and I yearn to count every one of them. All the various cuts I've made over the last twenty-four hours decorate her limbs, and looking at them causes my cock to twitch inside of my pants, and beads of precum to slip from the slit.

"Mon... ster," she slurs, as she attempts to force her head back up with difficulty, and her eyes try to focus on me. She gets an adorable frown on her face, and two little lines between her furrowed brows appear, giving her a look of innocence, instead of the rage she must feel. Her hand rises as if to swat at me, but the limb must feel too heavy in her drugged state, as it flops back onto her legs.

I bend down until I'm squatting in front of her and push away her matted auburn hair from her face. She is truly beautiful; in another time, sonnets would be written about her. She really is a sight to behold, and I'm so ecstatic that she is all mine. "Am I *your* monster, sweet temptation? How I desire to *devour* you." I press my fingers into her scalp, yanking on her silky, long tresses, and forcing her head to move towards me. My forehead meets hers, as I take deep inhales of her scent, the mixture of sweat, fear, and her natural flowery tone diluted by the mask, which makes me unreasonably cranky. I want to press my skin against hers, and feel its velvety, warm surface as it makes contact with my rough texture. I need to rub my lips on hers, taste her breaths and moans, and consume her screams until there is nothing left of her. It's a need that I can't seem to reason with. The desire to tame her, and make her mine, is the most overwhelming sensation I have ever felt, when usually I am frigid and hollow inside.

"You're everything I didn't know I craved, sweet temptation. I can no longer breathe comfortably without you. You have infected me, body, mind, and soul, and for you, that could have deadly consequences." The dark amber flecks in her eyes are stunning, and in their frightened depths, I witness apprehension but also enlightenment. She knows she will never leave here alive if I don't allow it. Right now, that doesn't seem likely, and for some bizarre reason, that makes me melancholy, an uncharted emotion for me.

I slip my arms below hers and wrap them around her torso, lifting her slight weight into my lap, and forcing her legs to wrap around my hips. Her cooled flesh puckers with my touch, and a shiver dashes across her soft flesh, as I sit back on the carpeted floor with her in my grasp. Her warm pussy rubs against my hardened cock, forcing a moan to leave my lips. I thrust against her, the material of my pants the only thing preventing me from being deep inside of her.

"Ahh," the garbled sound leaves her, in protest to my grip. Her eyes widen, with the feel of the tip of my cock stroking against her clit. Even though she's sedated, and her body is languid in my hold, it doesn't stop her breath from ratcheting up, and her breathing to become a husky tempo. Fuck, I want to tear into her and have my wicked way. I want to use her, every one of her holes, leaving her marked and full of my cum, until it's pouring out of her. "Are you wet, my pet? Does this pretty pussy wish to be stretched and filled by my cock?"

I release one of my arms from around her body, and trail my hand slowly down her heaving chest in the space between our bodies. Her rose-tipped nipples stand erect, awaiting my finger's ministrations, and her skin pebbles further with my touch. A low, garbled groan sounds from her lips, as my fingers strum and twist her nipple. Her body spasms against mine, and I can feel the heat of her core against my rock-hard cock. Fuck, I need to be inside of her, to feel her take me to the hilt, and clench around my thick length. I push her further back on my lap none too gently, and release my hold on her nipple to undo my button, and unzip my pants. My stiff cock springs forward, released from his imprisonment, covered in beads of precum. I press my thumb to my slit, coating it with my drips of cum, and then slip it to Chrissy's lips, painting them in my essence, like some amusing, depraved lipstick. Fuck, the mask is in the way of me licking myself off of her mouth. I desperately want to taste myself mixed with her flavor.

Soon, I can remove the mask and stop this charade, and allow her to see who her new owner is. Will she be surprised that it's me? I know that she's attracted to me; she wasn't as inconspicuous in her behavior at the strip club, or the diner. Will her confinement be easier to bear, knowing that the monster who has stolen her is known to her, or will that make her even more frightened? I can't wait to get my answers, but for now, this will have to do.

I push her body forward again, my cock rubbing against her wet pussy lips and slipping between their seam, as I begin a slow rhythm of thrusting against her swollen nub. A shudder rolls through her body, and her head drops to the side, limp, but still fully aware of what is happening here. One of my large hands grips her hip while the other braces her back, keeping her erect and forcing her to ride me. "You're drenched, temptation. Look at how your body responds to mine, how it craves my touch."

Her chest heaves as she tries to get enough air, and her pupils dilate with the desire that is coursing through her veins. A lovely pink blush rises on her chest, neck, and cheeks, and makes me want to add my fingermarks and a hand necklace to their stain. A part of me wants to hold off and play with her a bit more, but I'm slowly losing the battle for my control, and running out of time. I tighten my grip until it's punishing, and I know she's feeling pain, and with the next thrust, I impale myself inside of her warm pussy, balls deep. A growl rents the air as I bounce her lethargic body on my cock, forcing her to receive my punishing thrusts with no recourse. "Fuck, temptation! You feel so fucking good, so warm and tight; this pussy is mine."

Her head bounces back and forth, her gorgeous auburn hair cascading down her back, and over her shoulders. I pull her tightly to me, until my chest is pressed against hers, as I thrust up inside of her. My hand on her back pulls my mask up just past my lips, and I take the opportunity to bite down hard on the flesh of her shoulder. Her whole body seizes, her core tightening on my cock in a death grip, and she lets go, her orgasm ripping through her, as she soaks my lap with a garbled cry. My balls tighten painfully as a shiver slides down my back, and lightning snakes through my body, as my own release catapults me into bliss, and I cum deep inside of her pussy. "*Mine*," I groan, as I lick the drops of blood that have welled on the surface of her skin from my unhinged bite, and drag my mask back down.

    I pull back and partly release my tight hold, meeting her gaze. She looks adorable, all soft and relaxed. Her lips are set in a slight droopy, drugged smile, and her eyes are closed, with dark lashes against her high cheekbones. Sexy, that is what she is. A true temptation, one that I would love to spend the rest of the night fucking, but I have to go deal with this *'Ricky'* fucker. With an exasperated sigh, I place her sitting up against the wall next to me, my eyes divert to her pussy, and I watch as my cum slowly slides down from inside of her, and coats her pussy lips. I rise and grab hold of my semi-hard cock, and trail the tip across her lips and cheek, wiping my cum off on her skin before tucking myself away.

    I'm pissed that I have to end our session so soon. I want more of her; I want to spend all night buried deep inside of all her orifices, while she cries and begs me to release her. My gaze travels around the messy room, causing my OCD to soar at the state of mayhem she has caused with her tantrum. With a deep, agitated sigh, I set about rectifying the room's state, putting the upended mattress back on the bed, and the chair and dresser back in their correct positions, while I hum the melody to *'Santa Claus is Coming to Town'*. Once everything is finally back in its original place, and as neat as it's going to get, I squat down, slip one hand below her legs and the other braced around her torso, and lift her carefully onto the bed. Her eyes watch me from lowered lids, as I arrange her in the middle of the bed, and prop a pillow below her head. Her glistening pussy calls to me, and I can't resist getting a taste of her arousal and mine mixed together. I grab the discarded sheet from the floor and drape it over her face, leaving a corner open so she can still get air, and crawl onto the bed between her legs, before lifting the skull mask to my forehead, and diving in between her legs and licking her sweet pussy. "Fuck, temptation, you taste like heaven," I growl into her swollen skin.

Her musky, delectable, sweet taste mixed with my strong, salty cum is an aphrodisiac that I can't get enough of. I use my shoulders to push her legs open wider as I set to feast on her pretty pussy. I suck on her throbbing, swollen clit, and graze my teeth against its sensitive surface, before sucking one of her pussy lips and using my fingers to part her open, so I can shove my tongue inside of her core. I pull back and spit on her pussy, using my fingers to paint my name into her soft skin. All the while, little noises are muffled from below the sheet as she enjoys my actions. Her body tightens, the muscles in her stomach scrunching and spasming once again, and I'm rewarded with another gush of her delicious cum. The warm, sweet liquid trails down my lips and coats my chin, and I've never enjoyed eating anything more than I'm relishing consuming her. I suck and lick until she's clean, swallowing down both of our essences, and knowing it's the nourishment I need to go on my errand. With one final lick, I pull back with devastating regret, shove down my mask, and yank the sheet off her to cover all of her body, and expose her face.

Her lips are open in a silent gasp, but her eyes are closed. The sedative must be starting to wear off because I watch as her fingers curl into fists, and I know it will only be a matter of time before she can move all her limbs, and will try to attack me to regain her freedom. Unfortunately, it's time to go, and playing with her some more will have to wait.

I squeeze her breast over the sheet and rise from the bed, heading towards the door. "Don't trash the room, sweet temptation; it won't assist you in getting out of here, and the next time, I'll enjoy tanning your ass for your unruly behavior."

I close the door behind me, activating the lock, and head towards my car, knowing that Ricky Sanders is about to die a painful fucking death for interrupting my plans for the night. The taste of Chrissy lingers on my lips and tongue, and my cock juts out in front of me, begging to be returned to her warm hole. I fist myself through my pants and groan; soon I'll be back and have her all to myself, and fuck anyone who tries to interrupt my holiday plans. It's two days before Christmas, and all I ever wanted is already here and waiting for me to enjoy it.

A.L.Maruga

I decide to leave her with a bit of holiday music to get her in the spirit, so that when I return, we can really enjoy ourselves. I pull out my phone, and activate the hidden sound system that runs through the whole cabin. After selecting a few songs to go on a playlist, I press play and keep the volume low. *Merry Christmas, Baby* by *Christina Aguilera* starts crooning around the cabin, and I leave with a delighted grin.

Chapter 25

The Gift

The sunlight greets my tired eyes, as I force myself to sit up in the foreign bed. I drag my fingers through my rat's nest of hair and push it away from my face, as I grimace at all the light flooding the room. I really shouldn't have destroyed the blinds; that kind of backfired on me, and now I have to deal with the daylight like a vampire allergic to the sun. "Fucking hell," I groan. My mind processes the fact that there is still faint music coming from somewhere, and it's not just my delusional imagination. *Is that Sia singing about Mistletoe? What the ever living fuck? This guy really is insane.*

My eyes skate over the room's interior. I know the fucker told me not to destroy it and threatened me with punishment, but once I regained the use of my limbs, and that drug he injected me with wore off, I couldn't contain my rage and went to town, causing even more destruction, until I exhausted myself and crawled back into bed. My sore, swollen pussy reminds me that he's not small or gentle, and I'll probably pay harshly for being a brat. Ugh, gross, I feel the sticky wetness between my legs, which forces me to recollect that I was too out of it last night to think rationally and have a shower, and his cum is still inside of me and coating my legs. *Motherfucker.*

Thank fuck I have an IUD, otherwise who knows what could happen. I don't wish to be this psychopath's baby momma, nor do I desire to be featured in the next documentary on one of the streaming services, about giving birth to my captor's babies. *Fuck that shit, I'd rather die.* A shudder runs through me at the thought, and all the hairs on my arms stand on end. "You better not have any STI, motherfucker, or I'll rip your damn cock off!" I yell into the room, as the song changes to *Adam Lambert* crooning some shit about being home for Christmas. I quickly wrap the silky sheet around myself and head into the bathroom, slipping the chain to the gap at the bottom of the door and closing it firmly. Not that there is a lock or anything that would prevent the psychopath from coming in here to get me if he so desired.

A huge part of me is relieved that he didn't return last night to terrorize me some more. My emotions and thoughts are in complete turmoil right now in my head, and at war with each other. A part of me is terrified that I'm going to end up hacked to pieces, and buried in the woods in a shallow grave, or Christmas dinner for wild animals. The other part of me enjoyed him taking what he wanted from me, and using me for his depraved needs. That part of me fills me with self-loathing and disgust. How could I take perverse pleasure in being fucked by a madman who kidnapped me? There has to be something wrong with me, right?

I turn on the water as hot as it will go and step under the spray, allowing my skin to redden, and the soothing sounds of water to drown out my sobs. Will I ever see Toothless and Daisy again? How long is this psycho going to allow me to live, once he's had his fill of me? After a few moments, I grab the shampoo bottle on the shelf, which suspiciously is the same shitty brand I have at home, and wash my hair. The bastard could have at least provided me with better quality shit than what I can afford, if he's going to murder me anyways; some luxuries would be appreciated before I die.

After conditioning my hair and scrubbing my body down, the water is becoming frigid, and I have no choice but to leave the shower, and face my reality. I grab one of the towels from the floor that I threw around in my fury last night, and step before the mirror. The face that greets me looks pale as fuck and exhausted. I lean forward to get a glimpse of the bite mark on my shoulder, which is all red and inflamed. *Fucking vampire mauled me, I'm going to kill this asshole.* All of the bruises and cuts along the surface of my skin have me grimacing. How many more will decorate my flesh before this is all done with? The stupid metal collar and chain make it almost impossible not to choke myself as I move around, and it gets caught on stuff. Frustration continues to mount inside of me until it becomes tinder for a flame, and I start screaming like a wild banshee at the top of my lungs, until my voice is hoarse, and my throat is raw.

Tears burn my eyes and threaten to escape, but I refuse to unleash them. Crying has never solved anything in my life, and it's not about to start now. I square my shoulders, steeling my spine, and force myself to step out of the washroom and back into the bedroom, and when I do, my eyes widen with shock.

While I was in the washroom, the psychopath must have come in and tidied up the room. The remaining unbroken furniture is back in its place, and there are new dark blue silky sheets on the bed, along with a food tray with a plastic carafe, and a paper plate loaded with pancakes, fresh fruit, and plastic cutlery. My stomach instantly growls loudly, as the scents assault my senses, and remind me that I haven't eaten in over twenty-four hours. My eyes catch on a long, oversized white T-shirt draped on the corner of the bed. I hurriedly drop the towel and throw the shirt over me, feeling instantly more confident with clothing covering my skin. As a shield against him, it's weak, but at this point, beggars can't be choosers, and something is better than being naked all day.

I approach the food with suspicion, as some male singer asks faintly what he can bring me for Christmas in the background. How about my fucking freedom, asshole, or is that too much to ask for?

My gaze lands on the food, and my stomach rumbles loudly again. Is it possible he put something inside of it to drug me, so he can have his wicked way with me? A snort escapes me, as I think over how easy it was for him to drug me both times. He doesn't need to put shit in the food; the fucker can sedate me anytime he feels like it, from a distance, and there is very little I can do about it. I bring a piece of strawberry up to my lips, and the sweet flavor makes me moan out loud. Fuck it, if I'm going to die anyway, at least I won't starve. I've gone too many years barely eating, and certainly not being able to afford fresh fruit like this. I start stuffing my face like a wild, ravenous animal, until I've dispatched all the food, and drank the hot black coffee, and my stomach is full. I grab the empty tray and place it on the dresser before lying back down on the freshly made bed, and groaning with satisfaction. My tired eyes begin to droop as my body feels heavy and lethargic, and I burrow further into the mattress, my damp hair soaking the pillow, and the top of my shirt. Fuck, I should have dried it, but suddenly, I'm so tired that even the thought of rising from the bed feels too difficult.

The lack of sleep and the constant fear have done a number on me, and my body and mind are utterly spent. Maybe a quick nap will help me regain my strength, so I can fight against this asshole when he returns. I have no doubt in my mind he will be back; he's kidnapped me and brought me here for a reason. Could it be that he just wants to fuck me? Maybe this asshole is horrendous looking, and can't get girls in the normal way, and has to capture women to feed his sick, perverse needs. An image of the hairy beast from *'Beauty and the Beast'* enters my mind and makes me chuckle. Naw, that fucker was cute, but this guy must be hideous. The thought brings a moment of dismay that I've not only had this fucker inside of me once, but twice now. Ugh, fuck, maybe it's better that he keeps his mask on.

As I'm about to drift off to sleep, a thought pops unbidden into my mind. His eyes were dark silvery-gray last night, not black like the first time in my room. Was that a trick of the light, or did I imagine it?

I drift off to sleep with images of monsters, each one more grotesque and frightening than the last. This monster made one mistake by taking me: he thinks he's taken a helpless princess, when really I'm a warrior, and have no intention of not saving myself. Fuck him, he wants a fight, I'll give him one.

Chapter 26

The Gift

I groan as the sound of *Jingle-fucking-bells* makes my head feel like it's going to explode. Why is this asshole playing this shit so loud when I'm trying to sleep? I go to turn over on the bed only to realize two things: one, I'm no longer on the luxurious bed with its buttery soft sheets, and two, all of my limbs are tied down to whatever padded surface I'm lying on. "WHAT THE FUCK, ASSHOLE!" I scream as I try yanking on my arms to no avail. A quick look in the direction of my wrist shows me it's confined in a thick leather cuff, and attached to a wooden post protruding from the surface I'm lying on. This fucker drugged me again, *dammit*. I shouldn't have eaten the food.

The music suddenly lowers, and the pounding of my heart against my rib cage seems to intensify. "Naughty temptation, we really have to do something about that dirty mouth of yours. Maybe a hard cock lodged in your throat would fix it?" A husky, amused voice comments from somewhere behind my head, and apprehension races through my body. I attempt to strain my neck to get a glimpse of him, but the fucker has somehow locked down the stupid collar around my neck, preventing me from moving. "How 'bout I bite it fucking off, you psychopath?!"

"*Tsk, tsk*, my pet. I guess I'll have to teach you some manners." The next thing I know, my shirt is being forcefully yanked over my face, and cold water is splashing over the surface, in what feels like a never-ending cascade. I spew as I get a mouthful of water, and it begins choking me as I attempt to cough and breathe at the same time, and more water ends up going up my nose. *Jesus fucking Christ, this nut is trying to waterboard me!*

I feel movement around me, as I try frantically to move my head the small amount I can, to dodge the water. A heavy weight lands on my lower abdomen as he straddles me, constricting my breathing further, and the water suddenly stops. "There she is, my sweet little temptation. Are you going to behave, or do I have to continue with my lessons?" The shirt is pulled back off my face, and my terrified eyes meet dark gray orbs behind a black skull mask. "We can either enjoy your time here, my pet, or we can waste the holidays with me having to train you to behave. You know you're already on Santa's naughty list."

"You're... insane," I gasp as I spit water from my mouth, and it dribbles pitifully down my chin. A muffled, throaty laugh sounds from behind the mask as he lifts some of his weight from my stomach, and his bare hands go to the button of his pants. "True, but that fact only makes this more exciting, doesn't it?" My eyes widen as he pulls down his zipper and pulls out his long cock, and I get my first up-close look at what has been inside of me.

Holy fuck, he has a complete Jacob's ladder along the length of his cock, and it's girthy and long. No wonder I'm fucking sore, this asshole is the size of a gigantic fucking dildo. I watch as his huge, veiny hand wraps around the thick head and squeezes, before a shudder runs down his body and vibrates into mine, and he strokes himself from root to tip. "You see, temptation, here's the thing. There is not much you can do to fight against my wants and needs. In fact, if you want to stay alive, I'd advise against trying my patience; I have very little of it."

He shifts forward, straddling my chest, his meaty cock approaching my mouth, and his weight feels almost crushing. "Open up and be a good girl, and Santa will give you a treat." He cackles as the tip of his cock brushes against my bottom lip. I force my lips to seal closed, using my teeth on the inside of my lips to keep them shut, despite my terror, and my eyes glare into his face through the mask. A sigh escapes him, and he pulls back, his cock releasing from his hand and bobbing on my chin and neck. "I see we're going to have to do this the hard way. Don't say I didn't give you a chance to do the right thing, temptation."

Water immediately begins to pour over my head, this time without the barrier of my t-shirt in the way, and a scream rips from me, forcing my mouth open. A ton of water pools inside, and I begin to suffocate as my lungs heave. He pulls back, the water disappearing again, as his hand goes to my throat and massages the column, as I force myself to swallow, and water gushes from my mouth and nose. I realize the fucker is humming the tune to *'Santa Baby'* while doing all this psychotic shit to me. I'm going to die to Christmas music, how can this be my life right now? I don't even enjoy the holidays.

"Are you going to be a good girl now?" As much as I want to be defiant, I want to live more, and maybe playing along with this psycho will give me the opportunity to escape, or kill him; either at this point would be preferable to being tied down and waiting to die. "Yesss," I cough.

"Good, let's try that again, shall we?" He fists his cock and pushes it against my lips, and I open them wide, allowing his meaty, stiff cock inside of my mouth. His musky, salty taste hits my tongue as his metal piercings glide across the surface, and his tip hits the back of my throat. His other hand rises, and he trails his fingers along my cheek in a gentle caress, before his thumb rubs against my upper lip, and my lips tightly close automatically around his cock.

"That's it, my sweet, suck hard. Show me what a perfect slut you are." He hums again to the tune as he thrusts in and out of my mouth, each time hitting the back of my throat and making me gag. My tongue slides against his piercings, as I loosen my throat and hollow my cheeks, taking him further down the tight column. Heat and desire surge through me at his naughty words and the feeling of him using me, and I can feel my core weeping with arousal. "You're perfect, such a *good girl*. This mouth was made to swallow my cock," he groans, as a feeling of satisfaction bathes over me at his depraved praise. My whole body flushes hot and tingles. I can feel my nipples standing erect, with the need to have them stroked and twisted. My core feels empty without him inside of me, and a sickening truth fills me: I want this; what he's doing to me is straight out of one of my darkest fantasies.

He pulls back, his cock slipping from inside of my mouth, as he stares down at me. His expression is unreadable because of the mask covering his face, and a desperate need to see his features overwhelms me, but I'm terrified to voice the request. I clear my sore throat, feeling the mixture of my drool, and his precum, on my lips and chin. His flint-colored eyes meet mine, and a moment of recollection strikes through me; where do I know those eyes from?

"Please, let me go," my voice trembles as I croak the words. He rises off of me completely and squats down near my exposed pussy, his masked chin resting on my thigh, as his warm fingers trail up and down my leg gently, and the humming gets louder. "You have the prettiest, pink pussy I have ever seen." His middle finger slips between my pussy lips, and plunges inside my tight hole, and stills as I squirm. "I think that's not what you want, temptation. I think you're speaking from a place of fear rather than pleasure. Let me fulfill all your fantasies. Let me show you how much bliss I can bring you."

It's on the tip of my tongue to refute his words, but in the next second, he sinks a second and third finger inside my pussy and begins thrusting. "Look at how wet you are, my beauty, but it's still not wet enough for what I have planned." I hear rustling, then a cold liquid flows down on top of my vagina, and meets with his fingers inside of me. A fourth finger slides inside to join its mates as he stretches me, scissoring his fingers, and rubbing against a spot deep inside of my pussy that has my toes curling. "So close, baby girl, just one more to go."

"No, no, no, please!" I beg, as pain and pleasure mix inside of me at how tight the fit is, and my body desperately wants to writhe against the surface that I'm lying on, but can't due to the restraints. "OH MY GOD!" I scream, as I feel him push his thumb inside of me and thrust hard, stretching me impossibly wide until his whole hand is inside of my pussy, and rubbing against my walls. The pain is instant and sharp, but he brings his other hand down on my breast in a harsh slap, and it diverts my attention. His fingers tweak and twist my sore, hard nipple, adding more delicious sensation to the mix as he fists my pussy, slowly thrusting in and out of me, my body gushing and making it easier for him. I feel the beginnings of an orgasm racing along my skin, fire in its wake. "Please, please!" I beg, but I'm not sure if I'm asking for my freedom, for him to stop, or to make me cum... everything is a muddled mess inside of my mind.

His hand leaves my breasts and finds its way down to my clit. His thumb rubs hard circles on the throbbing surface, and my whole body tightens as his thrusts become wilder, losing some of their rhythm. "You look so beautiful right now with my fist deep inside of you. The only thing better would be to have my cock in your ass at the same time, temptation."

Oh my God, no! There is no way my body can take that. He's got to be wrist deep inside of me, with his large hand, and thick fingers, pressing against my sensitive walls. The stretch burns, but is pleasurable, as my body acclimatizes to his touch. I can feel my core tightening, the orgasm refusing to be waylaid, as it sizzles up my spine and all my limbs tense. Heat sizzles across my flesh, and I realize I'm making disturbing mewling sounds like an animal. He applies more pressure to my sensitive clit, and I explode with a guttural scream, my whole body shuddering uncontrollably against the surface he has me tied to.

He yanks his hand out from inside of me, my cum sliding down his digits, and in my post-coital state, I can't follow his movements clearly. I feel the restraints on my ankles give way, and without warning, he climbs onto the surface I'm lying on, pushes my quaking legs to his shoulders, and drags his hard cock down my slick pussy lips before thrusting deep inside of me. "Fuck!" I scream as he thrusts without mercy, and the sound of skin slapping against skin is loud in the air, along with my panting breath. "So warm, fuck, I love being deep inside of you, temptation."

He thrusts a few more times, then pulls back the wet tip of his cock, pushing against my puckered hole. "Sorry, baby, but this is going to hurt so good," he grunts, as he forces his cock deep into my asshole, and I scream as tears slide down my face. Before I can even catch my breath, his thick fingers are back at my tight hole, and three of them are slipping inside of me, thrusting along in time with his thick cock inside my ass. "TOOOOO MUUCCCHHH!" I shout as I try to regain my staggered breathing.

"You can take it, my pet." His masked face looks away from where he's impaling me and stares at me, and in his dark orbs, I see pleasure but also madness. All the sensations coursing through my body overwhelm me all at once, as he loses himself to the pleasure, and his masked head tips back against his shoulders. His body tenses, shoulders going rigid, and his chest rises and falls rapidly as he unleashes himself on me, and takes his pleasure out on my body. I cum with a vicious, shrill scream once again, my breathing ragged and my eyes rolling into the back of my head. "You're mine," he growls and thrusts one last time, before slamming inside of me, and I can feel the warmth from his cum filling my ass.

A.L.Maruga

He pulls out of me as I slowly regain my overstimulated senses. My head thrashes minutely against the surface I'm restrained against, and I get a glimpse of the space I'm in through my exhausted, slitted eyes. Its dark green walls look sinister, with shadows projected across the space. From the limited area that I can see, there is a wall across the room with various whips and canes against it, and that brings me trepidation that he'll use those on me. His manly scent of sweat, musk, and something clean like pine, fills my nostrils as he leans in closer, his skull mask brushing against the surface of my face. "I will never let you go, temptation. As long as your heart beats, you will always be mine."

Chapter 27

Santa

Her fatigued body lies limp against the padded bench I strapped her to, and I watch as she endeavors to look around my space. Her eyes widen dramatically as she glimpses all my whips, crops, floggers, and paddles against the wall. I have to bite my bottom lip to restrain my laughter. She doesn't look excited to see all my favorite toys that I've prepared for us to enjoy over our Christmas holiday. A pained moan leaves her lips, and her face scrunches up in distress. I scramble further back on the bench, getting a good look at her swollen pussy and her ass, that's dripping with my cum. I hunger for a taste of her, and I can't stop myself from sliding off the bench to my knees, lifting my mask to my nose, and burying my mouth against her puckered hole. I lick and suck all of her juices, mixed with my cum, off of her asshole before plunging my tongue inside of her pussy. I can tell she's sore, as she hisses at my intrusion and tries to flinch away from me. The rich taste of her pussy juices, my cum, and a hint of blood assaults my tastebuds. Fuck, I must have hurt her a little when I fisted her pussy. A part of me feels a sensation I'm unaccustomed to, and it makes me incredibly uncomfortable. *Is that remorse that I'm feeling?*

I pull back from her pussy, and watch as a lone crystal tear slides down her cheek, and disappears into her rich auburn hair. Is she crying because I hurt her, she's scared, or due to the realization that she will die here, and never leave me? "You're... a monster," she gasps, her lips trembling as more tears pool against her hairline.

I don't bother to respond and dispute her accusation, I am what she names me. Her petite body tries to twist on the bench, and it's comical to watch as she attempts to contort herself, but ends up further exhausting herself and out of breath. Her legs squeeze closed, and I know she must be in pain, all of the adrenaline and euphoria having now faded. I tuck my spent cock away into my pants and leave the room, ensuring to lock the door behind me, as her swearing follows me from the space. She really does have a dirty potty mouth, and I'm going to have to cure her of that. I walk down the corridor to the door that leads to my bedroom. I move within the space without taking in any of the details until I reach my destination. For a moment, I grind to a halt; what the fuck am I doing right now? Am I about to run a bath for my captive?

The part of myself that I no longer recognize snarls back that she's hurt and in pain, and reasons that we can't continue to fuck her if she can't take it. The part I do recognize counters that we shouldn't care, that she'll bleed a lot more before we're done. I rip off the mask and stare at my features in the large mirror. The man who stares back at me is becoming a stranger, and I don't like it one bit. Chrissy Cranbrook is changing me little by little, lessening the psychopath and making him feel. I don't want the void inside of me filled by anything, especially not emotions that make me rethink my actions. I like myself unpredictable and unconquerable. Why is this one tiny, foul-mouthed woman changing me?

A frustrated growl leaves my lips, as I move towards the large copper bathtub I have in the space, turn on the water, and pour some bath salts inside of it. I'm not being weak or unreasonable; I argue with myself. I want to enjoy her for as long as possible, and although I relish listening to her screams, I would rather they be in pleasure rather than in pain, but at the end of the day, none of that will matter when I tire of her.

When the tub is nearly full, and the rich scent of lavender and eucalyptus fills the air, I re-don my mask and head back to my playroom to get her. At the door, I press my head against the wood surface and listen, as her heavy sobs make their way through the surface. *Fuck, how bad could I have hurt her? Has she never been fisted before?* Based on her porn history, I find that highly unlikely. I enter the room, and the sight causes my chest to tighten. She's managed to twist her lower body on the bench until she's on her side, and her knees are drawn up against her chest. Her arms are still outstretched above her and restrained in my leather cuffs, and her face is all red from the strain and her crying. *Dammit all to hell.*

I lean down and press my masked face against her hair, not really sure how to comfort her. "My sweet temptation, are you alright? What is causing you to cry like this?" My voice is gruff and accusatory through the mask, and she flinches and tries to make herself smaller. I move over to my wall and grab a pair of metal handcuffs from a hook, moving back and securing one wrist in its metal band, before releasing it from the leather cuff, and repeating it with her other wrist. She doesn't even attempt to fight me; her arms go limp in my grasp, as she uses her fallen hair to hide herself from me. I push it away from her face, and stare into her dark brown eyes, filled with misery, before wrapping my arms around her and lifting her bridal style in my grasp. "Tell me, or I'll punish you," I demand as I move towards the door.

Her head leans against my shoulder as soft sobs wrack her body, and I tighten my grip on her delicate flesh. She feels right in my arms, as if this is where she has always belonged. The thought rips through me, and where fear should be present at such a vulnerable emotion, I only feel certainty. I press my masked nose against her hair, wishing I didn't have anything between us. "I... I'll never see Toothless again... he'll think I abandoned... him. You... left my baby... without his momma... at Christmas."

Toothless? Baby? What the fuck, she's balling her eyes out over that slobbering beast? I release a frustrated groan against her hair, as I make my way through my bedroom and into my bathroom. All the while, more tears slide down her face, and her skin pebbles from the cool air. I force her to slide down my body until she's on unsteady feet, and I hold her by her elbow. "Don't try to fight me or escape, temptation. I don't want to hurt you further today." I release my hold and grab my blade from my pocket, slicing down the front of the wet shirt and cutting it off her body.

Her pink nipples stand at attention, causing my mouth to salivate with the need to lick and suck them. I'm just about to say fuck it, and to do just that, when she flinches and tightens her legs, bouncing a little on the spot. "What's the matter with you?" I question, perplexed.

A flush of pink crosses her cheeks and neck, and a groan escapes her pouty lips. "I have to pee, asshole, and you have my arms tied up." *Pee?* A chuckle sounds in the air, and I realize with shock that it's coming from me. I grab her by the elbow and lead her to the toilet, forcing her to sit down against her mumbled protests. I stare intently at her, waiting for her to do her business, but instead, only silence greets me, and she bows her head, hiding her features from me. "I can't go if you're staring at me, creeper," she hisses.

I roll my eyes and turn away, but still keep her in my sight through the reflection in the mirror. When she's done peeing, I turn back around and grab some toilet paper, ready to clean her, and she starts screaming at me like a banshee. "What the fuck do you think you're doing?! You're not doing that to me! Oh my God, what is the matter with you!"

I lean down until I'm right in front of her, my amusement rising with her antics. "Little temptation, I just licked your ass clean not twenty minutes ago, you think a little pee is going to deter me?" I don't wait for her outraged response. I grab her shoulder, forcing her to lean forward, and wipe her clean. "You're an asshole!"

"If you don't quit yelling, I'm going to shove my cock back inside of your asshole without lube, then we'll see if you think wiping your pussy is the worst of my sins," I grunt, as I lift her in my arms carefully and carry her to the bathtub, and place her inside. A cooing sound leaves her lips as she leans against the copper surface, and sinks below the water, until only her face is exposed. My eyes take her in, as she closes her eyes and relaxes in the hot water, even though a predator stands next to her.

"Will you ever let me go?" she asks in a small voice, her eyes remaining shut and refusing to look at me. A part of me wants to lie to her, leading her to believe that there is a possibility she will get her life back. I want her to fight, thinking she can survive me, but I also don't want to give her false hope. "You will never leave me, not alive, temptation. Whatever world you knew before me is gone to you now."

She nods her head but remains silent, and a pang of pain hits me in my chest as I watch more of her tears slide down her intriguing face, and disappear into the water. Something about her silent acceptance doesn't make me feel like I've won anything. Instead, all I experience is a great loss. How can that be when I have my temptation here as my captive, and she's mine now? I have no answers, and as the silence thickens between us, for the first time in my life, I discern that I have truly wronged someone.

Chapter 28

The Gift

I'm back in my original room after that bizarre interaction with my stalker. He allowed me to sit in the stunning copper tub, until the water had cooled and all my muscles were jello. Other than the question that I asked him about letting me go, we spoke very little; he just mumbled words that meant nothing to me, and offered me no further insight into who he is. He handed me a bar of soap, and I washed myself under his scrutinizing gaze while still cuffed. When I was done, he lifted me carefully and gently out of the tub, and proceeded to dry me with a thick, fluffy towel, like one does a small child. I wanted to argue that I could do it myself, if he released my arms from the cuffs, but I was exhausted, and all the fight had left me. All I craved at that point was my own company, to be alone with my confused thoughts and fears.

Now, hours later, I'm lying on my back in the darkened room, going over everything that has happened so far, and what I know of my masked captor. I wrack my brain for answers on where I might know him from. Something about him seems very familiar to me. I don't know if it's the way he holds himself, his muffled voice, or the only parts of him that I have been able to see, his hands, eyes, and cock. I definitely don't know him by his cock; that thing is enormous and filled with metal, and I would undoubtedly have remembered if I had seen it before. Not that I've seen very many in my twenty-seven years, but one like that, yeah, you're not likely to forget. Maybe it's his eyes, they too are as distinct as his cock. There are not too many men walking around with stunning gray eyes. In fact, I can't quite place the last time I saw one.

This is hopeless; I doubt if I just asked him outright to remove the stupid mask, he would do it. I'm trapped in this room, in a house I don't know, far from the city I live in, with a psycho who has drugged and abducted me. The question I keep coming back to is, why me? There is nothing special about me. How did I get this madman's attention in the first place?

The door to the room opens without warning, allowing a sliver of light into the space before closing again firmly, and the soft footsteps across the carpet make his presence known. He stands next to the bed, a dark, ominous shadow, and instead of feeling fear, I feel relief at his presence. That alone should confirm that I'm losing my ever-loving mind. Is this Stockholm Syndrome, where I'm feeling affection for my kidnapper and abuser? I need to get my shit together and fight back against this monster, so I can regain my freedom, but right now, I'm so tired.

"I brought you some pain meds, and I want you to answer a few of my questions honestly." I snort at his request; how very entitled of him. "I have nothing to say to you. You want to drug me again, asshole? No thanks, I'd rather not take anything you're offering." A growl greets the silent and subdued room, and I bite down on my lip and tense my body, awaiting his violence at my rejection.

"I'd rather not have to drug you, temptation, but I don't want you to be in pain." His voice is so deep and low that I almost don't catch the last part of his statement. I turn over and stare at his large frame in the diminished light. He's got to be over six feet, which puts me at a severe height disadvantage. The old saying, *'The bigger they are, the harder they fall'*, obviously that twat never had to fight a man-bear like this one. "Everything you do causes me pain. You stole me from my life and my family; that's nothing but pain."

A sigh is his only response as I feel the bed dip at my side, and I wrap my arms tighter around myself, and try to inch my body farther away from him. "Don't run from me, I don't like it." *Run?* I would be lucky to make it two feet before he was on me. I know there is little to no chance of me escaping this room, and his clutches. Hopelessness fills me, knowing that what he told me is true; I will never leave here alive. "How many women have you abducted and kept captive?" I hold my breath, waiting for the answer that I'm sure will cement my future, or his refusal to answer, that will cause me further anxiety. Either way, it seems I lose.

"None. You're the first I've ever abducted and *kept*." I roll my disbelieving eyes at his statement and search him out, and I find him rubbing his hand against his mask-covered jaw. A memory pops into my mind of earlier when I was tied down, and he was eating me out; I'm positive I saw dark and silver scruff on his lower face, and I know I absolutely felt it against my sensitive skin. He can't be young then if he has gray hairs in his beard, despite his fit physique. Maybe he's middle-aged? "I don't believe you. You have definitely done this before." I don't bother to hide my accusatory tone; what would be the point? What's he going to do, kill me faster?

It's his turn to snort, and I feel his fingers trailing up the outside of my leg above the sheet. The sensation causes shivers to pulsate across my body, and I bite the inside of my cheek to stifle any of my sounds, and force myself not to pull away. I need answers, and right now, he seems willing to give them to me. "I didn't say I hadn't kidnapped people before, just that I hadn't kept them. I've never felt the need to hold on to my victims until you."

"So you've killed people before... *women?* How many have died at your hands?" I push the words out despite the trepidation that is filling me. My brain is yelling that we don't want that answer.

"Are you sure you really want to know, sweet temptation? Once you do, there is no going back from that; you will know exactly what kind of monster you're dealing with." His voice is solemn, and for a moment, I pity him. Is he lonely? He seems as if the weight of the world is on his shoulders. "Yes," the word leaves my lips in a breathy whisper, as I face my fears head-on.

"I've murdered thirty-three people, men and women." I scramble from the mattress, and tumble to the floor on the other side of the bed frame, with my heart hammering in my throat. *Oh my God, he's a serial killer!* He doesn't attempt to grab me, in fact, he doesn't move at all, as he watches me panic.

"You're a... " I can't bring myself to finish the sentence, as terror rides me hard and fast, and I see my death before my eyes. He's not just some lonely psychopath, who has a hard time approaching women, or enjoys playing out some sick fetish. This man is a killer, and he obviously enjoys what he does; why else would he have murdered thirty-three people?

"Serial killer?" He shrugs his broad shoulders as if that term means very little. "I guess I am, but I prefer not to have terms like that define me." He slides a small bottle of water, and two pills, across the top of the rumpled sheets towards me. "Take the meds, and I'll grant you a few more answers, sweet temptation. They're just over-the-counter painkillers, nothing that will sedate you."

His gray eyes meet mine and my breath stutters in my chest. "Just so you know, not once has it ever crossed my mind to keep any of those people alive a minute longer than necessary. You are the exception to all my rules, the ones I seem to be breaking over and over for you, temptation."

Do I trust that if I do as he's requested, he'll answer my questions? Can I even trust that he's telling me the truth, and that these pills won't knock me out, so he can have his way with me? *He doesn't need to knock you out for that, stupid. He can overpower you at any time, and do whatever he wants. Haven't you been paying attention?* My mind shouts at me. I reach forward and grab the pills and the water bottle, bring them to my lips, take a huge gulp of the water, and swallow them. The need to get answers to my questions overrides my good senses. "Why me? Why take me? To clarify; that's one question, so don't try to cheat me, asshole."

He laughs, and the hearty, rich sound has my core tightening. "You caught my attention, sweet temptation. Once you did that, I couldn't get you out of my mind."

"Where? Where was I when I caught your attention?" My heart thunders in my chest, and a cold sweat breaks out across my flesh. I'm so close to having a panic attack right now. If he lunges suddenly at me, I don't know what I'll do. There is nothing in this room I can use to defend myself. My hand tightens around the plastic water bottle, right now my only pitiful source of a weapon.

"If I really wanted to hurt you, my sweet, there is nothing you can do to stop me." He nods at the water bottle clenched in my hand. "I'm not here to cause you pain, at least not at this moment. To answer your question, you were working as a bartender at the strip club the first time I laid eyes on you."

My limbs tremble as I realize I must know this guy. Is this one of the regulars I've served over the last year that I've worked there, or just some creep who came in once, and I caught his attention? "Take off the mask. There's no need for it now; you and I both know I will never leave here."

For a moment, I think he will reject my request and tell me that question time is over, but to my tremendous surprise, he reaches up, grabs the mask from behind, and pulls it off his face, allowing it to drop to the mattress, and exposing himself to me. My breath gets choked in my throat as I get my first glimpse of him, and I can't believe my fucking eyes.

"Nic?"

Chapter 29

Santa

"**M**otherfucker!" She shouts, as she lunges across the bed and tackles me, with no regard for her safety, or any sense of self preservation. Her shoulder whams into my nose as I brace myself for her impact, cracking it hard, and instantly, a gush of blood pours from my nostrils. *Fuck, that hurt!* I attempt to grab hold of her as gently as I can, so as not to injure her more than I already have, but she's making it nearly impossible. "Fucker, cocksucker, monster, asshole!" She screams vivid profanity at me, as her arms swing in my direction in a cute attempt to pummel me. Her rage beckons to me, making me want her even more. Everything within me wants to throw her right over the precipice of madness that she's straddling, and follow her down to the depths of hell, where we can live happily together.

All of this is such a departure for me. A part of me wants to hurt her, as much as it wants to wrap my arms around her and cradle her gently, reassuring her that she is safe with me. That no one will ever be able to hurt her except me, and other than in our sexual escapades, I don't plan to either. She's a breathtaking disaster, an enigma to me, everything that contradicts how I've been living all these years in a hollow existence, just waiting for her to enter my life.

"Stop, sweet temptation, before you harm yourself." I grab one of her arms, and endeavor to prevent her from landing face down on the carpet, as she tries to bite my face like a rabid wolf. Her small fist slams into my cock, and has me buckling forward with a seething groan. "Stop calling me that!" She screams hysterically, as she grabs a fistful of my hair, and yanks. "Fuck, Chrissy!" I grapple with her legs and take her down with me, cradling her head at the last minute to prevent it from smashing on the floor, but my heavy body lands on top of her and knocks the air out of her lungs with a satisfying whoosh.

My stomach is rolling with nausea from the hit to my balls, and I'm struggling to catch my breath. "Please, temptation... stop! You're... going... to hurt yourself, and it will... get you... nowhere. I still won't let you... go."

"Now you're worried about hurting me, when you have been stalking and terrorizing me, fucker? All this time, it was you!" Her breathing is heavy, as her chest rises and falls with the exertion of trying to fight me. She's such a little thing, but filled with a fiery spirit, and I think that's partly what draws me to her. I bite my lip, to stop the grin that wants to crest across my face from rising. She's so cute when she's furious, and staring daggers at me. I'll have to remember to make that happen more often, as it causes a jolt of lust to race through me, and my cock to thicken, where I'm pressed firmly against her. I see the moment she realizes it too, as her eyes widen dramatically, and she tries to force me away from her body with all her might.

"Hell no, you crazy psychopath, stay away from me with that monster." She bats with her hands at the side of my face, smacking my eye in the process and making it sting.

"Monster?" I chuckle at her apt description of my cock, as I thrust against her warmth, knowing full well she has nothing underneath the borrowed t-shirt she's wearing, and disregarding her attempts to dislodge me. The action seems to enrage her further, as she tries to buck me off of her, but my heavy weight prevents me from moving more than an inch. "I'll kill you, I swear!" She huffs.

"Promises, promises, my sweet." My fingers trail up her rib cage, gently, almost reverently, as lust lights a fire within me, until I'm cradling her breast in my palm, and her stiff nipple is squeezed between my two fingers, as I twist it through the thin cotton fabric. A shuddering gasp escapes her, and the sound just eggs me on further, until I'm thrusting against her through the barrier of my pants. "Nooo, get... off me," she huffs.

Her rejection only spurs me on more as I squeeze the full globe hard, attempting to leave my fingerprints behind, so she can be reminded later of who she belongs to. "I need you to fight me, *my pet*. Give it all you have, it turns me the fuck on." I groan into her chest and regret giving her one of my shirts to wear after her bath. Right now, my mouth could be sucking and marking her ivory flesh. I bite down regardless, not wishing to be deterred, and she lets out a yelp.

"You're insane." She digs her fingers into my face, attempting to gouge my eyes. I have to release my hold on her breast to restrain her arm, bringing first one and then the other above her head, and transferring them to one of my large hands to hold her firmly. "Yes, I am. I make no apologies for it," I grunt, as I run my tongue down the side of her face. I've wanted to taste her lips for days now, feel her tongue brushing against mine, and there is no time like the present to feed my hunger. My mouth crashes down on hers as she attempts to keep me out, but I bite her bottom lip hard until she opens for me, and my tongue slips inside. Her rich taste is an explosion on my tongue, as I deepen the kiss until I'm hungrily ravishing her mouth, like a beast consuming his dinner. My tongue strokes against hers, then swipes the roof of her mouth, wanting to leave its mark and corrupt her. After a few seconds of her fighting against my hold, she gives in and kisses me back, her tongue moving against mine, and breathy little whines making their way inside my mouth, where I swallow them with pleasure.

My free hand trails down her side until I reach her thigh, and I force it to wrap around my waist, as I press my stiff cock against her sensitive clit and thrust, again and again. Her body surrenders to my touch, and she moves into the next thrust, pushing back against me. Fuck, I need inside of her now, regardless of how sore I know she is. I lift my pelvis off hers and, with frantic motions, unleash my cock from the constraint of my pants, shove the hem of the shirt out of the way, and bury myself inside of her tight heat with one go. Her gasp of pain and surprise melts into my mouth, as I begin a punishing tempo of pounding inside of her sweet, swollen pussy. Fierce growls are departing me, as I bite and suck on her tongue and lips, making me sound like a deranged feral animal, and that is precisely what I am where she's concerned.

She feels so good taking me hard, her soft body accommodating my harsher one. I pull back from her lips and stare down at her, as her glazed, brown, lust-filled eyes stare back at mine, challenging me to hurt her. Fuck, I will never get enough of her, and I know I'm completely fucked because of it. She's changing who I am, and what I believe about myself. With her, I don't wish to be the cold and callous killer. I don't want to murder her for sport. Instead, I see her in my future at my side forever. How can that be? How can, in such a short time, this woman, this little raged-filled hellion, have changed what I believe to be true about myself?

Her pussy tightens around my cock, eliciting groans, and tendrils of heated satisfaction, to race through me at how responsive she is. I release her hands to see what she'll do, if she'll attempt to fight me off, but instead, one of her hands buries itself in my hair, and the other rakes her fingernails down my back. I can feel her getting close, her body moving in time with mine as she meets me stroke for stroke. The obscene sounds of our skin slapping against each other, as I fill her to the brink, is the prettiest music I have ever heard. My face leans into the crook of her neck, drinking in her scent, and I can't help myself. The desire to mark her up is a madness inside of me. I bite down on the soft skin of her neck, and she arches it back with a scream, yanking on my hair in an unyielding grip.

"Ohmygod, ohmygod," her harsh pants are further encouragement, as her core spasms around my cock and grips me like a vice. "*Mine*, God can't fucking have you, and I'll murder the fucker if he tries," I gasp into her skin. She explodes with a scream on her lips, her body arching into mine, as I continue to pound into her like a man possessed. The heat searing up my back, and moving through my body, is a nuclear bomb waiting to go off, and with one more stroke, I unleash myself deep inside of her, as ropes of my cum fill her pretty pussy.

We both lie there, staring at each other, while our breathing returns to a more natural level. I glimpse the moment that regret and doubt fill her, at her participation in our lovemaking, and she decides to fight again. She grabs my hair and yanks hard, as she uses her knees to push me away from her. "Get off of me, cunt!" My cock slips from its new favorite place with sorrow, as I force myself up and away from her. The sight of my cum glistening on her swollen pussy lips is a temptation to a starving man. The overwhelming need to get on my knees and worship her causes me to hesitate. I'm quickly losing control of myself with her; she's corrupting me. "Why bother fighting against what is inevitable, Chrissy? We both know you enjoy what I do to you."

"*OH MY GOD!* Are you for real, you psycho? You drugged and kidnapped me! This is not a bad date gone wrong; this is a fucking nightmare!" She stands and scurries away from me, pressing her back against the furthest wall as she yanks the hem of the shirt down, and hides her pussy from me. "You took me away from the only family I have, and confessed to murdering people. It doesn't matter if I find you hot, or if I enjoy the way you fuck me. You're insane!"

All I hear from her screeched words is that she finds me attractive, and enjoys fucking me. That's a start; I can work with that. Soon, I'll have her begging me to let her be at my side. "You'd better get used to being here, and your situation, sweet temptation. You won't be leaving it any time soon."

Chapter 30

Santa

What the fuck am I doing right now? I question myself, as I push the rickety grocery cart down the pet food aisle, while a shitty rendition of *'All I Want for Christmas'* plays in the background. I grab various treats from the shelves, not having the faintest idea what a hellhound eats as a snack, besides small children, and the souls of those who displease him. I can't believe I'm actually considering kidnapping that fucking beast to make Chrissy happy. I have to admit to myself that I have now sunk to a new low. One I didn't think possible, considering I'm a serial killer.

It's been twenty-four hours since I fucked her into the floor in her room, and she admitted to finding me *'hot'*. You would think, with that admission, and what we shared, it would have allowed us to get past the whole *'drugging and kidnapping'* shit, but you'd be wrong. It seems my sweet temptation can hold a grudge like nobody's business, and despite the fact that I could force her to be with me, I find that I don't want to, much to my aggravation and disbelief. Chrissy hasn't eaten or drank anything in over a day, refusing to touch anything I bring her. She also won't speak with me, and flinches whenever I enter the room. I was losing my mind, and ready to pull out my own hair, as I watched her crying, huddled in a corner of her room, the pitiful sound breaking the heart I didn't realize could feel anything for anyone.

"That's a lot of treats; you must really love your furbaby!" A woman attempts to flirt with me, giving me a full body perusal, as she stops her cart and admires mine. I stare at her bleach-blonde hair in thick waves, and the pound of makeup caked on her face, as she attempts to look demure and bats her fake eyelashes at me. In the past, she would be an easy target, one I could use to soothe my bloodlust, but right now, however, only revulsion and annoyance fill me at the sound of her voice. "Unless you want to end up in his cage, *fuck off* and mind your business," I growl and keep moving, grabbing a massive bag of kibble and throwing it into the cart. I hear her gasp and the sound of her scurrying away. Goddammit, I'm losing my shit, and that's fucking dangerous. I need to get my shit together before I end up behind bars.

My phone vibrates in my jacket pocket, and I pull it out only to see my brother's number across the screen. Fuck, what does this asshole want now? Can't I have more than one day without him or my father getting neck-deep in manure? "What?" I blare into the phone, and frighten another patron as they walk by.

"Wow, you're in a very festive holiday mood. You do know tomorrow is Christmas, right? You better act right, or Santa will only leave a lump of coal in your stocking," Micah chuckles, and I grip the phone tighter, wishing it was his neck.

I force myself to count to ten in my head before responding, and trying to calm the need to go murder my brother painfully. "What do you need, Micah? I told Dad I need a few days. I already have shit on my plate that has all my attention."

A deep sigh sounds from his end of the line, and I hear his footsteps moving quickly across a hard surface. "Your shit wouldn't have something to do with the pretty redheaded waitress that is missing from that diner, would it?" *What the fuck? How would he know she's missing?* "What are you talking about, brother?"

"I went back to the diner yesterday, and it seems that the pretty redhead is missing, or so her crotchety coworker told me. She never showed up for work, and her roommate reported her missing to the police, not that they even took it seriously. I checked with one of Dad's contacts at the closest police precinct to the diner, and it seems young women go missing all the time from that neighborhood, and very little is done about it. You wouldn't know anything about that, would you?" His smug voice relays through the phone, and I picture stabbing his eyes out in my mind.

"Why would you go back there, Micah?" Furious rage soars through me, and I clench my hands tightly around the handle of the grocery cart, until the whole thing jolts and lifts off the ground at an angle.

"I wanted to see what was so special about her to have caught your attention, and not in the way you usually fixate on something, and honestly, I wanted to know if she was alive." *Motherfucker, I'm going to kill him.* He didn't go just to scope her out. The asshole is super competitive, and he went there to seduce her, just so he could serve that knowledge to me later. I breathe through my nose, compelling myself not to give him the reaction that he wants. Micah is like a shark when he smells blood in the water, and he won't stop until he gets what he wants. In that sense, we are much the same.

"I don't know anything about her being missing, and I haven't seen her since the last time I ate there. Micah, I urge you to find something else more interesting to occupy your time, unless you would like me to make body parts appear as your Christmas gift." The fucker's response is to laugh at me, and not just a little chuckle. It sounds like he's laughing so hard he can't breathe. *Asshole.*

"Whatever you say, *brother*. Dad wants you for a photo op on Christmas Day, and he says it's not optional. Don't decapitate the messenger, oh and Nic, have fun with your little redhead, but make sure you don't get caught with your pants down." He hangs up the phone before I can even respond, and it infuriates me further. Who does this little shit think he is, warning me about bad behavior? He's the one always getting himself into scrapes I have to clean up. Oh, how the tables have turned, and I'm not liking it one fucking bit.

I pass the junk food aisle and throw a bunch of goodies in, hoping that something will tempt Chrissy to eat. When I'm approaching the checkout line, I spy a small Christmas tree display, all lit up, and a bunch of obnoxiously bright decorations in a bin. I've never decorated for any holiday at my cabin; I usually avoid them and the season like the plague, only participating in whatever my father forces me to. *Would Chrissy like this? Would it make her happy to have a Christmas tree and presents?* A part of me can't believe I'm even worried about what my captive would like; it's not like she should get an option. The other part of me is busy throwing the boxed tree and a bunch of ornaments into my cart, knowing I've completely lost my senses.

"Oh, someone is in the last-minute holiday spirit!" The elderly cashier exclaims, as he starts ringing in my items on the checkout conveyor belt. "You know what you're missing, son?" He looks at me with excitement, and my eyebrow rises with curiosity, looking at all the useless shit I already have here. "Wine, boy, and some eggnog! You can find those in aisles four and seven. Go off and grab some, and I'll start bagging your items while you do."

I don't even realize I'm following his instructions, and heading in that direction, until I'm entering the wine aisle and I come to a complete stop in front of the red section. I drag my hands down my exhausted face. I have no idea what kind of wine Chrissy likes, or even if she likes wine. What am I doing? Where is the psychotic killer that lives inside of me? Have I lost him somehow in all this mess, along with my mind?

Fuck it. I grab bottles of red and white wine, and head to grab the stupid eggnog. At this point, I may as well go entirely overboard into the realm of my insanity, where I play house with my kidnap victim.

Chapter 31

The Gift

It's Christmas Eve, and I'm sitting in the dark, utterly exhausted from crying, feeling lost and terrified about my fate. My mind is still grappling with the reality that the man I found incredibly sexy, and alluring, at the diner, is the asshole who drugged and kidnapped me. Let's not even talk about what he did to me with my vibrator, and in the glory hole. The truth is I'm sitting here wrestling with myself; a part of me wants to escape and bludgeon him, and the other part desires to climb him like a thick tree, and fuck him silly.

A shiver races down my spine at the memory of him fisting me, and then yesterday when he fucked me ruthlessly into the floor. My traitorous, sore pussy tingles and weeps with thoughts of those piercings, which adorn his massive cock, and the pleasure that they bring. "Fuck, get it together, bitch, he's a serial killer," I mumble out loud. Ah yes, that seems to be my biggest hardship to get past, not the fact that he lied, stalked, and took me, or that he has my neck in a metal collar, and has me chained to a wall once again, but the fact that the psycho enjoys killing people. That's the part I can't get my mind to wrap around. He looks so ordinary, pretentious, and snobby as hell, but I would have never guessed he could have killed thirty-plus people. Jesus, I really do know how to pick them, don't I?

My eyes slide across to the surface of the bed, at the tray that is laden with food he left hours ago, when he once again tried to speak with me. My stomach thunders with hunger, but I hold back, refusing to take anything from him. It's the principle of it, I tell myself, as the bowl of fruit tries to seduce me from my spot on the floor.

I lower my head on my drawn knees, pulling the sheet I'm wrapped in closer to me, to prevent looking in that direction anymore, and think over his words before he left, frustrated and furious with me.

"You can't keep doing this, temptation. I don't want to have to force you to eat, but I will. I'm not above shoving a fucking tube down your throat, and a needle in your veins. Just try me; you won't like the results."

"Be reasonable, woman! So what if I kidnapped you? Can you sit there and tell me you were enjoying your life? I can give you anything you desire. Anything you dream about, I can make happen for you. You don't have to struggle anymore; give in to me."

"Sweet temptation, you're really pissing me off with this silent treatment. You don't want me to have to get creative to hear you speak. I would much rather have a civilized conversation with you, than torture you to hear you scream, but I'm taking nothing off the table until you act like a grown-up."

"Please, Chrissy. I just want to know if you're okay. Are you in pain? Do you need something?"

That last interaction almost had me caving. His voice was so soft and distraught, and his dark gray eyes were lined with sorrow. He looked like he hadn't slept any more than I had. His broad shoulders were rounded, and a look of utter defeat graced his handsome face. Despite the need to go to him and comfort him, I held firm and refused to speak, or take anything from him, and after a few hours of just sitting there across from me, he left without a word. I wonder if he'll kill me, now that he has no use for me.

Is he right? Did I have nothing to look forward to? Yes, my life was hard, but there were happy times too; it wasn't all hardship. Memories of when I first met Daisy at a bus stop enter my mind. She was a runaway living on the streets, who had stolen a bag of chips from a local grocery store, and was hiding as the manager searched the street for her, with a bat in his hands. I saw how her tiny body trembled with fear, and how she attempted to make herself disappear, contorting her tiny body into a corner behind a metal bench. Her soft blues looked up at me and pleaded for help, and in that moment, I found a kindred spirit, and knew I would never let anything happen to her. *Did she sometimes drive me insane, with her outrageous and reckless behavior?* Sure, but she was my family, her and Toothless. Found family, rather than blood.

Toothless, my poor baby, is out there, not knowing where I am. He counts on me for his survival. Daisy is a scatterbrain. I love her dearly, but she is, and I wonder if she's even noticed I'm missing yet. Is she feeding him and letting him out to potty? Does he have his favorite toy, and has he gone for walks? My chest tightens with the fear that I will never see the sweet pup that I rescued from a dog fight again. The memory of his beautiful large eyes begging me to save him from the monsters hurting him ripples through my mind. That was the first time I ever came close to murdering someone. Watching that horrible man beat on a small black dog, and allowing other dogs to attack him. I don't know what came over me, but before I could stop myself, I grabbed a discarded piece of wood from the ground, and bashed it against the back of his skull. Then I grabbed Toothless, and ran from that alleyway and never looked back. We have been inseparable ever since, except for now.

Deep in my heart, I know I could have killed that man, and that makes me wonder if I'm really any different than Nic. We all have those moments where rage takes over, and our predatory senses come to the forefront; his just seem more extreme. Maybe the people he killed were all bad, perhaps they weren't, but all I know is, at any point, he could have killed me or Daisy, and he didn't.

Does that mean I can put aside what he's done to me? I don't know; my mind and heart are warring against each other. There is something about him that draws me to him, and has from the very beginning. I remember the devastating sensations I felt, when he was interested in Daisy rather than me. *Holy shit!* Is he actually interested in Daisy, or was that a way to string me along, and make me not suspect him as the creep sending me the text messages? I need answers, and I need them now. One thing is for sure: I have no intention of letting that slide.

I get up from the floor, walk over to the bed, sit myself down, and start eating. I'm going to need my strength to pummel him, so I might as well not let any of this go to waste after all.

Chapter 32

Santa

Stalking is an art form, or at least it used to be to me, before I found myself in this mess with Chrissy. I squat down behind a group of trash bins on their neighbor's side, and a huge, ugly rat crosses in front of me, utterly unfazed by the large, menacing human standing not two feet from him. Fuck, I'm really getting tired of not being seen as a predator anymore. Have I lost my mojo? Do I need to go on a killing spree, so people and animals take me seriously again? I feel like I'm losing more of myself, and my swagger, every moment I don't slice someone open and take their life. It reminds me that bathing in someone's blood is also an art form, and I haven't done that in a while either. *Time to remedy that shit.*

Instead of being back in my cabin, fucking the shit out of Chrissy, and filling all of her holes with my cum, or going to murder my spoiled shit of a brother, I'm hiding here in frigid temperatures, risking being found by law enforcement, and waiting for that oversized slobber fest to take the bait, and eat the peanut-butter-covered sedative I left him on Chrissy's back porch. "Come on, asshole, just fucking eat it," I groan. The damn rat stares at me, as if I'm disturbing his peace and quiet. "Fuck off, cunt, or I'll feed you to a cat."

I hear a growl through the warped wooden fence, and I know the demon beast has located where I'm hiding. I peer through the boards, ensuring to keep him away from my limbs, and his sharp teeth, and glowing eyes greet me. Fuck, the things I'm willing to do for this girl. It's Christmas Eve, and I shouldn't be here. I should be somewhere having top-shelf scotch, and drowning my sorrows, or covered in blood, celebrating the holidays in the way I do every year, with murder and mayhem. A groan escapes me, and the fiend next door lets out a vicious growl. I swear to fuck, if this thing bites me, I am going to tan Chrissy's delectable ass with my flogger, hang her from my

chains, and use every one of her holes as I see fit. "Here, nice demon, go and eat the yummy treat Santa left for you."

Because I'm not taking any fucking chances, I throw another laced treat over the fence at Toothless, and pray I don't end up overdosing the huge thing. Think Chrissy might forgive me if I do, it was the thought that counts, right? I was trying to bring her oversized baby to her in one piece, even though I think this thing is not really a canine at all, but some alien creature from the beyond.

He runs for the treat, and I release the pent-up breath I'm holding. I pull out my phone and bring up the cameras, expecting to see Chrissy still huddled on the floor and looking distraught. I don't find her immediately on the bedroom camera, and my heart rate skyrockets before I reason with myself. How far can she have gotten? The door is locked, and her collar chains her to the wall. I think I really need a stiff drink right now, or maybe ten. The last couple of days have made me a frazzled, pathetic mess, with emotions and feelings that I don't understand how to process.

Honestly, I don't fucking get it. Someone could take a gun and point it at my father's head right now and pull the trigger, and I would shrug and walk away without a care in the world, or a backward glance, and that asshole raised me from birth. Yet everything about Chrissy causes a reaction. She's sad, *I lose it*. She doesn't eat, *I become unhinged*. She's in pain and doesn't tell me, *I want to rip out my own hair*. She's crying, *and I want to level the whole world*. Where the hell is all of this coming from? Is this what they describe as love? Am I in love with this girl? I've never loved anything, to my knowledge. The closest I have ever come was to tolerate something with slight affection, and that's my brother, Micah. Even on a good day, I would probably shoot him without the slightest hint of remorse.

My head begins to spin, and my hands go clammy with the possibility that I am in love with Chrissy Cranbrook. It's not possible. I'm not capable of processing those emotions, and yet everything about her makes me feel. What if she tries to leave me? What if I end up murdering her in one of my blind rages? The very thought has me stumbling, and I have to grasp onto the fence to keep myself upright. I can't lose her, not even to myself.

I force myself to stand and take deep breaths, as I focus on the here and now. I can put steps in place to protect her from me when I'm losing my mind, while still keeping her by my side. In time, she may grow to have those same feelings for me. We can be happy together, just the two of us, and fuck, I guess the hellhound can come too, as long as he doesn't try to eat or hump me. I can get us far away from here, and my father's malicious and power-hungry grasp. We can disappear. I have more than enough money to support us lavishly for the rest of our lives. She would never have to work again, or put up with slimeballs wanting to touch her. Our lives will be perfect as long as no one attempts to separate us, and they won't, because I will painfully murder anyone who tries.

With my little pep talk complete, I realize I no longer hear Toothless in the yard, and Daisy must have come home and let him in. Daisy is going to be a problem. I don't think Chrissy will take it too well if I murder her roommate, but I can't allow her to stop me from taking Toothless, or recognizing me and reporting me to the police. The little pest already went and made a missing persons report on Chrissy, despite being wanted on charges herself. That was both brave and stupid of her. Luckily for her, I made that disappear the minute Micah made me aware of it.

I climb over the fence stealthily and make my way to their back door, hoping the sedative is already working on Toothless. She's left the door carelessly open, and I can hear her talking to the beast. "It's okay, sweet baby, your momma will be home soon. Santa wouldn't let her be away from you on Christmas night. You'll see; she'll show up, she never lets us down." Toothless whines at her words, and I watch from the shadows as she gives him another treat. *Spoiled shit.*

"I'm just going to run to the corner store, Toothless, to get us a frozen pizza, so when your momma comes back, we have something to eat. Be a good boy, and don't destroy anything. I mean it, Toothless, leave my shoes alone!" I hear her moving towards the front door, and then it opens and closes, and I release my anxious breath. This is perfect. I'll be able to get the monster out the back door, and to the van I have on the next street, while she's gone. I don't look forward to having to carry him, but I won't let anything stop me from making Chrissy happy.

I hear a groan and then a thud, and peek inside to see Toothless down on his side, his big mouth open and his pink tongue exposed. Thank fuck, I was starting to think I was going to have to tranq the fucker again. I slip inside the house and stand over his snoring body. How am I going to carry this fucker out of here without being noticed? It's not like it's a regular everyday thing to see a large man holding a massive cane corso over his shoulder. Fuck, I'll need to wrap him in a blanket or something. I make my way out of the kitchen and towards Chrissy's haphazard bedroom, grab the worn comforter off the bed, and return to the kitchen. I bend down, laying the blanket on the floor next to Toothless, and prepare to roll the demon like a burrito, when I feel something hard press against the back of my skull and a very distinct clicking sound, letting me know someone has a gun pressed to my head.

"Where the fuck is Chrissy, asshole, don't bother lying. I know you took her, and are trying to steal Toothless too!" *Ah fuck, Daisy.* How did I not see this coming?

Chapter 33

The Gift

It's been hours since I last saw Nic, and my anger has turned from a small blaze to an inferno of rage. Has the fucker forgotten about me and left me here to die? This psychopath kidnapped me from my life, and then left me here to rot? Well, I'll show him. The minute I figure out how to get this collar off of me, it's game over for him, and I'm going to make him wish he never laid eyes on me.

I'm just about to wrap my fist in a towel and break the bathroom mirror, when I hear the electronic lock being disarmed. I race back out of the bathroom, the annoying metal chain rustling behind me like a damn leash. If there is nothing else about this situation that conveys how unhinged Nic really is, the damn chain and collar around my neck speak volumes. I could almost look past all the rest of the shit he's done, but not that. I'm not his fucking pet to keep chained, shit, I would never allow an animal to endure this type of callous treatment.

I'm ready and waiting to give him a tongue lashing, and throw hands at him, when he stomps into the room, his fists at his sides and a scowl across his handsome and fearsome face. Then my jaw hits the floor as Daisy appears in the doorway right behind him, wearing a bright red, ugly Christmas sweater and reindeer ears, and holding a gun to the back of his head. "Hey, babe! I missed you!" She grins and winks at me.

Have I entered the twilight zone? Maybe I hit my head somewhere, because this can't really be happening. I can't actually be seeing my bubbly spaz of a best friend holding my stalker hostage. "How? Where? Shit, how the hell is this possible?"

My eyes soar between Daisy's and Nic's, and that's when I realize that there is a third person, this one hiding in the shadows, and if I'm not mistaken, he's got a gun pointed at Daisy. "Hey ya, gorgeous. Long time no see," he calls out, and forces both Daisy and Nic to move further into the room. *Micah*. What the hell is he doing here, and why is he pointing a weapon at my best friend? This is getting stranger and more bizarre by the moment.

"I can explain," Nic growls, as he side-eyes Daisy and his brother with menace. Daisy's smile just gets broader and more devious at his remark, and even Micah looks ridiculously happy with whatever fuckery is happening here. "Girl, why are you chained up? Ah, he's a *kinky fucker*, isn't he?" Daisy wags her eyebrows at me as I stare at her with disbelief.

Oh my God, hole in the ground, please open up and swallow me whole. Of course, she would think this was fun, and part of some sexual escapade. I feel my body flush with heat and embarrassment, as Micah's eyes slide over me, from my bare feet to the top of my head, and everywhere in between, that the thin t-shirt I'm wearing doesn't hide. I can tell exactly what he's thinking, based on his lascivious grin. "Stop fucking looking at her, Micah, or I'll rip your eyes out!" Nic growls and steps towards his brother, his fist raised, and an unhinged look in his eye.

"Hey, I'm in charge here!" Daisy yells and attempts to grab Nic's arm to restrain him, and all the while, she's pointing a gun that I hope is not loaded, and perched on her stupid skyscraper heels. Nic releases a fearsome snarl, that has the hairs on my arms standing on end. "Don't touch me. I've humored you so far, but nobody gets to do that except her." He nods in my direction, and my eyebrows shoot up at his admission. *Me? Why the hell do I get to touch him?* Not that I don't want to, well, at this precise moment, I'd like to touch him with a tire iron.

"Why is that exactly, *huh*, Nic? What makes *Little Red Riding Hood* over there special?" Micah inquires, his gun held precariously in his hand, as if he doesn't care if he shoots someone or not. All three of these idiots are going to get themselves killed in an accidental shoot-out with each other. I would like to point out that I take offense to him describing me as a fictional character who lacked common sense, and got herself almost eaten by a wolf, but I'm too tired to argue with all the crazies in the room. My head ping pongs back and forth between them, and I'm starting to get dizzy from all the insanity.

"BECAUSE I FUCKING LOVE HER, AND SHE'S MINE, CUNT!" Nic howls, all the veins in his neck protruding, and he swings his fist toward his brother, regardless of whether one of their weapons could be discharged at any moment. His fist lands with a crack against Micah's cheek, who in turn releases his hold on his gun, and it goes bouncing across the carpet toward me. Daisy gets pushed out of the way, and falls against the dresser with a scream, and the two male gorillas start throwing punches at each other, and breaking what's left of the furniture. *Sweet baby Jesus, what the fuck!*

I dive for the gun, grasping it tightly and rising unsteadily to my feet, and pointing it at both of them, but there is no way to get a clear shot as they grapple, and honestly, I don't know which one of them to shoot. "STOP, FUCKERS!" I fire into the air, hoping to get their attention, and both of them freeze in place, as pieces of the ceiling plaster land on my head. Two sets of large gray eyes turn to stare at me, and for a moment, I forget what the hell I'm doing, as I get overwhelmed by their attractiveness. "You show 'em, babe!" Daisy cackles, and moves closer to me and away from the two psychos, who are giving off nothing but toxic masculinity.

I'm about to start questioning all of them, but a loud barking gets my attention, and I turn my gaze towards Daisy with horror. "Toothless?" She nods her head, as if it's no big deal that my massive cane corso has also found his way to my stalker's house. "Yeah, I made that asshole carry him inside. It was too cold in the car to leave him." Yup, 'cause that makes perfect sense right now.

"One of you start explaining, or I swear to fuck, I'm going to start shooting at all of you." I release a huge sigh, knowing whatever is about to be spoken is going to blow me away, while confusing me further. I keep running Nic's words through my mind, and I don't have a way to make sense of them. *He's in love with me? How is that possible?* A warm feeling radiates through my chest at the thought that maybe he did all of this because he feels that strongly for me. It still doesn't excuse drugging and kidnapping me, or murdering all those people, but at least it's a start. Do I feel more than just attraction for him, well, besides anger at the whole 'keeping me captive' scenario? On the surface, I want to answer immediately that it's all hormones and physical attraction, but in my heart, I know that's a lie. I couldn't stop thinking about him, and it's always been more than just attraction.

Something about him has always drawn me in, even when I didn't know it was him behind the mask. Does that make me as insane as he is? *Maybe.*

"Sweet temptation, please put the gun down; I don't want you to risk getting hurt," Nic utters in a soothing and placating voice, as if he is speaking to a wild animal, and not the woman he has chained to one of his bedroom walls.

"Oh my goodness, he calls you that, girl? *Swoon!*" Daisy giggles, and I'm forced to roll my eyes."I can't wait to hear your explanation for all this shit, and how you think you're getting out of it," Micah groans as he swipes at his bleeding lip, and pushes Nic away from him.

"Go on, explain, and make it good, or you can go explain to the devil why I shot you," I hiss.

Chapter 34

Santa

My eyes meet Chrissy's furious brown ones, and in their depths, I witness how serious she is. She'll fire that gun if I don't give her a reasonable explanation. The problem is I don't know if I have one; I can't even make sense of all that has happened. In all my years of murdering people, never once have I found myself in a situation like this. In fact, up until half an hour ago, no one, including my asshole brother, even knew where my cabin was located. Now, it feels like all my secrets are being ripped open like a festering wound, and everyone can see all the darkness I so carefully hide. I look over my shoulder at my brother, and the fucker has the audacity to stick his tongue out at me like a juvenile. "Temptation, I promise I'll answer all your questions, but first, I want to know why my brother was hanging around your house." Chrissy's lips open, I'm sure to deny my request, but I give her a pleading look, and she acquiesces by nodding, but her eyes narrow in my direction in warning that I'm trying her patience.

"Well, fucker, how did you even know where they live?" I'm furious that this asshole knew where to find my temptation. What was his game plan? Was he planning on trying to seduce her, or bribe her? The mere thought of him hitting on Chrissy has my blood pressure rising, and I have to cross my fisted hands over my chest, to prevent from lashing out at him. My body is wired tight with aggression, and with one wrong move from him, I'm likely to end him. This little fucker has been causing me nothing but trouble since the moment he left our mother's womb. There is nothing that I have that he doesn't covet, except maybe a work ethic.

"I got their address from the missing person's report that one filed," he nods his head in Daisy's direction with a grimace. "It's not like it's hard to get access to those files, even without your hacker skills."

"You're a hacker? That's very cool!" Daisy interrupts with excitement, and I blatantly ignore her approval. "Get to the part where you were hiding in the damn shadows, *cunt*. What was your plan?" I demand.

Micah sighs, and slides down the wall until he's sitting with his back against it, his knees drawn upwards. "Honestly, there wasn't one, at least not a sinister one. I just wanted to know what you were being so secretive about. I've never seen you possessive about a woman, and I was curious." He shrugs his large, lanky shoulder, as if that's a reasonable explanation for hiding and pulling a gun on not one, but two people, and then insisting on going along with kidnapping.

"Geez, I wonder why I don't believe you?" I cock an eyebrow in his direction, letting him know that I think he's full of shit.

"Okay, so maybe I was going to hit on her, and get her to sleep with me, film it, and send it to you as a Christmas gift. Now are you happy, asshole?" Micah throws his hands up in the air, in a sign of defeat as an obnoxious, taunting grin crosses his lips, and I'm flying across the room, before I can even think about it, and cracking his head with my fist. "She's *mine*, I'll fucking end you if you even think about touching her."

"Babe, I think you have to stop him. He's gonna kill his brother, and it's Christmas; there should be no murdering kin at Christmas. Santa would disapprove," Daisy screams behind me, as I kick and punch my brother as hard as I can. This fucker has been ruining, and stealing, my shit from the moment he was old enough to crawl.

Fingers grab onto my hair, yank hard, and pull me off of him. "This is getting us nowhere!" Chrissy yells, as I finally release my hold on Micah and stumble back on my ass, almost taking her down in the process, when I get tangled in the chain attached to her collar. Fuck, I should release her from that. Shit could go south, and one of these assholes could set fire to this house, and she wouldn't be able to escape and save herself. Loud, rancorous barking sounds in the background, and it's only a matter of time before that hellhound breaks out of my bathroom. I'm running out of time to get control of the situation. The only thing that matters is that I can't lose her.

I wrap my arms around her waist, surprising her with the action, and forcing her to land on my lap. The barrel of the gun ends up lodged between us, and even though I know I could end up taking my last breath in the next moment, I can't do that without telling her how I feel. Whether she accepts my truth, or murders me, after that, is something I'll deal with as it comes. *Here goes nothing and everything at the same time.*

"I hate everyone, temptation, people as a rule, annoy me with their scheming, manipulative natures and rampant emotions. I take immense pleasure in bringing others pain. You started out as a means of revenge, for kicking me out of your strip club, and then something inside of me changed. You changed me like a fucking virus I was powerless to fight. You infected me." I raise my hand, halting her attempt to respond. "I've never understood what love is, never felt the emotion or questioned whether I would, until you. I'm not sure if I am obsessed with you, or if this overwhelming feeling that is driving me insane is love. It feels volatile and dangerous, like it could destroy me completely."

I release a deep sigh, watching as her eyes become larger and larger with my words. Does she think I'm just spewing nonsense? I'm starting to think I've utterly lost my damn mind, not that there was much sanity to begin with. "I'd like to think that I fell in love with you the moment I saw you, but the truth is, I think my heart has always been in love with you, and it was just waiting to meet you. *You*, Chrissy Cranbrook, are the reason it beats, and without you, there is no reason for me to keep breathing." I bite down hard on my bottom lip, as anxiety rises within me at her silence. She just sits on my lap and stares, her mouth opening and closing, like a fish out of water, and no words leave her at my confession. Shit, I fucked up, and she's going to leave me the second she gets the chance to run.

Sniffling noises can be heard beside us, and I raise my eyes over her shoulder to look at Daisy, who has tears running down her face. I don't bother to look in my brother's direction, not wanting to see his judgmental face. Every single word I uttered was the truth. Somewhere along the line, I must have realized that she was what I always wanted. A world without Chrissy Cranbrook is not a world I want to live in. "Please, say something, *anything*," I beg.

Before she can utter a single word, alarms start going off around the house, and I quickly rise to my feet, dragging her up with me. "What the hell is that noise?" Chrissy questions, as she brings her hands to her ears, the gun still precariously clutched in one of them. I quickly disarm her, much to her fury, and pull my phone out of my pocket, bringing up the multitude of cameras I have around the property. What greets my sight is my worst nightmare. Various cars come to a halt just outside of my cabin. Doors open and close, and a horde of men dressed in tactical gear surround the property. My eyes quickly look toward my brother, who has rapidly gotten to his feet, despite the beating I just gave him, and shock registers on his pale and swelling face. "What the fuck did you do?" I shout.

"Fuck! I might have mentioned to Dad that you were abandoning us for a woman, and acting out of character." Micah's eyes meet mine, and I witness the fear in their depths. He's realizing what he's done; our father is a paranoid psychopath. Anything that might be a threat to his power base, and control, must be eliminated. If my father thinks I might betray him, or stop serving his cause, he wouldn't hesitate to kill his oldest child. His actions and words have signed mine and everyone in this room's death warrant, including himself. My father wouldn't hesitate to use our deaths to gain political sympathy from the public. He'll spin it so he looks like the grieving father. Meanwhile, he'll wipe the slate clean of the two people who know all of his secrets and misdeeds.

My fingers work quickly on my phone screen, activating the various defense methods I have hidden around the property. With one push of a code, I disarm the collar around Chrissy's neck, and it falls to the ground with a clang. "My father's here to kill us all. We have to get ready to defend the cabin, or none of us are making it out of here alive."

"Who the fuck is your father? Why would he want to kill us?" Chrissy asks in a panic, as she grabs the gun I forgot from the floor, and rubs at the red mark on her neck left behind from the collar.

"He's a fucking deranged psychopath, with control and trust issues," Micah yells, as he makes it out of the door. Toothless' barking, and his body hitting the bathroom door, are getting louder despite the alarms blaring. That fucking beast is moments away from tearing out of there, and then we will have a new threat to deal with. I hope Chrissy can get him under control before he tries to rip out my throat.

"My father is Governor Brantford, and he'll stop at nothing to keep his grasp on power, including killing both his sons who know his secrets."

Chapter 35

Santa

"What the hell do you mean your father is the *governor?*" Chrissy's panicked voice follows me out of the room, as I start making a checklist of all the weapons I'm going to need, and arming the electrified windows. There is no way my father came here just to have a chat, the asshole saw this as an opportunity to clean house, and means to end my life. I have no intention of allowing that to happen, especially with Chrissy inside the cabin. He must have had Micah followed, it's the only explanation for him knowing where we are.

My thoughts are confirmed when I spy two of his henchmen for hire, Chris and Henry, on one of the cameras, trying to approach the back of the cabin. Those two fuckers will be the first to die, simply because they've always pissed me off with their shitty, alpha male, toxic behavior. "NIC! Are you even listening to me?" Chrissy grabs onto my shoulder and forces me to halt in my tracks, and for the first time in my whole life, I don't feel revulsion or rage at the uninvited contact. In fact, if I didn't have to deal with all this shit at my door, I'd press her against one of the walls right here in the hallway, and fuck her brains out. It hasn't escaped me that she never responded to my declaration of love. I'm just choosing to place that on the back burner for now, but we will be having a chat the minute I have parted my father's head from his shoulders.

"What's to explain, *Red?* Daddy is an asshole at the top of the state's food chain, with incriminating blackmail information on the president, and has a hard-on for getting what he wants. It's best to let Nic do what he does best right now," Micah chuckles as he follows us out of the room, with Daisy on his heels. Chrissy turns around and gives him a scathing look, filled with the promise of pain. A smile breaks across my face as he takes a step back from the angry look on her features, and crashes into Daisy. "What is it that he does best?" Daisy peeks around Micah's shoulder, with her eyebrows up by her hairline, and the ridiculous reindeer antlers she's wearing bobbing on her blonde head.

"Kill people," Micah says.

"Murder," I reply.

"Stalk, and decapitate body parts," Chrissy answers at the same time. Daisy looks between all three of us with shock, and motions for us to proceed walking. "Sorry I asked," I hear her mumble.

I press a code into a door at the end of the hallway, and it slides open with an electronic beep. It reveals the massive arsenal I have collected over the years. A part of me always knew something like this was bound to happen, the minute I started resisting taking orders from my father, and I wanted to be prepared to fight back. "*Jesus*, Nic, how long have you been stockpiling this stuff?" My brother steps into the room, and runs his finger down a stainless steel hunter's bow.

"You know how to use all this stuff? Who the hell trained you, *'Rambo'?*" Chrissy demands as she looks around with both awe, and apprehension, across her delicate features. "The United States government did; Nic used to be in the special forces, just think of him as an unhinged *'Captain America',*" Micah chuckles, as he picks up a rifle and starts playing with it, not realizing the fucking thing is loaded, and could blow his head off. I grab it, yank it away from him, and start strapping weapons and ammunition to my body. "You'll shoot your eye out, idiot."

"I can help. Give me a weapon," Micah whines, and I roll my eyes at his childish behavior. "I can fight too. You are not leaving us as sitting ducks inside of here, while you go out there and play *'Call of Duty',* asshole."

I can hear Toothless slamming his immense body against the door at the other end of the hall, and I don't want to be in his vicinity when he finally escapes. Somehow, I don't think the demon will forgive me for drugging him. *Fuck, I don't have time for this shit.* Very soon, we are going to have a bunch of thugs breaking into my home, intent on murdering us all. I hand Micah and Chrissy each a loaded handgun, equipped with a silencer, and a blade, and Daisy; a bat. Somehow, the little psycho managed to tuck the original gun that she used to kidnap me with into the top of her pants. My money's on her being the most useful; something about her screams *'unhinged'*. "Point and shoot at anyone besides us. Don't hesitate; if you do, you're dead."

My hand wraps around Chrissy's neck, and I yank her into my body, my mouth crashing down against hers with fierce hunger, and filled with promises of the depravity I'm going to punish her with later. "You stay safe, sweet temptation. Don't forget that you belong to me." I stare at her, knowing that she's as broken inside as I am, and all of her sins and darkness call out to mine and beg me to stay, beg me to grab her and run from this place, and live the next fifty-plus years by her side. However, I can't delay it anymore, even though nothing within me wants to be parted from her, but I have to go murder these men before they get to us. It's the only way to ensure she survives. I pull away from her as pain radiates inside of my chest, and has my breath struggling to escape. *Fuck, I love this woman. This can't be our ending; it's just our beginning.*

I stop in front of my baby brother, who, despite being the bane of my existence, and the reason we have been discovered, is the only other person besides Chrissy that I even remotely care about. I press my forehead against his, his gray eyes staring into mine with worry. "Don't die, fucker, and Micah, protect them with your life. If something happens to her, you won't be taking another breath when I find you."

I race for my computer room in the basement, and the hidden exit that will release me into the wooded area behind my house, so I can hunt my prey without another glance backward. My father has made a big mistake, if he thinks I would just stand by and allow him to murder me. The cunt has consistently underestimated my abilities, and my willingness to be an orphan. He's about to learn I'm the biggest monster in these woods. A quick glance at one of the screens confirms that Toothless has been released, and is currently getting lots of kisses from the girls; *lucky bastard*. I almost feel sorry for whoever attempts to breach the house and go after them. He's going to rip them apart one vicious chunk at a time.

I sprint for the tunnel that will bring me outside, climbing the metal ladder, and hesitating before I emerge. I pull up my hidden cameras that line the property, and give me eyes on where everyone is located. I can see Chris not more than twenty feet ahead of me, and stalking towards the side patio door. The fucker doesn't know it's electrified and armed, but he's about to find out. I search the area for the other asshole, Henry, and spot him heading for the side of the house. He's closer. I'll take him out first, but I need to do it up close, and in person, so as not to announce my presence to the rest of the men my father has with him. It's best if they think we are holed up inside, instead of me about to pick them off one by one.

    I use the shadows provided by the giant evergreens surrounding the cabin, to move stealthily toward Henry, and pull out one of my large needle-style blades from the harness strapped to my thigh. When he's busy peeking around a corner, and not watching his back like a fucking amateur, I slide up behind him on silent feet, and before he can utter a sound, I slam my hand over his mouth, and push the blade through the back of his neck until it protrudes out the front. His mouth opens on a gasp below my palm, and his eyes widen as his blood gurls up his throat, and slides down his face. "You fucked up, Henry. Whatever he promised you to kill me, it wasn't nearly enough," I whisper into his ear, as I pull back and grab a smaller blade from my thigh strap and thrust it into his eye, before yanking it out and doing the same to the other side. His warm blood sprays and coats my face, and it only heats my desire for more death. I'm taking it very personally that these assholes came here to murder me at my father's orders, and I want to ensure I send a message, in case any of them manage to escape. Although I have my doubts about that, since I don't plan to leave any of them breathing. Henry drops like a sack of shit to the ground, and his body shudders before going still. *One down, lots to go. It's playtime.*

Chapter 36

The Gift

He kissed me like it was the last time he might see me, demanding that I stay safe and remember that I belonged to him, and I didn't utter one fucking word. *Why didn't I say anything?* He might die out there, trying to protect us from his father, and I chose that moment in my life to remain silent. *What the hell is wrong with me?*

This man has all my emotions tangled up inside of me, and wrapped in dark chaos. Blood, mayhem, and unhinged violence, surround him like a thick layer of steel that is impenetrable, and yet he sat there and showed me a weak spot in his armor. I no longer comprehend if the world is up or down right now; all I do know is, that was the hottest kiss I've ever received, and the sweetest words anyone has ever spoken to me, and I let him go. Is this what it feels like to be genuinely wanted and cherished? To be overwhelmed by passion, and lose yourself to your emotions? All of these feelings are foreign to me, and they terrify me down to my guarded and mistrusting soul.

My hand tightens on the gun he gave me, as I stare sightlessly ahead to where he stood mere moments ago. I feel like I'm not seeing anything in front of me, just a haze, and instead, only the image of his serious expression, and those dark, stormy gray eyes as he declared that he loved me, remain. *"I'd like to think that I fell in love with you the moment I saw you, but the truth is I think my heart has always been in love with you, and it was just waiting to meet you. You, Chrissy Cranbrook, are the reason it beats, and without you, there is no reason for me to keep breathing."*

Who the hell says things like that? Who declares their love to a person they kidnapped, during a siege, and then walks away? Instead of replying to his words, I sat there stupefied and overwhelmed, staring into his gunmetal gray eyes filled with expectation and hope. No one besides Daisy has ever told me they love me, and she certainly doesn't mean the type of love that Nic is implying. All I could think about was whether this was what it felt like to be wanted. No one besides Toothless and Daisy has ever needed or wanted me. They have always been my only family. I spent my childhood and teenage years alone, with no one to count on besides myself, and I have always had to fight to protect myself from the monsters who would enjoy hurting me.

My heart soared with his words, and the earnest expression on his face. I wanted to wrap my arms around his neck and kiss him back, but instead, I froze. When he begged me to respond, I couldn't make the words form on my lips. I wanted to tell him that I felt something for him too, that it wasn't just one-sided, but nothing left me, as my throat closed up with dread. What if he's just saying all that to keep me here, playing me for a fool? I didn't want anyone to see the constant self-doubt and vulnerability that lives within me, the one that never adds up to others' expectations, and constantly causes me to feel like I'm lacking, or less than them. I've been hurt too many times because I trusted others, and they used that to exploit me. I refuse to allow anyone the opportunity to destroy what's left of me.

A loud bang, as the door at the end of the hall splinters, and a black ball of fur races down the hallway toward me, reduces my current thoughts to ash. "Toothless! Hey, baby!" The sweet boy almost takes me down to the ground in his eagerness to get to me, and I wrap my arms around his thick neck. He's happy and distracted for a mere second, before Micah makes the deadly mistake of moving. Before I can restrain him, he's darting out of my arms, using his body to protect me and Daisy, and growling ferociously in Micah's direction. "SHIT! Call off your beast!" Micah shouts with panic.

"I don't know, I say we let Toothless eat him; he's a dick," Daisy shouts above the barking, as I grab onto the large dog's collar, and am almost taken off my feet. "Stay, Toothless, friend!" *Though I doubt that very much.*

Toothless instantly heels, but continues to growl aggressively at Micah in warning, and honestly, I'm okay with that. I don't trust the slimy fuck, he went to my house with nefarious intentions, and he's the reason his psychotic father is here now. Who's to say he wasn't in on this plan from the very beginning? The only ones I can trust are

Daisy and my dog, and actions always speak louder than words. *We can trust Nic; he's out there trying to save us,* my mind supplies.

The sound of gunfire outside of the cabin gets all of our attention, and for a moment, I'm not sure what to do. I want to go help Nic, but he made it clear we're not to step foot outside of the cabin, and to shoot anyone besides him who comes in. "We have to do something; we have to help him!" I yell at Micah, who has the audacity to point his gun towards Toothless. "Trust me, Red, my brother doesn't need our help outside. He'll have them all dispatched to hell shortly, so all we have to do is worry about anyone getting past him and inside."

Just as he finishes his statement, we hear the sound of glass shattering, and painful, shrill screams from the other side of the cabin. I don't hesitate to move in that direction; my self-preservation lost amongst all the noise, my gun firmly in my hand, and the blade shoved into my back pocket. I can hear the thundering footsteps of Micah, Daisy, and Toothless behind me, as we reach a large oak kitchen area, and see the glass all over the floor from the shattered patio door. A man is shuddering on his hands and knees, his body contorting grotesquely as electricity soars through his limbs. *Jesus fuck, what the hell have I found myself involved in?*

Toothless doesn't hesitate to barge past me, growling deeply in his throat, as he places himself between us and the threat. The guy suddenly stops shaking and makes a move to attempt to stand, and before I can stop him, Toothless launches his muscled body at him, and bites into his upper arm, tearing into him. The screams are right out of a nightmare, and so is the blood.

My eyes meet Daisy's, and where I thought I would see identical fear and disgust, instead, I'm rewarded with sparkling eyes, and a mischievous smile across her pixie face. "Daisy!" I shout to get her attention, but she hesitates to pry her eyes off the scene before her to meet my glance, and all the while, screams of terror and ripping sounds are happening, that cause bile to race up the back of my throat. "*Good boy,* Toothless! You show him who's boss!" She cackles with glee, and claps her hands like a small child. I search for Micah, thinking the fucker must have escaped in the chaos, but I find him pressed against the furthest wall, looking a little green, his gray eyes wide with dread. "Keep... that... monster away from me!" He turns to the side and empties the contents of his stomach. I can't really blame him; I'm close to doing the same.

A shadow moves from the corner of my eye, and before I can scream out a warning, a man dressed in dark camouflage grabs hold of Micah. His large arm wraps around his neck, and a gun is drawn to Micah's temple. "Your daddy's not too impressed with you, *boy*," his southern twang fills the air, and I have to grab Toothless, and haul him back with all my might, before he attacks the newcomer. "In fact, the governor has issued an order to kill you and your brother on sight. You must have really pissed him off."

"I'll... double... whatever he's... paying, let... me... live," Micah gasps as his face goes red with strain, but the response is a deep, rumbling chuckle from the man with the gun. "I don't think you have that kind of money, boy. I'll take my chances with the governor." His dark eyes trail over Daisy and me, and my skin crawls with revulsion. "I'll be taking those sluts as spoils of war too." He tilts his chin in our direction. *The fuck, he will! I would rather die.*

I raise my hand with the gun, and it trembles in my grasp. "Whatcha gonna do with that, girlie, hmmm? Why don't you put that down before you get yourself hurt," he calls with a grin. I can almost read his disgusting thoughts, and I know that if this creep manages to kill Micah, and make it past Toothless, Daisy and I are going to wish for death. My finger twitches against the trigger as I take a few deep breaths. I'm only going to get one shot, before he fires that gun and kills Nic's brother, and I've never in my life shot a gun at a person. While I'm busily contemplating what to do, and how accurate my shot needs to be, an explosion sounds from my other side, and the man's head blows back against the wall and explodes like a crimson balloon. "Don't call us sluts, you dirty old cunt!" Daisy's shrill voice meets my ears, and I turn slowly to stare at her in awe, my mouth dropping open in horror.

The man's body drops like a sack of stones, and he releases his hold on Micah, who is covered in blood splatter and trembling. "HOLY SHIT!" He gasps, as he bends forward and grabs his knees, as he attempts to breathe. "Jesus, Daisy, how the hell did you learn to shoot like that?" I grab her arm, which is still pointing the gun in that direction, and force her to meet my eyes, all while Toothless whines at our side.

"Girl, I was raised on a farm, you know that. My daddy was an abusive asshole, but he made sure we all knew how to shoot." This is the first I've heard of her knowing how to handle a weapon besides a bat, and I've lived with the brat for three years. We can't stop to discuss this now. There are sounds of shots being fired in close proximity to the house, and I'm afraid more men like that asshole, whose brains are coating Nic's kitchen walls, are coming.

"We have to get out of here!" I utter, as I look for a possible way out of the cabin. How the hell did Nic get outside?

"You, missy, aren't going anywhere," a strong, male, authoritative voice catches my attention, and has my neck craning around, to stare at a man in his sixties, wearing an expensive wool coat, and pointing a gun right at me. He has the same gray eyes as his sons, but more wrinkles line his aged and fake-tanned face. "Hello, son, I see you've made new friends. Pity all of you are about to die."

Chapter 37

Santa

I'm covered in the blood of my enemies, and feeling exhilarated, as my heart pumps with excitement in my chest. I yank my blade across the neck of the asshole that tried to jump me from behind. His blood coats my hand, and trails down my arm in rivulets, as his blood arcs and sprays everything around me, like a morbid sprinkler. The ground is littered with the dead, and their crimson moisture is soaking the ground, and turning the small amount of snow into red slush. Who says the holidays aren't pretty?

I wonder if Chrissy would let me fuck her amongst the bodies of my victims? She would look so lovely as I drape her on their silent corpses, her ivory skin glowing, as I use their blood as lube and fuck her raw. I'm getting hard just thinking about it. We absolutely have to try that sometime; she'll learn to love it. I know that she has dark and disturbing fantasies, ones that I mean to cater to, for as long as we both shall live.

See, while I've been killing my father's pathetic men, I've also been thinking. It doesn't matter that Chrissy didn't immediately answer me back when I told her my feelings. Even if she doesn't yet have the same emotions as me, she will in time. How do I know that with certainty? Because I have no intention of ever letting her go, or allowing her to ever love anyone else. It's me or no one for her, and no, I don't think that's selfish or unreasonable. I saw her first, and she belongs to me. She's my sweet little temptation.

I look around with disappointment, a scowl crossing my face, as I don't see anyone else for me to send to the underworld. *Pathetic.* Where did my father even get these guys? From what I can tell, they're primarily street thugs and amateurs, who don't even know how to handle basic weapons. He should be fucking embarrassed to have come at me with these men, thinking that he would win. Speaking of the soon-to-be-dead fuck, I haven't seen him for a bit, and I want to have a word with him before I rip out his cold, beating heart from his chest. I got a very brief glimpse of him before I was overrun by men wishing to die, and the rat disappeared.

I move cautiously amongst the dead. Cockiness is a sure way to die, and although I know I'm good at killing others, I have no intentions of being a victim, just because I was too vain to pay attention to my surroundings. I steal a glance through the trees at my cabin, and notice that the patio door has blown out, and I can see right inside my house. Fucking Chris must be smelling like fried chicken right now. *Idiot.* No sounds make their way to my ears, and even the forest creatures know to be silent when a predator is moving amidst them. I approach the house on quiet feet, reloading my gun, and preparing myself to take anyone on who needs killing.

A gunshot reverberates through the air from the direction of the interior of the cabin, and it has me running across the last fifty feet of dense trees. My heartbeat pounds in my ears, and dread slithers through my veins. One of them got inside. Was that shot fired by my brother, one of the girls, or an enemy? I refuse to consider that one of them may have been on the receiving end of a bullet. A brief image of Chrissy lying in a pool of blood enters my mind, and a dark red haze slides over me, promising death to everyone I encounter if she's hurt. She has to be alive; I would know if she wasn't. I would fucking feel it in my pitch-black soul, the one that belongs to her as much as she belongs to me. I can't lose her now, not after finally feeling something after all the miserable, lonely years I have been alive.

As I scramble onto the back patio, I press my body against the wooden logs and stone that make up the exterior of my cabin. I can hear the low murmuring of voices, but I'm not close enough to discern what they're saying. The whooshing of my blood in my ears isn't helping either. I've never felt fear like I'm experiencing right now. I guess I've never had anything to lose before. I can't lose her now that I found her; I won't survive without her. I'll burn this world down to ash before I join her. Death would be a kindness I don't deserve if she's gone.

I take another few steps, my chest feeling heavy as I attempt to control all the unwanted emotions soaring through me. Concentrate, fucker, we have to get to Chrissy and save her. "Hello, son, I see you've made new friends. Pity all of you are about to die." The voice that utters those words has ice formulating in my veins. My father has survived, and made his way inside of my home like a cockroach. It's too bad for him that he won't be living long enough to make himself comfortable. He'll be lucky if there is enough of him to scrape off my floors for a state funeral.

"Dad, how could you do this to your sons?" The sound of deep growling accompanies my brother's ragged voice. Shit, the fucking demon hound is loose. What are the odds that furball is going to attack me as I kill my father? *Pretty good odds are my guess.* I keep moving forward as a plan formulates in my mind. Here's hoping my idiot brother isn't blocking my shot. I peek up and stare through the window above the sink. I would have preferred to have used my phone to locate their positions through my cameras, but some cocksucker back in the woods shattered the screen with his overly large forehead. My eyes catch a glimpse of Daisy and Chrissy to one side, closer to my position, and Toothless protectively positioned between them. Daisy has a gun pointed in the direction of my father, but Chrissy is standing there frozen, and the expression on her face tells me she's terrified. Both the gun and blade I gave her are long gone, and she's weaponless.

I force my eyes away from her, after cataloging that she's not injured, and slide them across the room, where I spy my father pointing a gun at my trembling brother, who's covered in blood. Fuck, is that his blood or someone else's? "You were both disappointments. You're weak, Micah, and your brother is an uncontrollable psychopath with a penchant for killing. I can't allow either of you to tarnish my legacy. I'm still young enough to have other sons to carry on my name. I plan to be president one day."

Motherfucking cocksucker, while I don't realistically dispute his assessment of both Micah and me, fuck him for thinking we're replaceable. He's the reason we are who we are. Nurture over nature, and all that bullshit. He thinks he gets just to create a new line of sons, because the ones he currently has are a little defective. *Fuck that shit;* I'll make sure that his name ends right here, even if I have to die in the process to make it happen. Nothing matters except that Chrissy is making it out of here.

"Wow, you're just winning daddy of the year, aren't ya?" Daisy's voice inquires as I prepare to throw myself through the patio door opening. "Are you the whore that has caught Nic's attention, or is that the other one?" My father nods his chin in Chrissy's direction. "Maybe I'll keep one of you alive, and in a cage, to remember him by." The asshole must find his comment amusing, because I can hear him chuckling to himself. No one is keeping my temptation in a cage but me. Rage as I've never experienced, in my thirty-three years of living on this detestable planet, roars through me, and my body trembles with the need to see my father's blood smeared across my flesh. When I'm done with him, there will be nothing left to identify him by.

"That whore would be me, and the only cage I'll be in is a prison cell after I murder you, asshole," Chrissy mouths off, and a part of me wants to laugh and groan at her comeback. Oh, sweet little temptation, we are going to have to work on your responses. "Pity, the other one's prettier," my father sighs. I hear movement, and then another growl, as I catch sight of Toothless aggressively snarling at my father, as he pushes Micah forward.

I don't get a chance to make a move, before he shoves Micah at the snarling dog. Toothless immediately lunges forward and attacks my brother, as my father fires in the girls' direction. Painful screams, and gunshots, are all around me as I force my way past Chris' dead body, and another male, and storm into the room to witness complete mayhem. Chrissy's throwing things from my counters at my father, like my toaster, and Daisy's firing her gun. A bullet whizzes past me, and embeds itself into the wall inches from my head. My eyes narrow on Daisy. Is she trying to kill me or him? I see her grin at me, and I know the little psycho was partially aiming at me.

"Save your brother!" She shouts, and fires in my father's direction, getting him in the arm as he ducks to avoid getting smacked with my coffee maker. He's attempting to shoot at the girls, but his aim is off, and all he's managing to do is destroy my kitchen cabinets. Bet the fucker's mad he never took me up on my offer to teach him how to shoot now. I take my eyes off them unwillingly, to assess how to get Toothless to stop eating my brother. My eyes glance at my gun, and just as I consider shooting the hellhound, Chrissy screams out, "Don't you fucking dare hurt my baby, Nic!" Well, there goes that idea.

"NIC! FUCK, HELP!" Micah demands, and Toothless swings him around like a ragged chew toy. Jesus fuck, the things I put up with for this woman. "Here, demon boy, come and get me!" I shout, and throw one of my broken chairs in his direction, to get his attention. His luminous eyes stare up at me as his teeth clamp down on my brother's bicep, and blood pours from his mouth. His black lips curl back in a snarl, and I realize the fucker must recognize me because, in the next moment, he's releasing Micah and charging at me. *FUCK!* All his body weight hits me in the chest like a freight train, and I stumble back through the patio opening, as he tries to rip off my face. My hands wrap around his large head, trying to prevent him from eating me, but also trying not to hurt the beast that so gallantly defended the girls.

"Toothless! Come here, pretty boy, come to momma! Toothless, release! Release!" Chrissy's frantic voice fills my ears, as she grabs onto his large leather collar and tries to pry the bane of my existence off of me. Slobber and blood coat my skin, and for once in my life, I am completely grossed out. Toothless finally heeds Chrissy's command, and they back up, but he continues to bare his sharp teeth at me. Other sounds make their way back to me, and it sounds like crying. *What the fuck?*

I rush back inside the kitchen, and my brother is curled like a baby on the floor, clutching his limp and bloody arm, and my father is on his knees, with his arms above his head, blood running down towards his shoulder from a bullet hole, as tears pour down his face. "Say it louder, so both your sons can hear you!" Daisy demands, and she holds the gun pointed at my father's face.

"I'm... the worst... father... in the... world," Governor Brantford sobs, as snot slides from his nose, and his body trembles with fear. If I'm not mistaken, that rapidly growing puddle below him is piss. Holy shit, this is unexpected and yet incredibly satisfying. My power-hungry, male chauvinist, entitled father, brought to his knees by a small woman, and a stripper at that. "Hey, Nic, your daddy and I were just getting acquainted." Daisy smirks but never takes her eyes off my father.

"Son! Please save me! I'm your father; you can't let her end my life!" Chrissy steps up beside me, and I don't see Toothless near her, but I can hear him running outside on the patio. If I, by chance, left anyone alive out there, they won't be in a minute after meeting that beast.

"What do we do with him now?" Chrissy questions as she runs her hands across my body, looking for injuries. "If you don't stop touching me, temptation, I'm going to bend you over my counter and fuck your ass, no matter who's watching." I take her hand in mine. "I promise I'm unhurt." Happiness fills me that she's worried about me, and as much as her expression indicates that she thinks I'm joking, I'm not. Violence and bloodshed turn me on, and my cock is painfully hard. I'll rip up that shirt and fuck her hard right now.

"Son! Please!" My father begs, and the sound hurts my ears, and makes me remember all the times he's been an asshole to me. The way he's used me as his personal assassin over the years to do his dirty work. "Not a chance, old man, you will die here today."

Chapter 38

Santa

I wash my bloody hands in the sink, as I stare into the mirror at my reflection. My face and skin are still covered with my father's, and his henchmen's, blood. The coward died begging for his life, as I slit his throat, while Micah and the girls watched. There was never any doubt that he would die at my hands; I earned that right after all these years of having to put up with his shit. After patching up my brother from Toothless' gnawing, and restraining the massive beast without losing a limb, I ended my father's life right there in my kitchen while they watched. It was anticlimactic at best. He died still thinking there was a chance one of his sons would save him, and neither one of us had any desire to see him continue breathing.

My brother called in the reinforcements to help clean the scene, and stage it to look like an attack on the governor by gangs, who was spending the holidays with his beloved sons and their girlfriends. A tragedy is what the news is calling it: *cue an eye roll*. Having blackmail information on most of the influential people in the state, and country, will help cover our tracks, and anyone who dares not cooperate will find themselves at the end of my blade in the middle of the night. A snort leaves my lips, as I remember how my brother spun his web of lies, and even somehow managed to wrap Daisy up tight in them, as his girlfriend. I give it twenty-four hours before she shoots him. That girl is as unhinged as I am.

A noise catches my attention, and I watch through the reflection as Chrissy closes the bathroom door and makes her way towards me. She's wearing one of my hoodies and a pair of my oversized sweatpants, and honestly, she's never looked sexier. Her dark chocolate eyes meet mine in the mirror, and I witness the worry in their depths. I find it humorous that she's worried about me, after I killed my father, and over ten men, in cold blood. Has she forgotten that I drugged and kidnapped her?

"Are you okay? You didn't let the medics check you," she questions, little lines appearing between her eyebrows. No, I didn't; the only hands I want touching my body belong to her. Everyone else can fuck right off. My arm reaches out and encircles her waist, pulling her against me despite her little gasp. I press my nose against her rich, auburn hair, which is all tangled and in a messy bun, and my cock twitches in my pants. She smells like sin, sunshine, and heaven. I don't think I will ever be able to get enough of her; she calls to my inner demon, the monster that craves bloodshed, destruction, and her. She is what I never knew I wanted or needed, and now can't even fathom living without.

"There was no need," I breathe into her hair, and my hand trails up her ribs below the hoodie, and towards her breast. "I have the cure to all my ailments right here." My fingers meet her hardened nipple as I tweak it, and her breathing begins to ramp up. She's so tiny compared to my six-foot-three frame, that I have to bend my knees to accommodate our height difference. She's my little, slutty Christmas elf. Fuck, now I'm picturing her in one of those skanky elf costumes, while I fuck her tight pussy and cover her in my cum.

My other hand slips down her hip and grabs a handful of her perfect, perky asscheek, forcing her body flush against mine, so she can feel how stiff and ready my cock is for her. "Mmmm," she moans, and I can't help myself. The need to kiss her is a demanding tempo in my blood. My head lowers until my mouth is mere centimeters from hers. "You will never leave me, temptation, and you need to understand that now. I'm not a good man, and I don't plan to change that, but I can be good to you. You will never have to be frightened, or want for anything ever again. I will always protect you from everything but myself."

"I'm not afraid of you, Nic. I should be, but I'm not. You're a monster, but I find I can't resist you, or your crazy. If I can't leave you, then the same goes for you." She leans forward, and her teeth sink into my bottom lip hard, and draw blood. "Don't think I won't go on a killing spree if you fuck around on me. I don't share, *ever.*" Her words are my undoing, and I slam my mouth against hers with a groan. My tongue slips inside and tangles with hers, until both of us are losing our minds. My hand squeezes her breast, and my fingers pull on her nipple, until she's gasping into my mouth. Fuck, she's wearing too many clothes. I need to feel my skin against hers. It's a fever searing through my body, and causing sweat to bead along my temple.

I pull back from our kiss, and her breathing is harsh as I take inventory of her. Her lips are swollen and wet from our kissing, and my blood is smeared on their surface. Her alabaster skin is flushed with a pretty pink hue, and her brown eyes are wide, pupils blown with lust. She looks like a fucking goddess ready to receive her tribute. Somehow, the image of her on a pedestal pops into my mind and makes a chuckle leave my lips. As much as I want to serve her, and I will, right now, I need her down on her knees, showing me how much she wants to stay with me. I release her breast and pull my hand from her shirt, trailing it through the space between her breasts before wrapping my fingers around her throat. "We don't have much time; the officer said we have to leave, Nic," she moans, as my fingers tighten around the delicate column until she chokes on her next breath.

My home is now a crime scene, and we're being kicked out, much to my aggravation, but not before I get what I want from my sweet temptation. "I suggest you be a good girl, and get on your knees for me then." I use my grip on her neck to force her down to her knees before me. My other hand slides into her hair and grips her bun. She looks up at me with unabashed lust across her stunning features, and at this moment, I know that I'm the luckiest son of a bitch to walk the earth. "Pull out my cock, and spit," I instruct her, my grip on her throat warning her not to sass me.

Her hands dig into the waistband of my pants, and she releases the button and yanks down my zipper. Her small, warm hand reaches inside and grips my hard length, her soft palm rubbing against my piercings, as her thumb slides through the beads of precum forming on my tip. Fuck, that feels so good, and as much as I would like to allow her to continue her torture, she's right. We're pressed for time, and someone will eventually come looking for us. Her head moves forward as she follows my instructions, spits on my crown, and uses it as lube to slide down my rigid length. "That's a *good girl*; now open wide, baby, and take me to the back of your throat," I demand and tighten my grip on her hair. Her lips wrap around my cock as she hollows her cheeks, and I thrust into the back of her throat, causing her to choke and gag. The sound makes my balls draw up tight; I'm so wired from all the bloodshed, and how sexy she is, that it won't take me long to blow.

I start a punishing rhythm of thrusting into the back of her throat, over and over again, without mercy, as she chokes and gags on my cock, and saliva and tears run down the sides of her face. All the while, she's keeping eye contact with me, her hands gripping the back of my thighs, her nails digging into my flesh, and it's almost my undoing. I can feel the orgasm racing up my spine and electricity soaring through my veins, causing the hairs on my arms to stand on end. She feels so good, and as tempted as I am to blow, I want her to cum with me. "Slip your hand down your pants and fuck yourself on your fingers, temptation. I want you to fill your pussy with at least three of them," I groan.

Her hands leave the back of my legs and slip to the waistband of the joggers, yanking them down to her knees. I watch with rapt attention as she spreads her legs as much as the fabric will allow, and slides her fingers between her pussy lips, groaning as she makes contact with her needy clit. Two fingers slide inside her tight hole, peeking back out so I can see how drenched she is. "Fuck," I moan, as I watch her slip them back inside, and she hums against my cock. I yank on her hair in warning not to fuck around, and she grins around my cock, and slams three fingers inside of herself, matching the rhythm I'm producing inside of her mouth. A fourth finger slips inside, and she rides her hand the way she would my cock, her hips moving in a relentless motion, and her throat closes tightly with her gasps around the tip of my cock. It's my undoing; I thrust harshly against her mouth, forcing my cock as far down her throat as I can, until her nose is pressed against my pelvis, and tears are sliding from her eyes. I grip her hair mercilessly to hold her in place, as I cum down her throat, and she's forced to swallow every drop I give her, as her breath stutters.

Her whole body tightens, and she pulls against my restraining hands as she explodes from her orgasm, her eyes sliding to the back of her head as her body deflates, and a scream rumbles against my hard dick. Fuck, I just filled her throat with my load, and I'm ready to go again. The thought of filling her pussy with my cum, and watching it drip out of her, has me pulling out of her mouth, using my grip around her neck to force her to her feet, where she stumbles against the cabinet with a bang. I push her face roughly down on the stone counter, my hand slapping harshly against one asscheek and then the other, as my cock slams inside of her drenched pussy and fills her.

I don't wait for her to acclimate to my large size, before I pound into her in punishing thrusts, forcing her lower body to slam again and again into the wooden cabinet. The sound is loud in the small space, as if we were going to war against each other. "That's it, temptation, take all of me. You were meant to be my slut. Look how well your sweet pussy swallows my cock."

"Fuck, fuck, fuck," she pants as her cunt tightens around me, and another orgasm rips through her. Her whole body trembles and tightens, her hand gripping the edge of the sink for dear life. Her mouth opens on a scream, and the sound pushes me right over the edge with her, as she clenches like a vice as I cum inside of her pussy. "You're mine, Chrissy Cranbrook, forever."

I pull out of her pussy, and lower myself to my knees as her legs tremble, and aftershocks take her over. I'm ready to pay tribute to my goddess, who owns my pitch-black soul. My eyes narrow on her slick folds, and I can see my cum already attempting to make its way out of her. I use my thumb to push it back inside of her and lean forward, allowing my tongue to swipe between her swollen pussy lips. I suck, lick and bite until she's once again writhing against the counter, and little desperate mewling noises are escaping her. My tongue slips inside of her tight hole, and I eat her out, getting the full body taste of my cum and hers on my tastebuds. *Delicious, best shit ever.* I'm just about to suggest that I fuck her ass next, when a furious pounding on the door interrupts my thought process, and places an angry scowl on my face.

"Chrissy! Nic! Jesus, come quick, Toothless has bitten a cop, and he's threatening to shoot him!" Daisy's panicked voice sounds through the door, and Chrissy jumps up, yanking her pants back to her waist and attempting to move around me. "That fucking beast is a menace, and a cockblocker," I groan.

"If you love me, you have to love him. He's my baby, Nic. We come as a pair, and with Daisy as an attachment." She doesn't wait for my response, as she slams open the bathroom door and races from the room, leaving me on my knees, with my cock still semi-hard and exposed.

"Nice metal, dude. You better help though. Chrissy will end up in jail if that guy touches Toothless!" Daisy exclaims as she follows a screaming Chrissy down the hall.

Merry fucking Christmas to me; Santa really did bring me everything I could have ever wanted.

The End.

If you're interested in more depravity, why not jump into another one of my worlds?

Casbury Prep Series: Dark academia, why choose, bully romance with a secret identity and a strong dose of revenge: Start with **Reign of the Queen**, download it here!

If you are looking to dive into something darker, even more unhinged, and utterly depraved, take a look at my **Be My Sinner,** but get ready to get on your knees for the **Brotherhood of the Sacrament**. Get it here!

A.L.Maruga

If you just need another obsessive, morally gray psycho who stalks and kidnaps you for his depraved needs, come meet Diego Cabano in *The Queen's Serpent*. Get it

Acknowledgments

This was my first holiday-themed book, but I can tell you it won't be the last. I had so much fun with these characters, and honestly, I'm really sad to see them go. I know this wasn't your typical Christmas romance story, but I had to do it my way. I hope you've enjoyed this ride down the chimney with me, and you get to sit on a bearded man's lap for the holidays.

To the readers: Thank you for continuing to read my work and sharing it with others. Without your support, there would be no books.

My ride or die: Thank you for not even questioning my wanting to make a dark and dirty Christmas book; you really are Prince Charming.

To my daughter: My Christmas elf, who read this in protest 'cause I was going to ruin Christmas romances for her. I couldn't continue to do this without you, I love you, *little momma*.

To my handsome son: You didn't blink an eye when I said I was writing a serial killer, Santa. Thanks for not caring what I write. I love you, puppy.

To my P.A.: *Darcy Bennett*, thank you for not losing your mind when I told you I was writing this book instead of the one I was supposed to. Your continued support means so much to me.

Mia Fury: Where do I start, you are my cheerleader, sister of my heart and you make me a better writer. Thank you for being by my side and pushing me down the hill, screaming during this journey!

Katelin: Woman, I love you! You are always ready for a quick read, and your comments are invaluable. I am honored that you willingly read my depravity and enjoy it. Thank you for being an amazing human. Love ya, big time, with lots and lots of Timmies on the side.

Sinner Street Team: Ladies, you are life! You make every day better, keep me sane, and make me want to write. *I love you all.* Thank you for filling my days with smiles, naughty memes, laughter, and all your support. I am forever honored and grateful.

Sinner Bitches & All The Words Bunch, You ladies are amazing and so inspiring. I am grateful to have met you all. You keep me laughing and striving to get better at the craft. I am privileged to call you my friends. Thank you for being but a click away.

My lovely members of the *Queen's Lair* on F.B., You make me smile & keep me sane every day, and I am honored to have all of you in my group! Please keep up the naughtiness!

To My ARC Team: Thank you from the bottom of my heart for supporting me and helping me promote my books! I appreciate everything you do and all the time it takes. I could not continue to do this without your help and don't think I don't know it for one second.

Thank you to the other fantastic book community authors, PA, and readers who have been very supportive, inclusive, and patient with me.

To both my four-legged demon spawns: You're both assholes, but I can't live without you. You both are the best doggies a momma could have.

Thank you to the amazing J. Armstrong from **Furious Editing** for painstakingly helping me edit this book. I'm getting better with those commas, right? (Just go ahead and lie to me)

2025 is going to see new worlds from me, as well as a few surprises and departures into new genres. I hope you join me on my journey.

I love ya, lovelies!

A.L. Maruga, xoxo

About the author

Author A.L. Maruga grew up in Toronto, Canada, reading romance and watching Buffy the Vampire Slayer. She always seemed to fall for the villain, not much has changed.

Her love of all things romance and paranormal has stayed with her over the years, and she continues devours books and writes about the unhinged characters in her head!

Drinker of gallons of coffee, a lover of all things chocolate, and a collector of broken souls. You can find her wandering around her small town in Southwestern Ontario with her trusty writing furbaby assistants 'Daisy and Rayo' or spending time with her two grown kids and her soulmate, Mr. Maruga.

2022 was her debut as a romance author with her first book, *Reign of the Queen*, a dark enemy to lovers' bully, why choose romance. 2024 will see her close off the year with a total of 10 books published and so many more to come.

She writes about demanding, unapologetic, possessive, dark alpha a-holes and the strong women who bring them to their knees.

Made in the USA
Las Vegas, NV
16 December 2024